Dear Len,
To a great
and fellow car guy!
Keep motoring and hope
you enjoy my tale.

Sincerely
Bob

Waiting For Einstein

A Novel

Robert J. Majeski

simply francis publishing company

North Carolina

Copyright © 2022 Robert J. Majeski. All Rights Reserved.

No part of this book may be reproduced, stored in a retrieval system or transmitted, in any form or by any means-electronic, mechanical, photocopying, recording, or otherwise-without the prior written permission from the publisher, except for inclusion of brief quotations in a review.

All brand, product, and place names used in the book that are trademarks or service marks, registered trademarks, or trade names, are the exclusive intellectual property of their respective holders and are mentioned here as a matter of fair and nominative use. To avoid confusion, *simply francis publishing company* publishes books solely and is not affiliated with the holder of any mark mentioned in this book.

This is a work of historical fiction. Any real persons depicted in the book have been fictionalized for dramatic purposes.

Written permission has been granted and or attribution given for the use of all photographs in this book not taken by the author.

Library of Congress Control Number: 2022918794
ISBN: 978-1-63062-042-4 (paperback)
ISBN: 978-1-63062-043-1 (e-book)
Printed in the United States of America
Cover and Interior Design: Christy King Meares

For information about this title or to order books and/or electronic media, contact the publisher:

simply francis publishing company
P.O. Box 329, Wrightsville Beach, NC 28480
www.simplyfrancispublishing.com
simplyfrancispublishing@gmail.com

DEDICATION

To my wife Henny, who has been the love of my life, my guiding star and best friend throughout this life.

To Katie Barton who totally enriched my life.

To Julia Ruth Stevens who showed me that making new friends never gets old.

AUTHOR'S NOTE

"Nothing happens by accident. Everything happens for a *good* reason no matter how bad it seems at the start."

That has been my mantra for every event in my life and even on a larger scale, including many events in world history. The people we meet and the experiences that shape our lives through the years have purpose in how we grow and develop as citizens of our towns, countries, and the world.

The events that I am about to relate to you here may seem impossible, but are they? The following pages will reveal *possibilities* that many of the greatest minds, over the centuries, have contemplated and even tried to prove scientifically. What happened to my grandson, Adam, and me will seem incredible. We are still trying to figure out if this was a gift or a curse. However, if my beliefs are correct, at a minimum, this must have happened "for a good reason."

So read our story and you be the judge. Gift or Curse? True or False? Plausible or Implausible? Reality or imagination? Or just maybe we have stumbled upon a doorway to a world of limitless possibilities.

Unidentified co-worker (left), Jules Majewski, driver (right), circa 1933

CHAPTER ONE
Brooklyn
March 1933

The Brooklyn Borough Hall building looked impressive as it towered over Court Street. The Greek Revival fluted columns stood tall and straight with a few spotty areas of mismatched grey cement to repair cracks that had developed over the decades.

It was unseasonably warm for early March, hitting close to sixty degrees, and we had our car windows partially rolled down. The few small trees that seemed to sprout out of the sidewalks near the curbs were still leafless, without the slight signs of light green that would start to pop if the weather continued to stay this warm. But the warmth brought out that earthy aroma that damp trees and earth emitted whether you were near a city park or in country settings all over the world.

I was jolted from my sight-seeing by the sudden clang of the trolley bell behind me. The conductor leaned out the left side window of his trolley cab, his hand clutching the thin cord attached to a bell, and yelled, "It's not gonna get any greena, Buddy!"

I already had our little Chevy in first gear and let the clutch pedal up smoothly as the car rolled forward to the next light on Court Street. The trolley, committed to the direction of the tracks, turned off to the left behind us toward Fulton Street. It was not easy for me, having to fight the steering wheel, to keep the narrow front tires from following the tracks embedded in the street.

Chapter One

A neat, black '32 Chevy Cabriolet, with the top down, pulled up on our left. Two young men, looking very smart and important with their light-colored fedoras cocked over their right eyes, gave the impressions that they were on serious business. One wore a smile while the other looked stone-faced until, suddenly, they both looked to their right and I got a full-face view of them. I immediately noticed the driver's striking light blue eyes as the hair stood up on the back of my neck and I felt the blood drain from my face. I knew that face all too well, and I swear I had seen that exact pose in an old snapshot which I had retrieved from a box packed with photos that had been under my parents' bed. That old Abraham & Strauss Department Store box was a treasure trove of images which gave me a peek into their lives before they met and for years after. Many of the pictures were taken way before I was born and were full of images that chronicled their young lives.

My grandson, Adam, spotted the change in my demeanor. His eyes tracked my line of sight to the driver on the left and back to me just as the traffic light changed. The roadster jumped forward and cut in front of where we were stopped and eventually took a right turn down Atlantic Avenue toward the Brooklyn Navy Yard.

Adam's a smart kid and is very perceptive when he wants to be.

"That guy looked so much like that picture of Great Grandpa that you have on the wall in your living room."

Then it hit him.

"That's not possible, is it?"

I stated with the same feeling of incredulity, "That's my DAD, your Great Grandpa, Julian Majeski."

Cheshire, Connecticut
March 2013

I had just taken my 1933 Chevy coupe out of its winter storage and wanted to let the wind blow some of the dust off. I had called my oldest grandson, Adam, to ask if he wanted to go to Blackie's Hot Dog Stand for lunch and he amazingly said it was fine. Since he had started high school, his social calendar was packed between swimming, school theater projects, and studying. To get any time with a sophomore in high school was pretty amazing. I felt lucky and was not going to squander my limited time with him.

I picked him up in my vintage 1933 Chevy coupe. I liked traveling the backroads with the car. It replicated what it was like, driving the Chevy back in the day when it was newer. As we approached an old brownstone arched trestle, which supported the abandoned rail bed of the Waterbury-New Haven Trolley Line, we saw a bright light on the other side of the tunnel. Despite being blinded by the light, I maintained my speed, driving through the one lane opening, knowing it was too late to slow the car while accelerating up the steep grade. I would have stalled dead in the opening, making matters worse if someone was coming from the other direction. I looked at the speedometer with the needle pegged at forty-two miles per hour. Honking my horn a few times, I braced for a possible impact with whatever was causing the light but nothing happened as we rolled through the brownstone arch.

I swerved to the right as soon as I got through the narrow passageway. We looked at each other and Adam observed that it

Chapter One

must have been the sun that got in our eyes. However, as we continued up the road, I became a bit confused and disoriented.

All the houses that I knew along this stretch of the road were gone, until we came to the first intersection at Plank Road and Matthew Street. I spied what I called 'The Nelson House' on the left. I had called it that since the mid-70's when I redid the roof for the then-owner, Rick Nelson, not to be confused with the '50-'60's rock-n-roll legend. That's when I had learned from Rick that the house had been there since the late 1700's.

We rolled another hundred feet to the corner where an old Victorian house sat on the right corner between a brook and the road. My wife and I almost bought that house in '72 but it needed more work than we could afford. It did not sport the same colors that it had after the restoration a few years later with multiple colors to accent the 'gingerbread' trim. It was all white.

At the stop sign we turned right onto Plank Road and did not see any houses again until we got to the next intersection at Plank and Summit Roads. Adam was not familiar with this neighborhood road and did not notice the differences that I was seeing. A Victorian farmhouse appeared on the right corner at the next stop sign. It had not looked like this since the late '70's when a careless remodeler removed all the trim to update it. Here, it still sported a porch and lots of gingerbread trim that later owners had removed. How could this be?

We turned right onto Summit Road, braking most of the way down the steep decline. A left onto East Main confirmed the sinking feeling in my stomach. There was no interstate overpass to drive under. There was no Interstate, I-84, a major highway built in the '60's, that crossed overhead going east to west across the state. It was the same thing all the way to Blackie's Hot Dog Stand. There were no houses, I estimated, built after the 1930's anywhere, just open fields, hills, and trees. Neither one of us said anything. Adam just looked straight ahead and I simply drove keeping my eyes on the road.

Then I really panicked as I came to the corner and our destination. No Blackie's! Old cars passed us when I pulled over to the side of the road. They were all from the mid-twenties to early thirties vintage. The realization hit me like a ton of bricks. These were not 'antique' cars. They were simply cars, everyday cars, the transportation of an earlier generation.

"That's a REO! Oh my God, here comes a '29 Nash. Adam, I don't know what is happening but I have an idea where we are and it's not good."

Adam replied with a worried look, not sure why he should be worrying about the answer.

"What are you talking about, Pop?"

"Well, we are still in Cheshire, Connecticut. What I don't know is 'WHEN', but I have an idea. There's a picture in Blackie's that says they opened in 1934. I think this may be sometime before then."

We were looking at the trees and the hill where Blackie's should be standing. It was certainly there when I lunched there a week ago. However, it was obvious that they had not broken ground yet. Now, Adam looked very scared trying to comprehend what I was saying.

"You're kidding. Right?"

"I wish I was, Buddy."

I had to stay calm and not further frighten Adam. He has always scared a bit easily. After a short discussion and keeping my internal panic hidden, I finally convinced Adam that, although things seemed confusing and a bit scary, I was sure that there was a logical answer. It just might take a little time. The

Chapter One

look on his face told me I was not really convincing him of that. We headed down the road toward the center of Waterbury until we saw a roadside diner that looked like it was converted from an old railroad car and pulled into the dirt parking lot. I remembered the 1920's vintage $20 bill that I had found under the Chevy seat years ago. It stayed hidden there as a good luck piece. I realized that the smaller modern bills in my wallet would be useless. After we parked, I popped up the seat cushion and retrieved the old bill to get us something to drink while we tried to figure out what was happening.

"I'd like a coffee and Coke to go," I said to the waitress behind the counter as we took our seats.

"To go where?"

I realized my *faux pas* and quickly said that we would drink them here. But when I pulled out the antique twenty dollar bill the waitress rolled her eyes.

When I gave the waitress the twenty to pay for the drinks, she did not look happy.

"Don't you have a dime on you? The drinks are only a nickel each. If I have to break this it will clean out my register."

"I'm sorry, this is the only money I have on me."

She turned and headed toward the register.

"Hey Frank, we got the Rockefellers here today," she said as she waved the bill over her head.

Just as she started to rifle through her cash register drawer to make change, I looked over her shoulder and spotted a calendar sporting a picture of the "New 1933 Ford" with the March page stapled just below. All the dates were scratched off 1 through 11 leaving Sunday the 12th unmarked. I pointed to it.

"Well now we know what year it is."

Waiting for Einstein

Adam looked at the date and turned pale. "This has to be a dream, a nightmare."

"Whatever is going on, we have to figure it out fast before we are missed."

The waitress slapped my change down on the counter without cracking a smile. There was three fives, four singles, eight dimes and ten pennies. I'm sure she had some quarters but I think she was trying to make a point. I simply folded the bills and stuffed them in my back pocket. I slid the pile of coins off the counter's edge into my open hand and put them in my left side pocket.

We finished our drinks without conversation. We needed more privacy than the small diner afforded to continue any conversation. Picking through the clump of coins, I left her a dime tip for her troubles. I thought that would make her happy since that was a 100% tip. Not feeling welcome, even after my act of generosity, we decided to find some other place to talk and try and come up with a plan.

We continued along the road toward the center of Waterbury. Heading down East Main Street we came to the Waterbury Green where I spotted Drescher's. This was a famous German restaurant and I remembered when they moved the entire brick building off the Green to a side street back in 1975. It was a monumental task and I got to witness it over a few days on my lunch hour. At that time, I was managing a little Health and Beauty Aid store around the corner on Bank Street. Consumer Value Stores was a small chain that had just broken out of the Boston market and had about ten stores in Connecticut at the time. Most people don't remember that was their name, but they sure know what CVS is all around the country nowadays.

There was a half dozen cars parked along the street in front of Drescher's. I know my cars from that period better than those

Chapter One

made in our century and found it amusing that our eighty-year-old car was the newest one in the line as I pulled into a parking space. They ranged in age from a mid-20's Model T Ford pickup to a '31 Buick sedan. I could not help but notice a long-gone marque, a 1930 Durant. If this wasn't the beginning of a nightmare, I'd be having the time of my life with all these cars around.

We found a seat and the waiter came over with a clean white towel over his left forearm. "What can I get for you gents?"

"We'd like to see the lunch menu."

He took two menus from under his arm and handed them to us. He was dressed in a black suit, but the jacket was cut short and he wore a black satin cummerbund that was working hard to hold in a substantial stomach. We ordered from the menu, and then watched the waiter head toward the kitchen to place our requests with the chef. We were finally alone and out of earshot to brainstorm.

Adam is such an amazing kid. Some would call him an "old soul." At fourteen, he already towered over me by four inches, not that I was any way a challenge, being only five feet, five inches. He is broad in the shoulders and that would make you think he was a line man on his school's football team, but you would be wrong. He was on the swim team, but he was all about singing and theater. A gentle soul in every respect. I think if he had to tackle a kid in any sport, he'd always be apologizing to him as he helped him get up. He was a member of "Best Buddies" at school and was a mentor and friend to some of the physically challenged kids in his class. I am sure that he would have just done this on his own whether there was a club or not. It's just the way he is wired. No grandfather could be prouder by the way he was turning out. The fact that he was a straight 'A' student didn't hurt either.

We talked for what seemed like hours as we assessed our situation and tried to come up with some plausible solutions. In the end, with no idea on how to get back to our time, I hit upon an idea.

"Let's go through the trolley trestle again and see if we can get back to our time."

He liked that idea.

"That could work."

It was only a twenty-minute drive back to Mixville Road where we had stumbled into our situation. We drove through the tunnel repeatedly, in both directions with no success. I knew this from the absence of the more modern houses on either side of the tunnel. I made sure I was even doing exactly forty-two miles per hour, like we had been doing when we traveled back in time. There was no light at the end of the tunnel with every attempt. Pun intended. I relayed that thought to Adam but he was not laughing. There was shear fright in his eyes and I even saw them watering up as if he was going to start crying at any moment.

Finally, after much soul searching, I presented an alternate plan to Adam. It was a time-consuming solution and a big leap of faith, but I could not think of a better answer to our dilemma. Sweet and simple, we needed Einstein's help. Yes, The Einstein. I had always been interested in Albert Einstein and had read many books about his life and work. I knew from my early readings about him, that he would not get to Princeton, New Jersey until October of this year, that is 1933. I conveyed my thoughts as confidently as I could.

Chapter One

"Pop! What are you talking about?" Adam started to count off numbers using his fingers. When he stopped, he was holding up seven fingers.

"That's not for another seven months! I must get back to school! We can't wait around that long!"

With each sentence his voice got louder and more agitated.

"My folks will go crazy not knowing where we are! We can't wait that long! There must be a better way!"

"I can't think of anything, Buddy. I truly believe that only an Einstein can come up with an answer for us and luckily, he will be around soon. Okay, maybe not soon, but months are better than years, or worse, never. Right?"

Adam began to grasp at straws.

"What about going to that museum where that DeLorean from *Back to the Future* is? That might work."

"Come on, be serious, none of that existed in 1933. And even if it did, that was a movie prop. It wasn't an operational time machine."

"No, but somehow your old Chevy is? What are we going to do? I don't want to be stuck here, away from my family. They're going to be worried sick if we don't get back soon. They're probably already worried and have the police looking for us. Why we may be the lead story on the Evening News!"

"You don't think I'm not worried about that? And your Grandma, she is going to be frantic. She'll think we were kidnapped or worse, murdered or something."

Henny and I had never been apart for more than a few weeks since my Basic Training and AIT at Fort Knox right after we married. It was definitely the longest five months of our lives, but she knew where I was. If my idea actually worked, we would be apart for months with her thinking we were dead or something. None of the scenarios were good. But what alternatives did we have? Adam had to trust me about this. I had no clue why this happened, but I felt good with my plan. And I had an idea where we could wait until Mr. Einstein got to Jersey.

I just put it out there to Adam.

"Hear me out. It makes more sense to wait for Einstein down in Brooklyn, New York. After all, we will have to head in that direction eventually, and I have little to no knowledge of Connecticut in 1933. However, my knowledge of Brooklyn is extensive because of the many hours I spent listening to my parents and relatives speak of their childhoods in Brooklyn. When I was a kid, my family drove into the Bay Ridge Section of Brooklyn at least monthly to visit Grandma and Pop Majeski. Other trips into the City ended at my Grandma Kennedy's place in the Flatbush section of Brooklyn."

"But that's their history," Adam countered.

"You forget that I also went to high school, St. John's Prep, on Lewis and Willoughby, in the Bedford Stuyvesant section of Brooklyn in the mid '60's, followed by four years at St. Francis College over on Remsen Street in Brooklyn Heights near the Brooklyn Bridge. Therefore, my knowledge of Brooklyn is pretty extensive. Are you feeling better about my plan, yet?"

"Not really. Those are your memories, not mine."

"But coupled with all that, my home repair skills, as well as life-skills, the plan can work. Brooklyn is the logical choice."

"There is nothing logical about any of this, Pop."

"*Touché*, but it's a plan with a solution." I almost said "possible solution" but thought I needed to sound more positive.

In Manhattan, they were constantly tearing down buildings for new ones. This was decades before Jackie Kennedy

Chapter One

championed the Historical Preservation Movement and stopped the demolition of Grand Central Station. However, Brooklyn had remained relatively untouched since the late 1800's with most edifices standing for well over a century. I also figured that I had a better chance of finding work with my carpentry and handyman skills in the city than in the country. After all, as my Dad would tell me, more people meant more buildings and more buildings required more repairs. He sold storm windows and added, "And more houses and buildings mean more windows."

And again, Brooklyn was halfway to Princeton, New Jersey, where we hoped to catch up with Einstein in October. But Adam was not convinced. He was scared that if there was a "time tunnel" or worm hole that we stumbled upon in Cheshire, we should stay close by to check it out regularly to see if we could get back. My comfort level in Brooklyn was in no way reassuring for him. Now he would be far from home in time and space.

"Pop! We have to stay in Cheshire. All our family is here. The tunnel is here. My parents will be looking for me."

He was almost frantic.

I hugged him and simply said, "It's going to be Okay. I've got this. You'll see."

"I'm not liking this plan at all."

"I don't like it either but being the adult, I am going to take the lead and I need you to stick with me on this. I will get us back home. I promise."

"You don't know that! I'm scared."

"Duly noted. I admit that I have no experience to draw on, but I have a good feeling about this plan. I don't know why, but I think we need to hang out in Brooklyn.

"I'm not getting that same feeling. I just want to throw up."

"That's not going to solve anything. Either way, staying here isn't going to solve our problem either. We've tried to find that 'time tunnel' and that did not work."

So late that evening I turned the Chevy south, with my very reluctant passenger, toward Brooklyn with the hope of finding lodging and work for the long wait. Adam sulked the whole way.

We traveled down the Waterbury Cheshire Road to Main Street in Cheshire. We stopped at a gas station on Whitney Avenue in Hamden and tanked up for the trip at eighteen cents a gallon. It took $1.44 of our cash and we had to be careful if our money was going to last until I could find work. I also realized that I had no knowledge as to when the bridges, that I normally took to Brooklyn in our time, were built so we stopped at a Shell gas station and picked up a map of the Metro New York area and two others for Connecticut and New Jersey. Maps were free in 1933, given as advertisement and a courtesy, so it did not hurt our cash reserve. We studied the map carefully. Wow, there was no Whitestone Bridge yet. We would have to drive through the Bronx over a small Bridge into Manhattan and eventually take the Manhattan or Brooklyn Bridge to get onto Long Island. What a pain.

We drove until we hit the entrance for the Merritt Parkway toward New York. The Merritt became the Hutchinson Parkway in New York. It was all local roads to a small bridge into Manhattan, and then we had to cut across to the Brooklyn Bridge.

Driving during the nighttime worked out better since Manhattan would have been a nightmare if we had to cut across it during the day. Even in the 1930's, traffic was an issue. We arrived in Brooklyn about two in the morning and found a parking space on the street near Prospect Park. It wasn't long

Chapter One

before we were fast asleep from the emotional and physical drain of the drive and our situation.

It was not comfortable sleeping in the tight cab of that little Chevy but we got enough shuteye to re-energize ourselves for the tasks ahead of us. While we waited for the rest of the world to wake up, I took the time to remind Adam about the economic situation we had been thrust into when we leapt back in time.

"What did they teach you about the Depression in school? Because right now, The Great Depression is in full swing."

"Not much. We study mostly about what happened after World War II. That's a lot to study. After all, most everything that affects us happened in that time slot. Why study that old stuff? It's just history."

Adam chuckled at his pun.

"Well, any other time, I would let you get away with that attitude, but there is a lot of truth in the adage that, 'If you do not learn from history, you run the risk of repeating it.' And in our case, you need a short course, if you are going to survive it, since we are actually living in the middle of 'history.' They called it The Great Depression for a reason. So, listen up. This is important stuff."

Adam realized that our situation demanded his attention.

"The Roaring Twenties were a time of prosperity, and everyone seemed to be doing great. Farmers were growing produce in record amounts. Investors were playing the market and winning big. Factories were in full swing making goods for here and overseas to sell to hungry buyers with all this new money. But it all hit the fan in October of 1929."

"What happened?"

"More accurately what didn't happen? Like most disasters, tornadoes, train wrecks, whatever, the Great Depression was caused by a host of things that made the perfect storm, financially, that is. If my memory is correct, a bill was passed by Congress earlier in '29 called the Smoot-Hawley Tariff Act. It was a tariff on goods coming in from Europe. That made those countries very unhappy with us and they followed suit, imposing tariffs on our products. On top of that, many of the investors had borrowed money to get into the stock market, making much of the wealth hollow, with no foundation in real money. So, overproduction on the farms and in the factories coupled with a shrinking marketplace in the world left goods and food unsold everywhere. The money had already been spent to grow and make this stuff and suddenly there was no return on investment. All the elements were there for a financial disaster, but no one in banking or the government reacted or understood the consequences. Even the Federal Reserve, which was founded just fifteen years earlier to prevent such things, was so new that they either did not have the skills or understand their powers to stop the impending disaster."

"Didn't anybody see it coming?"

"Not that I recall. October of 1929 comes, and on, what my history books called, "Black Thursday," the market crashes. After just four days of trading, the market loses 23% of its total value. On Wall Street, guys are jumping out of windows to their death as entire fortunes are wiped out overnight. People start running to the banks to get their money out, all at the same time. Because many of the banks speculated on the market with their customers' savings, they didn't have the money to give back to the depositors and they started defaulting and, banks all over the country and world banks started to fail. Your namesake, Adam Majewski, your great-great Grandfather, had amassed a small fortune fixing up and flipping houses during the teens and

Chapter One

twenties and had put all his money in a bank for safe keeping. He lost it all in a few days. It changed our family's history for decades."

Adam looked truly interested when he heard how the Depression had touched our family.

"That's awful. He took a big risk on the market."

"That's just it, he didn't. He never invested in stock. He earned every dollar he saved. He worked hard for that money and thought the safest place was a bank. It returned a small interest rate but was stable. However, the bankers were using his money as well as millions of others' playing the market and lost it all. He was a victim of all that greed."

"That's so sad," Adam was almost tearful.

"There's more - 1929 is not the worst year. Unemployment hit its worst at almost 26% in 1933, and we are smack in the middle of all that, as we speak. We have our work cut out for us to find jobs, since over one-in-four American workers are out of jobs, with us."

"You're not saying anything that makes me feel like we are going to be doing Okay. What happens if you cannot find a job? You said we will be here for months."

"You are getting ahead of yourself. I'm not proud and will do any job that will pay the rent and put food on the table. AND that goes for you, also."

"What are you saying, Pop?"

"In 1933, you are of working age. If we are going to survive, it will take our combined incomes to make ends meet. My Dad started working right after grade school. He never went to high school. He had to help support the family, being the oldest boy."

"Pop, the most I've ever done is dog and house sit. I don't have any skills to get paid for. We're screwed."

Waiting for Einstein

"There is plenty that you can do. I've been working in one way or another since I was twelve. I bought my own bike when I was twelve after doing odd jobs around the neighborhood for a year. Then I put myself through Catholic high school and college working as a golf caddy and at the college library and going to school full time. I'm no smarter than you. My Dad instilled in me a work ethic that has served me well over the years. You're going to have to tap into those genes as well. You're a Majeski, and we are workers. You can do this. I'll help you. We are smart and with hard work we will survive, meet with Einstein and get back home. I promise."

"I trust in you Pop, but I'm still scared."

"We got this, and with your help, we can do it."

Our hands met in a fist bump.

The fact was, I had no clue how we were going to pull this off.

We started looking for a room to rent first thing.

Many people were being evicted daily because they had no money to pay the rent. Landlords had 'Apartment for Rent' signs in the windows even before the old tenants' furniture was put at the curb. Sadly, there were many renters who just left their furniture behind since they had no other place to move to and even less money for moving or storing their possessions. We felt guilty to be benefiting from this situation, but we were in no way able to help others in our current situation.

We walked past piles of furniture on every block as we walked down Flatbush Avenue. There were families sitting on the steps of apartment buildings with mothers comforting crying children as the fathers begged with landlords and building managers to just give them a few more days to get the rent money. It was gut wrenching to watch. We started looking for a place where we

Chapter One

would not see the family that we might be displacing. We could not bear the thought if we had to step around such poor souls to get a place of our own. The thought that we might be in similar circumstances in a few weeks crossed my mind as well.

We eventually found an apartment at 693 Flatbush Avenue on the corner of Winthrop Street. It was over a restaurant and was noisy until they closed each night but it was furnished and had two bedrooms, a bath, living room, and a tiny eat-in kitchen. It reminded me a lot of my Grandma Kennedy's place which I knew had to be in close proximity to our place. We could rent by the week. It was forty dollars a month but they agreed to let us rent weekly at eleven dollars. I really had to find work fast. We had less than six dollars to our name after we paid the first week's rent.

In the middle of all this I was still trying to wrap my head around the fact that we were time travelers. Did we get chosen by some all-knowing and powerful being? Was there a secret society that we were drafted into? How were we chosen? What was the purpose or meaning of this experience? Was there a mission? If so, what was it? Would we recognize the purpose if the facts were revealed? I went to sleep hoping I'd wake up in the morning and Adam would be back in my son's house and I'd be in mine and roll over in bed and see my wife, Henny, sleeping soundly next to me. This couldn't be happening.

The next morning, however, we were still in Brooklyn and it was 1933. Adam and I woke up in our rented, furnished apartment and over the small kitchen table we started to plan our day and how we might survive until we could figure out how to get back to our time, 2013. I tried to make it seem like the adventure of a lifetime that we would laugh about when we got back, but deep down inside I was scared. I think I did a good job hiding it from Adam because he seemed pretty calm and confident that I would get us back somehow.

"Pop, do you have any idea how scared you look right now? I know you're worried, big time, like when we got stuck in Pennsylvania when the generator fell apart on the old Rambler. I'm not afraid to admit that I am. My iPhone is useless here. I have no idea how to get information that might help us. I wish I could Google 'how to get back home from time traveling in the universe.'"

Well, so much for the good job of hiding the seriousness of our situation.

I looked at him and tried to ignore his accurate assessment of my state of mind.

"First, this isn't anything like breaking down in Pennsylvania. Second, even if the Internet existed here, I doubt we could get much help on how to get out of this mess. There's no app for accidental time travel that I'm aware of. We are going to have to find our way back on our own."

Anything I knew about time travel I learned on the History, Discovery, Sci-Fi channels, Jack Finney novels, and the movies. I could clearly hear Morgan Freeman's voice as he discussed worm holes that could transport a person through time and space in theory, but I never paid much attention to the details. These were not exactly the in-depth scientific studies that gave me enough information about how this happened and how we could get back.

Also, I never saw any real proof that time travel had been experienced by anyone credible. All talk was always slanted to the possibility but not the reality. What I did remember was that many of the shows referenced Einstein and his theories about

Chapter One

time travel. The injection of a genius' belief in the possibility of time travel was there to support the possibility, not the reality.

Adam and I, however, were now living proof. We had first-hand experience that it could be done. That realization though was not getting us closer to getting back home to our time. Somehow, we had to link up with Einstein and recruit his help. This was our only hope. Other than that, I did not have any idea where else to begin.

When I bought the 1933 Chevy from my longtime friend, Andy Johnson, I had researched that year from every angle: sports, politics, theater, celebrities, and science. I've done this with every car I owned since I like to assess how the society of the times influenced the design and functionality of the contemporary automobile. It was also an excuse to do historical research, which I enjoy, and buy things on eBay that I really didn't need but liked to have. I confess that I am a collector and only need the slightest excuse to start amassing more stuff. Give me a theme and I am off and running.

I retain lots of facts from my rummaging through the dusty halls of history. This information had vital importance to our situation. I knew that 1933 was the year that Einstein fled Nazi Germany. The new Nazi government was rounding up intellectuals and educators and sending them off to concentration camps if they didn't murder them outright. It was at this time that Einstein fled across the English Channel to Britain with much fanfare. After a short stay he continued to America going to California first. He returned to Europe but came back to the States in October. If my memory serves me well, he finally took up residence in Princeton, New Jersey to head a think tank near or at the University.

Waiting for Einstein

If we could get down to the Garden State Parkway and find a way to meet him, maybe he could figure out a way to get us back. I would think that his amazement with our story would get us in the door and he would be more than glad to help. It was a long shot but it was the only chance we had if we were ever going to return to our family in *our time*. I reviewed this plan with Adam since I thought that it would keep him focused and his spirits up.

"How can I argue with this plan? I love you Pop, but you're no Einstein. I'm pretty sure that it will take not just *an* Einstein but *THE Einstein* to get us back home. But, what do we do until October?"

"Survive," was all that I could answer.

CHAPTER TWO
Working with History
March 17, 1933
St. Patrick's Day
"We have nothing to fear but Fear itself."
Franklin D. Roosevelt

Considering the enormity of our situation, I was deeply concerned with how we could make our stay in Depression Era America sustainable and possibly comfortable. We were initially saved by that 1928 twenty-dollar bill I had kept under the Chevy's seat for good luck after I purchased it from our closest and dear friends, Andy and Nancy Johnson. Andy had been an usher at our wedding. They were the third owners of the car after Guy Roese had sold it to them in 1987. I suspected that Guy left it there as some kind of good luck piece. I was equally thankful that Andy had also left it untouched. Why he did, I never asked, but it became a lifeline none of us anticipated.

I knew that the modern bills I had in my money clip were useless since they were a different size and design and printed in a series dated in the early part of the 21st century. We would surely get arrested for trying to pass 'bogus' bills. I buried them under the seat when I retrieved the, now current, twenty. The last thing I wanted to do was accidentally pull out one of those new bills and bring unwanted attention to us.

Our apartment was furnished since the previous owners could not afford the storage fees and probably sold the furnishings to the landlord for a fraction of the original cost. So, we had a furnished place and the landlord got two dollars more a week. I hoped that he paid them enough to at least get a few months rent at a cheaper place but I worried for them when the money ran out.

My Grandma Kennedy moved to Flatbush with my future Mom, Dorothea and her two younger brothers, Jack and Bobby after she and my Grandpa divorced. They had to be close by and I wondered if I would bump into them on the street.

It was amazing how much that old twenty-dollar bill bought us with the low cost of things in 1933 but the money was running low, and we needed to find some income. In 2013, I was making good money as a Registered Nurse. That's an okay profession for a man in the future but in 1933 that was not going to fly. Men did not go into nursing since it was not considered a man's profession and nurses made next to nothing. It was considered a vocation and not a profession. You could not support yourself on a nurse's salary.

I also had visions in my head of hundreds of men on "bread lines" waiting for hours for soup and bread. Pictures of these broken men were frequently shown in any documentary about the Great Depression. In my mind, I always thought that I would rather spend my time looking for work. Now that I was actually here, the thought that I could end up on any line looking for free food scared me to death. I could not let this happen to us. No, I figured I would have to rely on my skills from an earlier career as a carpenter and all-around handyman if we were going to continue to eat and have a roof over our heads. It was during that time that my own personal history found us the most unlikely allies to survive in the past.

Chapter Two

Adam was not sitting around for me to come up with all the answers. He had also been analyzing our situation and coming up with possible solutions. He also looked at his own situation and we discussed everything. We knew that truancy was not an issue since children were only required to attend school until eighth grade. Many kids got jobs to help support the family after grade school. It was Adam who realized that there might be another solution to our immediate employment problems. We were sitting at the small table in our tiny kitchen planning our next move. Adam had an idea of how we might survive until we could catch up with Einstein.

"Pop. I was thinking. You do know lots of people that are here right now in 1933!"

"I do?" I answered, not yet seeing where he was going with this line of thought.

"Think about it. We have already bumped into your Dad. What about that lady you always talked about who was married to that Broadway star? She's got to be here. We just have to find someone and maybe, just maybe, you can reintroduce yourself or introduce yourself. Jeez, it gets confusing. Anyway, then they can help us out." He almost shouted as he added, "It'll be easy. OUR PROBLEM IS SOLVED."

Ah! Youthful optimism! Why didn't I think of that? On the other hand, he made me realize that I truly did know people who were living in 1933. Now that my mind had been opened up to this realization, I started to think of all the people I knew in my lifetime that had to be walking around in our new "present." My parents were here even though they did not know each other yet. That wouldn't happen until 1937. Many relatives that I knew on both sides and even some that died before I was born were working their way through everyday life today, just like us. On the other hand, how could I possibly approach these people to help us based on a relationship that technically wasn't going to start for another thirty years?

"Hello. You don't know me yet but I'm going to be your son or grandson in 1949."

That was a fast track to psychiatric ward at Bellevue Hospital, assuming that it was even open by now. My trivia knowledge had not extended to the history of mental hospitals yet.

Then, I have to admit that I saw the possibilities that caused some of Adam's optimism. We were not alone anymore. I just had to figure out how to tap into this other generation so that we could survive until it was time to meet up with Einstein.

We started to write down all the names of family members that I knew were alive in 1933. That was a long list made up of family members on both my Polish and Irish sides. We made another list of acquaintances that I also knew would be co-habitants of the Depression Era. Well, it wasn't a list, it was a single name. Katie Barton.

"Okay, Buddy." I stared at Adam. "If you were to do this, who do you think you would approach first, family or friend?"

"I like trying to connect with your friend first," he answered without hesitation.

"You sound sure about that. Why?"

"Because, if there was some reason that you become friends with her in the future, like, because of your similar personalities or something deeper, wouldn't that exist even now? I would think that same connection could still exist."

Smart answer.

"And a true friend just might believe you."

With Adam's keen observation about a basis for true friendship, our direction was set. I retold Adam the details of my

Chapter Two

relationship with Katie so he could help me figure out how best to approach her.

Katie Barton entered my life in 1963. I was fourteen, the age that Adam is now. To say that she was a character would be an understatement, and that was one of the many qualities that endeared her to everyone she met. Katie Mullin (Penman being her stage name) was a former Ziegfeld Follies chorus girl who married one of Broadway's royalties. It was a vivacious Irish Katie who captured the heart of James Barton, one of the giants of the Great White Way, during the early part of the 1900's until his passing in 1962.

She was the greatest of storytellers. I would spend hours listening to her life adventures in front of and behind the curtains of the great theaters of New York. The thread that ran through her life was her unending love for Jim. She bragged about her husband when he was a dashing young Vaudevillian, babysitting her in her parents' dressing room while they performed on stage. Even at the early age of five, she had promised herself that she was going to marry this talented Irish teen hoofer. Her stories gave me a backstage glimpse into the Golden Age of Vaudeville. I was hooked and could not get enough of her tales.

When she wasn't at my home mooching a Sunday dinner with my Mom's famous mashed potatoes, I was bicycling over to her place and walking the halls and rooms looking at all the pictures and movie stills that covered the walls celebrating the incredible life and times of her husband. It was exciting to me to look at enlarged movie scenes showing Mr. Barton with legendary performers such as Gregory Peck, Harry Morgan, Mitzi Gaynor, Gordon McRae, and a teenaged Debbie Reynolds. Little did I know that our mutual affection for each other during the 1960's, until her death in 1989, would now be the key to Adam and me surviving in these extremely hard times.

The next day Adam and I drove from our Flatbush Avenue apartment toward Nassau County and Mineola Park. We drove along Jamaica Avenue in Queens and continued east toward Floral Park, just over the city line. We immediately passed under the train trestle, that ran up to Creedmoor State Hospital, a few miles north just as a supply train was crossing over on it. The huge black steam locomotive belched out thick smoke blocking out the sun for a moment until the man-made cloud fanned out and gradually allowed the sunlight to re-emerge. The road name changed here to Jericho Turnpike. I was amazed at the sights that I was seeing. There were old store fronts on both sides of the street which was narrow with only one lane in each direction. The road was camel-backed, arched higher in the middle, designed to help keep the oil dropping from the cars and rain water running toward the curb and sewer grates. It brought back my childhood memories of the 1950's Floral Park that I knew as a grade school student.

    The Floral Park Theater came up on the right. Like most Vaudeville Houses of the turn of the century, this theatrical gilded gem had been converted to a movie theater with the growing popularity of motion pictures in the 1920's. I had spent many Saturdays there in the fifties and sixties when a quarter could buy me a double feature, two full length movies, with additional cartoons and movie previews.

    My friends and I would spend the entire afternoon there assuring our Moms that we would be home in time for dinner. Another dime could buy enough candy and popcorn to keep our appetites at bay until supper. Even at an early age I was

Chapter Two

interested in architecture and old buildings. It was fascinating to see the huge organ that sat unused on the left side of the stage. The keyboard was multi-leveled and formed a semicircle around the long-retired organist with foot pedals too numerous to count. It was years later that I found out it was probably installed during the silent movie era. Films came to town accompanied with a musical score to be played along with the film and timed to enhance the dramatic moments in the story line. Hollywood had not figured out how to put sound on the film yet.

As a grade school student at St. Hedwig's, a nearby Catholic school, I remembered the nuns herding the entire student body three blocks, along Jericho Turnpike, to the theater during Easter Week to see Victor Mature in *Demetrius and the Gladiators* and *The Robe*. There were no parental groups back then objecting to kids seeing movies with too much violence. If it had something to do with Jesus it must be okay. Unlike the boy taken to the cockpit in the movie *Airplane*, who was asked if he liked gladiator movies, no one ever asked us for our opinions. But we DID like gladiator movies. Why wouldn't we? We got out of classes for the entire school day. Later, the boys would play gladiators at recess for the next few weeks until it got boring.

My attention returned to navigating the traffic with the parked cars slightly leaning toward the curb on either side. I drove slowly past the butcher shops, bakeries, German delicatessens, clothing stores, shoe emporiums, and pharmacies on the north side of the Turnpike. I knew that they would be demolished by 1960 to widen the road to four lanes. The town never regained that old town charm after the more modern sixties and seventies architecture slowly refilled that side of the Turnpike. It always looked as if two different towns slid together until they crashed at Jericho. I was reminded of how busy it was in the decades before malls became the shopping meccas of a new generation. The sidewalks were full of pedestrians and shoppers. Adam noticed this as well.

"Why is it so busy? It's like a mall on a Friday night," he observed.

"That's an apt comparison. This is the mall of the thirties. This is where everyone goes to shop unless they want to take the train into the city to shop at Macy's, Gimbel's, or A&S."

Adam looked at me and asked, "Gimbel's and A&S? Are those big stores?"

"Gimbels was Macy's biggest retail competitor and Abraham & Strauss was the reason no one from that tip of the Island crossed the Brooklyn Bridge to Manhattan to shop at Macy's and Gimbels. I worked at the original A&S on Fulton Street in sporting goods on the 8th floor when I was in college, back, or I guess I should say forward, in 1968. Did you ever hear about a Mr. and Mrs. Strauss who perished on the Titanic in 1912? They were the co-owners of that store."

Adam just rolled his eyes thinking, 'He knows all that without checking it on an iPhone. Not that I can fact-check him anyway.'

We soon passed my old grade school. I still don't know what my mother was thinking but she had, for some reason, decided that my older siblings and I should attend a Polish school. Granted, our name was "Majeski" but she was Irish, a "Kennedy/McLaughlin" no less. So, Martha, Linda, Raymond and I all attended St. Hedwig's Grammar School, a Catholic parish founded by the surrounding Polish community. We hiked past Holy Ghost School in New Hyde Park, which was only a few

Chapter Two

blocks from our home, and traversed another mile to where the Felician Nuns taught, with Polish Language as one of the required subjects. You might say that my mother wanted us to get in touch with our European roots. You'd be wrong. The "devil be paid" if we used Polish in the house as my Dad was bilingual having grown up with immigrant parents.

"So, you don't want your Irish mother to know what you're talking about?" she'd cut in with her husky smoker's voice in a decided Brooklyn drawl.

Polish was limited to school and occasionally used at Grandma and Pop Majeski's Sunday visits. My brother and sisters and I quickly forgot what we learned except for the "Sign of the Cross" and "Hail Mary," which were drilled into our brains from the daily repetition at the beginning and end of every school day. Neither was enough to have a conversation later in life.

Driving down the Turnpike we came upon New Hyde Park Center just past the start of Lakeville Road on our left and Covert Avenue on the right. All the old buildings had the retail stores that I remembered as a kid twenty years into the future. The clothes store, Altman Ross, sat predominant due to its size, being three times bigger than most stores in the town. My older sisters, Martha and Linda, worked there as salesgirls during high school in the mid 50's. The Park Theater, a smaller version of the Floral Theater with an identical provenance, towered over the street. The marquee was lit up. '*KING KONG* with Fay Wray, Robert Armstrong, and Bruce Cabot.' What a year for movies!

A food market came up on our left just before Ingraham Lane. I remembered the market being called Associated Market in the fifties. During my pre-school years, I went shopping there with my mother. Across the street we passed Christ Plumbing and Supply. In my youth, this was one of the last clapboard buildings left with the original wooden sidewalk from the days when the Grand Prix Vanderbilt Cup Race cars careened down the Turnpike during the first decade of the 20th Century.

Being a car nut, I had learned that the races were annual events from 1904 until 1910 sponsored by William K. Vanderbilt, Jr., a member of one of the wealthiest families in the world and an avid automobile enthusiast. They were the first international motor car races in the United States. Of course, the best year was 1908 when the American built Locomobile #16 won the race. "Old 16" was in the logo of the car club, the Vanderbilt Cup Region, AACA, that I joined when I was eighteen just before I bought my first car, a 1928 Nash in 1968.

We finally passed the Town Hall, crossed New Hyde Park Road and came up to the Barton home just over the town line into Mineola. My head was still finding it hard to comprehend that I could see all the way to Hillside Avenue to the North. All the neighborhoods that my friends lived in when I was a kid were open fields at this time. I remember my Dad telling me that, in 1946, when Grandpa Kennedy's house was built on New Hyde Park Road, halfway to Hillside Avenue, potato farms dominated the entire tract. My Grandpa's home, where we celebrated every Christmas Eve in the 50's and 60's, would not be built for another thirteen years.

CHAPTER THREE
A New Old Friend

As we rolled up to the curb, Katie's house looked different from the way I remembered it, mid-century. By the sixties this area along Jericho had been developed as retail and commercial real estate surrounding the Barton home and restaurant. By the 1950's, the house, which was only fifteen feet from the sidewalk, had been surrounded by a six-foot-high cyclone fence with an unlocked gate leading to the walk that brought you to the front door. Landscaping with different kinds of evergreens had been allowed to grow higher than the window sills to allow privacy from the foot traffic along the sidewalk.

In 1933, the shrubs were much shorter with lots of low ground cover making the home more trim, attractive, and inviting. There was no fence. The big block-like Castro Convertible Showroom of the 50's, that cast a huge shadow over the Barton house, was not built yet allowing us to see the house easily as we drove up to it.

"Barton's Place" which would become "The Dublin Pub" when Katie rented it out after Jim's sudden death in 1962, sat next door just past the house and looked the same as it did in the future except for the original name in neon in the large front window. It was a busy establishment with what looked like a large lunch crowd.

In this time, the 18th Amendment, prohibiting the sale of alcohol, was still in force. I was proud of the vintage metal plate I bought on eBay that I had mounted on my trunk which read

"REPEAL THE 18TH AMENDMENT FOR PROSPERITY." Another antique plate attached above this one said "WIN WITH ROOSEVELT." The recently inaugurated President, Franklin Delano Roosevelt, also known as FDR, would not be able to keep his campaign promise to get rid of this unpopular Constitutional Amendment, until December of this year. My plan was to be home before the repeal.

Adam and I spied an open field surrounding the two buildings with parking off road on a gravel covered area on the side and behind the establishment. The mix of car makers surrounding this eatery told you that the patrons came from all economic levels with a truly democratic mix of classes. I pointed out to Adam a huge Packard convertible sedan, an air-cooled Franklin sedan with side mounts, two Cadillac sedans and even a Pierce Arrow limo among the Fords, Chevys, Dodges and Studebakers, and Nashes. FDR would be extremely pleased to see that the Bartons welcomed and attracted people from all classes. Our little Chevy coupe fit in nicely. This parking lot would make one heck of a car show in 2013.

I could not stall any longer. I had to initiate an introduction that could sink any hope of surviving here if it went south after I told our story, if we would even get that far. It was time to introduce myself to Katie again, but this time I'd be fifty years older than the first time we met back, or I should say forward, in 1963.

I strolled up to the Barton's front door after directing Adam to wait in the car. We didn't want to scare Katie since during these hard times two strange men coming to your door could seem threatening. Although he is only fourteen, Adam appeared more like a young man than the young teen he really was.

I swung the big knocker on the front door.

Chapter Three

"I'm coming," I heard a young woman say from inside. I could hear the sound of high heels approaching as someone came to the door. I had butterflies in my stomach hoping that my rehearsed presentation would convince Katie that we were friends in the future, and hopefully translate to some kind of friendship in the present. The knob turned and the door swung open. An attractive, well-dressed woman in her late twenties stood in the doorway.

"Can I help you, sir?" said a voice that was so sweet that she almost seemed to sing the question.

"I'm looking for Katie Barton, ah, I mean Mrs. James Barton."

"My friends call me 'Kitty' but I don't believe we have ever met."

I almost fell backwards on my heels.

With all my rehearsing of how I was going to approach Katie, I never gave it thought about how she might look in her youth. It threw me off because I never imagined that she would not look the way I remembered her. She was youthfully beautiful with a sweet voice I had never heard from her lips before. She was wearing a stylish dress for the 1930's with a loose V-neck top that was belted at the waist pulling the dress in to enhance a waist that could not have been much more than twenty-five inches. The skirt went to mid-calf and exposed silk stockings and two-inch ivory heels that matched the color of the dress. There was one large rose printed on the fabric close to the hem just below her left knee for dramatic effect. It worked. Couple this with a stylish short bob and she looked every bit like the movie stars I read about in a 1933 copy of *The New Movie* magazine I had found on eBay a few months ago.

This was not the gray-haired woman who wore loose fitting dresses to hide her pear shape with the raspy voice that I knew in the sixties. This person had a dancer's body and her dress was tailored to show her shapely figure to perfection. I remembered that Katie had told me in the sixties that she was thirty-years-old when she married Jim. She didn't look thirty. She still had the dancer's physique and carried it well.

Noticing my surprised expression, she said, "Are you alright? Is there something I can do for you?"

She asked with no sound of annoyance or impatience in her voice.

"You really are quite beautiful. I'm sorry. I wasn't expecting that." It came out before I could stop myself.

"I'll take that as a compliment, I guess, but you haven't answered my question."

I gathered my thoughts quickly and tried to get back to the task at hand. Taking part of a line from the iconic time travel movie from the late 70's, *Somewhere in Time* I replied. "Well, Mrs. Barton, you don't know me yet, but you will."

It worked for Christopher Reeves with Jane Seymour in that movie so why not give it a try.

She tilted her head slightly. "What did you say?"

I stayed formal for now.

"Mrs. Barton, I have an incredible story to tell you and I know you love hearing, as well as telling, stories."

"Oh really? I do?"

She raised one of her thin, arched eyebrows. This was a novel approach for a salesman. He surely was not dressed like one, with no dress shirt or tie, not even a jacket. Dungarees and a flannel shirt, and casual shoes. He didn't look like one of those aggressive Electrolux vacuum salesmen. If he put his foot in the door it would be broken before he got it out. Just before she was

Chapter Three

about to slam the door in my face I was able to get out one last comment.

"Yes, I'm very sure of that and you're our only hope if we are going to survive until a bigger problem we have is resolved."

I hoped that I did not sound desperate.

She stepped forward and stuck her head outside the door and peered side to side. "You said *we*. Who's *we*?"

She stuck her head out enough to see that no one else was with me. She still looked a bit nervous and I stayed as calm as I could not to scare her more.

"I'm sorry. My grandson, Adam is in the car. We thought that we might worry you if there were two strangers at your door. He's okay. He can wait."

"Well thanks for the concern but I can take care of myself quite well, thank you."

Her composure seemed to relax and then she surprised me.

"Don't make the poor boy wait in a stuffy car. Go get him. I have a feeling this is not going to be a short story. If I'm your only hope I want to meet him, too. This is no promise to help you, but you do have my curiosity stirred. Quick! Go get the boy and I'll wait here."

Mrs. Barton questioned her sanity as to why she was letting this go this far. He could be one of those Wall Street investors who decided not to jump out of the fortieth floor and was looking for a hand out. Maybe he was familiar with James' success on Broadway and was just looking for a handout. At least he did not look like the criminal element that had grown out of these tough times. She felt quite sure of that. He was just too soft spoken.

When I returned with Adam, I was not sure that Katie would still be there to welcome us but I remained hopeful. She did not disappoint us.

"My, you're a big one. So, you must be Adam."

She reached out her hand and shook his.

"I don't think I caught *your* name?" she added looking back at me.

I shook her hand.

"I'm Bob, Bob Majeski."

"Well, Mr. Bob Majeski and Master Adam, you have my attention. Please, come in and I'll have my housekeeper make us some coffee. Would you like some crumb cake? It's Entenmann's and it's fresh. The bakery just delivered it. No one can tell me that they don't make the best crumb cake in the world."

"I grew up on Entenmann's cakes and doughnuts. They were the highlight of every Sunday breakfast," said Bob.

Katie turned and we followed her into the house. She always loved to eat, especially when someone else made the food, like my mother. But the rest of what I observed was not the Katie I knew in my youth. As she led us through the foyer and into the front parlor it was hard not to notice her youthful appearance. What was I thinking? She's old enough to be my mother. Wait a second. I'm old enough to be *her* father! Whatever!

She directed us to the couch with a coffee table in front of it. It wasn't the same couch that I sat on many times in this same room years later. However, the baby grand reproducer piano in the corner was familiar. It was an amazing instrument for its diminutive size with the hand-painted oriental motif all over the fine cabinetry. I remembered Katie telling me that the reason Jim bought it for her was so she could hear 'Rhapsody in Blue' exactly as George Gershwin had played it when he debuted the masterpiece in New York City at Aeolian Hall in 1924. Katie would have been too young and not yet financially able to have

Chapter Three

been in the audience that historic night. Jim, however, had been there.

She had told me that reproducer pianos were unlike any other player pianos because they could play a musical composition exactly like it was played by a particular pianist on a specific day at an exact time. It captured all the subtleties and nuances of the artist and his performance as if he was there playing just for you. It was electrified to keep up a steady air pressure to accomplish this. Katie never got tired of playing that piece and even though the piano came with a dozen other piano rolls of other iconic performances, Gershwin's jazz masterpiece was the only roll I ever heard played in this room.

I wanted to hold Katie's curiosity and lay the groundwork for the bombshell I was going to drop on her.

"Your piano has always amazed me. Can I assume you have the 'Rhapsody in Blue' roll in it?"

I said this trying to give her a wry smile and a look into her eyes that said, *I know you and you know me.*

She looked quizzically at me with increased interest, but gave me no hint that she recognized me. I was not surprised or disappointed. How could I be? There was no expectation of her recognizing me. But I was more than sure that I had her attention.

CHAPTER FOUR
You May Call me "Kitty"

The housekeeper entered carrying a large serving tray that had everything needed for a delightful late morning snack. When I glanced in her direction, I caught a look that dared me to try anything stupid. A large knife that she must have used to cut the cake was left on the tray in plain sight as if to let me know that it could be used for more than culinary purposes. Her large frame and substantial height made me think that she had the power to protect her mistress with little effort. I think that she was doubling as a bodyguard in Jim's absence. She turned and headed toward the kitchen but not before giving me one more warning glance.

Katie poured coffee into the cups that the housekeeper had set out. Crumb cake squares were stacked on a plate creating a small, pastry pyramid. Cloth napkins were placed within reach to help catch the inevitable crumbs and powdered sugar that would fall from every bite of the incredibly delicious treats.

"I don't see a manuscript so your story must be in the planning stage. Are you hoping to write a novel or play, maybe a screenplay? You have dropped enough tantalizing hints to pique my curiosity. I hope, that you will not disappoint and will, at least, deliver an entertaining story. However, I'm interested to find out if it will be a great story because, as you so correctly stated, I do love a story."

"It's not like that at all. Before I get started, I want to thank you for letting us share our experience. The other thing I need to

Chapter Four

ask you is if I can still call you Katie? It's hard for me to call you by such a formal term as Mrs. Barton. Our story will reveal the reason why I feel that way."

She gave me a broad smile that made her younger version look more familiar, like the person I knew later in her life. It was a smile that I didn't realize, until now, that I truly had missed over the years.

"Why don't we keep it Mrs. Barton for now. I'll save my decision until after your conclusion. If your story entertains me, I may give you that privilege as a reward. Now, why don't you tell me how you know about my piano and my love of stories."

"I've been rehearsing how to start our tale and I'm still stuck at where to start. I can assure you that it still is as unbelievable to me and Adam as I expect it will be to you *and* we are the ones actually living it."

As I finished my stumbling introduction, I glanced over to Adam who was rolling his eyes like he did when he wanted me to get to the point in conversations. He dropped his head, chin to chest, in frustration. I was not doing anything we had rehearsed. I was taking way too long and he could not contain himself any longer.

Looking at my old friend, he jumped in.

"Mrs. Barton, what my Pop is trying to tell you is that you both have already met in 1963! He's told me many stories about you and Mr. Barton so that I almost feel like I know you as well. He's told me, over and over, how he was my age when you first met and how you both became close over the following years. I know it sounds unbelievable, but you must believe me when I tell you that *we are from the future, your future.*"

Waiting for Einstein

Adam found himself standing and his voice slightly trembled, anticipating that he might not be believed. He knew that everything hinged on Katie's believing our story.

Mrs. Barton was the one who was lost for words. We could tell by the look on her face that she was trying to process what Adam had thrown in her lap. Her delicate hand went up to cover her mouth as if she wanted to hide her shock at this revelation. It was also as if she didn't want to comment yet and wanted to hear more before she came to any conclusion. The woman I knew, in the future, always believed that almost anything was possible. What I didn't know was at what point in her life did she start to think this way and become open to all the possibilities that the universe might present. That would be key to how she would receive our current revelation. Was it possible that her experience with us was the start of her open mindedness, or was she always an accepting person who could embrace such a new reality?

She turned her attention to me.

"And how far in the future are you from, if I may ask? Your grandson said you and I met when you were the same age he is now. You've obviously grown a bit since then."

She giggled at her bit of humor. Her voice was steady and sure and did not give any indication that she was shocked by the possibility. It also hid whether she thought any of this was real.

I answered simply, "Two thousand thirteen."

Still seemingly unshaken, she continued her questioning.

"Did you use some kind of time machine or spaceship?"

The smirk on her face gave the impression she was starting to think that this was some kind of joke, and my honest answer did not convince her that we were serious.

Chapter Four

"We got here in an eighty-year-old Chevrolet. It's a 1933 coupe that I bought in 2008."

To fill the silence that followed, I added, "And it's still pretty reliable after all these years." I nervously laughed hoping that a little levity might keep her attention.

Mrs. Barton was never one to let me or anyone else get the last laugh. "Well, I would think so, after traveling back eighty years without a breakdown. You didn't break down, did you?"

She chuckled at her own little joke.

I nodded, "No."

I had to keep her focus on this as being really serious.

"Mrs. Barton, we haven't figured out how this happened yet but until we do, we need your help. We have some ideas but until then we need your help."

"If what you're telling me is true, and you haven't convinced me yet, I'm sure you need someone's help. However, my knowledge of time travel is quite limited. I doubt that I can help you go back to wherever you came from, even if, as you say, we are, or will become friends. First off, let's return to the primary issue. What proof other than your word can you give me of this incredible feat? Besides what you have told me about my piano, can you prove a relationship between us really starting in, when was that, oh yes, 1963?"

I was at a place I did not want to be. I had tons of information about the future. I knew when, where and how Jim Barton was going to die. Heck, I knew when she was going to die. Based on our future friendship I had already decided that I was never going to divulge any information like that. No one needs that cloud hanging over their head for decades. I knew it was hard enough for her when Jim died suddenly.

Waiting for Einstein

I have mentioned that I am a registered nurse. I guess it is time to say what kind. More specifically, I'm a hospice nurse. Over the last eight years I have cared for and signed more death certificates after the pronouncement of more patients than I dare to count. I don't enjoy telling family that the person they loved and cared for is gone but I have been told that I am good at it. With this enhanced sensitivity and training I had decided that I would never reveal any of these events in Mrs. Barton's future. I was determined to focus on only positive facts from the future to make my case. If it meant our being stuck in the past, so be it. My love and affection for this woman could never let me use this information in any self-serving way. It would be off limits and I had related this to Adam. To his credit he also agreed to keep this information close to the vest. He always amazes me with his caring nature. We would just have to navigate around these issues.

"Well. One of the first stories you ever told me was how you and Mr. Barton met."

Our hostess interrupted me gently.

"It's common knowledge that we met during our Vaudeville days."

"I know that was the story Jim put out there, but you told me the *real* story, your version. He babysat you backstage while your folks performed on stage well before you hit the boards as a chorus girl in your teens. Obviously, he had not been interested in you since he only saw you as a little girl. However, he didn't like people thinking that he robbed the cradle, literally."

She started to interject. I held my hand up.

"Please, let me finish. You told me that no one knew that story and I was the first person you had ever shared this with. That was in 1964."

Chapter Four

She looked at me with an increased realization that I might have actually heard it from her directly.

"I waited all those years before I told anyone?"

She was starting to sound like she was coming around to some level of belief.

"That is our secret history. Jim and I keep that story extremely private. He has never told that to anyone, not even his best friend, the Babe. Babe Ruth, that is."

"I know who you are referring to. Babe Ruth was, I mean, is Mr. Barton's best friend. You told me that your husband introduced Babe to his second wife Claire, who was a chorus girl in one of his shows."

"You certainly have done your homework."

She softly said this with some skepticism in the sound of her voice. That sounded like a lingering doubt.

"That was one of many things you told me about the both of you. Mr. Barton particularly likes to hang out with sports figures, but Babe is different. They're best friends."

I said this with utter confidence in my personal knowledge of this lady and her life as she had told me years ago. I could see that this tone might be chipping away at her skepticism.

I made direct eye contact trying to get her to lock eyes with me. I figured that if I looked her straight in the eyes, she would see that I was not making any of this up. Don't they say that when someone is lying, they cannot look you in the eyes?

"Do you believe me yet? What else do I have to do to convince you?"

Adam was thinking that his Pop and Mrs. Barton's mental duel was fun at first but the way he was seeing it there was a good chance it was heading toward a deadlock. Plus, it was just taking too long. His generation likes quick resolutions.

"Excuse me Pop, isn't our car a time machine?"

Mrs. Barton and I both turned toward my grandson. He had the floor.

"Let her see the car. Better yet, let her sit in the car."

I looked at him. "And?"

"AND let her see what's over the windshield."

"What a great idea!" I reached across the couch and 'high fived' him. Mrs. Barton looked on with some confusion. Do they 'high five' in 1933?

"Mrs. Barton, how would you like to see our time machine? I'm quite proud of it. I promise, you will come back and continue to partake of this excellent crumb cake in a whole new frame of mind."

She looked directly at my grandson and asked, "Master Adam, you really believe that your little Chevrolet will convince me that you're from the future? After all, they are plentiful. What makes yours, so special?"

"Oh, I think it will open your eyes, big time."

"Okay, young man, I'll let you lead the way."

We all got up from our seats and headed for the front door. I felt the rigid stare of the housekeeper on my back as we exited the house. We went past the restaurant to the parking area. I ran ahead of Mrs. Barton and opened the passenger side door. She placed her high-heeled shoe on the running board, demurely sat down on the worn but intact mohair seat and swung her legs in while keeping her knees together. She straightened her skirt to cover her legs.

Chapter Four

"Now what, young man?"

Adam simply directed her. "Look up."

She looked up and noticed the row of different pins attached to the small cloth panel above the windshield. The collection spanned the entire width of the car from door to door. She started reading the pins and buttons. Her brow furrowed giving her a definite look of confusion. Adam had done his job. Now it was my turn to start answering the questions that were definitely going to come.

The look on Mrs. Barton's face was priceless. Her jaw dropped in amazement. The first four directly above her were about the new President. A tarnished gold toned pin embossed with the word *Souvenir* had an attached red, white and blue ribbon which held a large button that hung down with a picture of FDR and announcing his inauguration on March 3, 1933. No big deal. This was not exactly news by this time. However, the next button simply stated *We Want FDR AGAIN*. The third button was a small molded white donkey with a white plastic banner hanging from it that read *AGAIN in '40*. The last one simply read *Roosevelt and Truman.*

The next button announced that the New York Giants were the *1933 World Series Champs.* And another pin showed a horse's head surrounded with embossed letters, *SEABISCUIT-1933-1948.*

Katie didn't say a word at first. Was that a good sign? By the look on her face, with eyes squinting, furrowed brow, and no smile, the things she read over the windshield had not had the effect that we had hoped for.

"Those could be more predictions than things that have already happened."

Adam and I looked at each other as if to ask, *How can we convince her?*

"Pop, THE MONEY!"

I gently nudged Katie to exit the car to gain access to the front seat. Adam had already run to the other side to help with lifting the cushion to get at our unusable currency from the future. If official U.S. currency could not convince her, then I had no arguments left.

I pulled open the Ziplock sandwich bag that kept the bills dry and handed her the more modern, smaller currency. "Please, Mrs. Barton, look at the date on these bills, where it says the Series."

"That's got to convince you that we are not making this up," Adam added with desperation in his voice.

She slowly unfolded the bills. She looked closely at the small print on a twenty flipping it over more than once to take in all the details of the engravings. She did the same with a ten, then a five, and eventually a single dollar. She went back to the first bill as if to look for something to change.

"They are quite small." She rubbed the surface of the legal tender, seeming to test the quality of the paper. "They feel like real money." She followed suit with each one. "They all feel like real money. I will admit that you have some compelling evidence here. Nevertheless, I am reserving my opinion, reserving my final decision for a time down the road as we get to know each other."

She looked at me with that smile that I had come to love years from now and said with her distinctive giggle, "Until then, you may call me Kitty, Bobby."

Chapter Four

A chill ran down my spine because no matter how much I complained about her calling me by that name in my teens she insisted on doing it anyway.

I looked at her a little stunned and confused.

"I think I'm a little old to be called *Bobby*."

"According to you, you're not even a glint in your father's eyes yet so *Bobby* fits you just fine."

Another giggle punctuated her observation.

"Let's go back inside and figure out how we can help you until the two of you can get back home. You do have a plan, I hope. I just love an adventure, don't you?"

The burly housekeeper removed herself from her post at the front window as we walked back to the house.

I also realized that I was going to have to get used to calling her Kitty after decades of always thinking of her as Katie. I did wonder why she introduced herself to my family as Katie so many years in the future. I also realized how unimportant that was at this time.

CHAPTER FIVE
The Joke
March 18, 1933

Katie, or now Kitty, was more than true to her word. She introduced us to her husband the next day without giving away our secret. My father gave me the best calling card to give Mr. Barton, a truly great Irish joke. Jim sat back in his chair at Barton's Place the next afternoon. Kitty knew that I would have to stand on my own with him if he was going to help us. I had to hide the fact that I was truly in awe of this man and his talent. Of course, that was mainly because of Kitty's influence on my younger-self years from now. I knew that he was yet to create some of the most memorable characters in Broadway history in *Tobacco Road*, *The Iceman Cometh*, and *Paint Your Wagon*.

If my Dad's joke failed, it might crush any chance I had to be in his company. No one told this joke better than my Dad. However, he was not around for comparison and even if he was here, I doubt he had heard the joke yet. My hope was that my interpretation would be entertaining and polished enough to convince Mr. Barton that we were somehow worthy enough to be kept around in some capacity.

"An Irish priest was stationed in a tiny Catholic parish in downtown London. Every Sunday he would verbally abuse the congregation." I continued in my best "Lucky Charms" Irish accent.

"And the British people be damned to hell! This whole island with all its British souls, living and dead, will be dragged to hell

Chapter Five

in a ball of flame and every British soul will rot for all eternity for what they've done to the Irish."

I continued with the story that the parishioners were so upset that they went to the bishop and complained. The next day the bishop summoned the priest to his office.

"Father Murphy, if you don't stop with all this IRA crap, I'll send you so far into the coal fields that you'll never see the light of day. To keep that smart Irish mouth of yours out of trouble, no more sermons! I want you to just read the gospel and get off the pulpit. I don't want any more complaints!

"Well, there was no way that the Irishman was going to let the bishop have the last word. The following Sunday was Palm Sunday. The priest started to read the gospel. And the Lord was seated around the table with all the Apostles and said, 'Today, one of you shall betray me.' All the apostles around the table repeated, 'Lord is it I? Lord is it I? Lord is it I?'"

Then in my best British cockney, I delivered the punch line. "Then that black-hearted Judas said, 'Blimey Gov'nor, ya bloody well don't think it t'was me?'"

Jim's head flew back with a hearty laugh and I knew that I was somehow in his good graces. My Dad's favorite joke saved the day.

"I never heard that one before. Did you write that yourself?"

"I cannot lie. It was my Dad's and I repeat it in his loving memory."

"I'm not saying it isn't a great joke, but in my family, we only tell originals, those that we come up with on our own. My Grandfather and Pa never handed down a joke and I live by that rule as well. I'm proud to say that I have upheld that tradition. You have a gift. If you use it to tell other people's jokes it's being squandered. So, come up with your own and then you can be a great joke teller."

"I appreciate the advice. I think I will leave that business to the professionals like you."

I was a little cowed by his critique, however, I understood his point. Either way, the joke broke the ice and was the start of a great friendship.

If generosity was central to Kitty's personality it was obvious what drew her to Jim. They were true soulmates. It did not take much to convince him to give me a job driving him to the different venues. The job included watching the stage door entrance at the theaters while he performed.

Jim was between shows in 1933. He had already finished a hit run on Broadway in *Sweet and Low* in 1931. He filled in the time before he would start his historic 1934 to 1941 run as Jeeter Lester in *Tobacco Road*, with frequent top billings at the Palace and the Cotton Club to name a few. Of course, at this time he did not know he would be approached for *Tobacco Road,* or that it would keep him occupied for the foreseeable future once he took over his record-setting lead role.

There were many large and small venues for dancers in the twenties and early thirties. They were all speakeasies since they all served alcohol in one form or another. Before Prohibition, there were about 16,000 saloons in New York City alone. Following the ratification of the 18th Amendment and the passing of the Volstead Act, speakeasies replaced the saloons, and the number grew to somewhere between 30,000 and 100,000. Granted, some were just a room with a table, a chair, a bottle of booze with a glass; many were much more.

Chapter Five

One of the crown jewels of this type of establishment was the Cotton Club in New York City which married great entertainment with drinking. What made the Club distinctive was the fact that the band was all black and almost every entertainer was an African-American while many of the patrons were white. In this era, African-Americans were called negros or blacks. These were really different times from our cultural sensitivity in the 21st Century. The concept of things being "politically correct" was not part of the vernacular yet.

White entertainers regularly performed in "blackface" in their acts. The most noted was Al Jolson, who was of Jewish heritage. I also knew that Jim Barton did blackface more than once. He even wrote and performed in a short film in 1927 titled *After Seben* in which he played a black man. Amazingly, all the other actors and actresses in the piece were black. He was the only white in the movie. I had seen it on YouTube just last year when I searched his name. That was the first time that I had seen how well he danced in his forties. It blew me away to see how original his dance routine was and how difficult the moves were. However, he made them look easy as he glided across the dance floor.

There seemed to be another motive for this short film because it also featured incredible dancing on the part of the black performers as well. Did he make this film for the black movie-goers to show them that a white man could dance as well as a black man, or was he trying to get a white audience to acknowledge the talent of the black performers? Whatever his intentions, I came to the realization, watching him dance, that he might have been the best 'white' dancer over all the others of that era. That's saying a lot when you think of all the hoofers on stage and screen.

Waiting for Einstein

Fred Astaire was at the height of his career and I was always stumped as to why Jim never got the recognition he deserved with the general public. His fellow artists definitely knew. Bing Crosby, one of the biggest stars of the '30's and 40's always said that Barton was one of his favorite top ten performers. The other thing that struck me was his makeup for the movie. Unlike most blackface makeup which was done with a wide white area left around the mouth and eyes, Barton's was done to make him look like an actual black man. It seemed to be more of a tribute to their talent rather than a comical parody. I knew for a fact that one of his close friends was Bill "Bojangles" Robinson and I could not imagine him mocking his talent in any way. If there is a code of ethics for time travelers it might include a level of tolerance, without acceptance, of the norms of the society we visit.

The first time I saw how well James could dance was years ago (in the 1960's) when Kitty called me and alerted me to when there would be an airing of the movie, *The Daughter of Rosie O'Grady* on television. He made this movie in 1949 when he was fifty-nine-years old and closed the movie with the most incredible dance routine, acting like a man on ice skates, when he was actually in dance shoes, slipping and sliding all over the stage, catching his balance every which way. He did this so convincingly that you really thought he was on real ice and it showcased only the tip of his incredible dancing ability.

One of my first nights driving Jim and Kitty to a performance was to one of the most infamous speakeasies of the era. Never, in my wildest dreams, did I think that I would get to see him perform in his prime. Yet, here I was, watching from off stage, as he glided across the dance floor at the Cotton Club with the grace of a gazelle and with moves that a double-jointed person would find difficult.

Chapter Five

I was in awe and somewhat confused that the theater public would somehow forget this incredible talent in the future. History is fickle. Bill "Bojangles" Robinson, Fred Astaire, Donald O'Connor, Sammy Davis, Jr., and Gene Kelly became dancing legends that most people recognized for decades as great dancers long after their careers ended and yet this incredible talent was somehow only remembered by the most dedicated theater and dance aficionados.

Then I spied Kitty sitting at a small table just off the dance floor. Her evening gown was a stunning lilac satin that draped over her narrow shoulders. It nipped in at the waist over her crossed legs onto the chair to the floor like it was liquid. The love and admiration showed in her every facial movement. She had insisted that I sit with her. I protested that I was not dressed appropriately and convinced her that I could enjoy the show from backstage. She kept loyal to her desire to see Jim perform as often as possible. She was the definition of what a great marriage should be. I never tired of being in her company. Her positive vibe permeated any room she was in.

I knew that one evening I wanted to bring Adam to see James Barton dance in person. Adam loved the theater as much as any kid could. My wife Henny and I enjoyed watching all our musical videos with Adam as he was growing up. *Yankee Doodle Dandy* with James Cagney was one of his favorites. His portrayal of George M. Cohan was the stuff of movie legend. Adam loved everything about the story. However, I was certain that he was more worried about seeing his parents, brother, and family again. Since he was here, in this time, why not try to enjoy some part of it and take his mind off our situation.

I had another concern about waiting months for Einstein while watching from the wings as Jim danced. I kept hearing my own mantra that every event has a purpose. I had been looking for something or someone that would give me a sign as to why we had been transported back in time. This could not have been a simple random cosmic accident. We were here for a reason.

If we didn't find the answer to my question, this could become the longest that either of us would be away from our loved ones. The last time I was away from Henny for any length of time was right after we were married, April 17, 1971. When we came home from our honeymoon in Pennsylvania my orders were waiting in the mail to report to Fort Knox, May 14^t, for my basic training and tank crewman school. This was the required training for the New York Army National Guard unit I had joined on Long Island.

We did not have much money and during our entire first summer as a married couple we could only afford to fly me home one weekend to be together between basic and advanced training in tank school. I was gone again until September 11. God, I really missed her now and I could not even entertain the thought that I might never see her again. I quickly pushed that thought out of my head.

Adam had been away from his family just last summer for two weeks as part of a "Friends Across the Ocean Program" which sends young students overseas to share time and stay with families in Europe. He had a great experience visiting with families in Greece, Italy, France, and Spain.

This was a different situation. We were not only away from our families measured in miles by being on Long Island, we were distanced by time measured in decades well in the past. And time was what we would have to endure until Einstein would finally settle in New Jersey in October. I still hadn't figured out how I was going to approach him or, more importantly, how I was going to convince him about the truth of our fantastical

Chapter Five

dilemma. My hope lay in the fact that I knew he believed that time travel was possible and that he would be delighted to meet a time traveler. I was equally certain that he had no idea how to do it or he would have published that information by now. He wasn't that modest of a man who would not want to take credit for such a discovery.

While I sat at the kitchen table in our rental every morning looking across at Adam, I wondered if this situation would be one of the great adventures of our lives, or that we were prisoners of time, never to see our loved ones again. I was determined that I would not let that happen. We would get back home.

Until then, I was going to find out what our situation had to offer and give Adam an experience that would keep his mind off our problems. The Bartons were the key to seeing some incredible things and meeting some of the major personalities of the times. I was sure of that.

Back in the future, Katie had told me stories about her life and she liked to drop names of theater, movies, and sports figures who she and Jim had known. He was not always seeking them out either. All these celebrities were old friends or simply fixtures in the New York City circles of the rich and famous. He truly was that big of a star. It was going to be interesting to see how Adam was going to manage this lifestyle. When we returned home, he would be the most knowledgeable kid on the planet about the 1930's, bar none.

CHAPTER SIX
Colors, Sounds, and Aromas
March 20, 1933

I was still trying to get used to seeing this world in color. Until now all my visual impressions of 1930's were in black and white or sepia through movies, photos, family archives, old newsreels or documentary films. I was also familiar with the sounds of the times from motion pictures, the same documentaries and records. The smells and aromas were a whole new experience. There were so many new scents and smells when Adam and I walked down the street and our noses were assaulted almost from the time we left our apartment starting in the hallway. There the smell of meals being prepared leaching out from the other kitchens on our floor as well as the restaurant below.

The street was another experience with the belching exhaust from the cars and trucks. Thick, choking clouds of oily exhaust hung in the air from vehicles needing serious ring and valve jobs. None of these cars had any emissions protection which was required for cars in our time. The horse-drawn junk wagon and, fruit-and-vegetable carts had an exhaust of a more solid nature as piles of manure were left behind on the street leaving a clear and odorous trail that you could step in if you were not paying attention when crossing the street. Vendors making all kinds of foods to lure pedestrians to eat, added to this man-made soup for the nostrils that defies description. If smell-o-vision had been invented for movies, all the cinemas would have struggled to survive.

Chapter Six

From our perspective of the mid-20th to early 21st centuries, it always seemed like a dark and dreary world which heavily punctuated the harsh realities of the Depression. In reality, it was just as full of colors as our time but magnified by a cacophony of sound and aromas new and different to our modern ears and noses.

The natural colors of this world were well appreciated. Then there was the explosive color that only theater can create with stage lighting. Thanks to the generosity of the Bartons, we were privy to that incredible spectrum created by the stage designers of New York theater of the thirties.

Cars crisscrossed the streets in a rainbow of colors. I felt that I was in a car-nut heaven as Packards, Franklins, Lincolns, Nashes, Hudsons, and Pierce Arrows tangled with Chevys, Fords, Dodges, Oldsmobiles, Grahams, Studebakers, and Pontiacs all vying for space on the Brooklyn roads. The ever-present trolleys added to the confusion. Brand names that had already been snuffed out by the Depression were still all over the place like Daniels, Kissel, Willys-Knight, Durant, Dort, and Star. The more expensive brands tended to have a wider variety of colors that spanned the color spectrum. The less expensive machines only sported bright colors on occasion since you would have had to pay extra for the optional colors. They were mostly done in somber colors like dark greens and blues and most in stark black. It took a few weeks before I stopped pointing these cars out in wonder to Adam, who was showing less interest as he became increasingly homesick and more concerned about our future.

Yes, it was true that there were real hardships for the masses with one-in-four men unemployed during the Depression. Given my salary from James Barton, we were able to afford housing and have food on the table without any difficulty for the time being.

Waiting for Einstein

We were paying our rent on time, buying food and putting fuel in the gas-guzzling Chevy that I needed to commute to wherever Jim needed me. Most of the time, I simply drove to his home in Mineola and then I drove him around in his huge beautiful 1933 Lincoln. Jim paid me fifteen dollars a week which was more than anyone else was paid for a similar job. With that amount, we were doing well.

To his credit Adam was not going to sit around and do nothing while we waited for Einstein. He got a job selling newspapers on the street. He was lucky to get a corner on Flatbush Avenue selling the *Brooklyn Eagle* getting a penny for every copy he sold. At this time, the *Eagle* was one of the top selling papers in America by volume. I'd say he was lucky to get this corner because these *newsies* were extremely territorial and would fight tooth-and-nail to defend their turf. Adam's predecessor had moved away and Adam had just been in the right place having gone to the paper's headquarters looking for work the same day. The distribution manager just got word that he had lost another paperboy. He turned around quickly spotting all the boys waiting for him to notice them. It was easy to spot Adam who was a head above any other kid.

"Hey, you, kid. How old are ya?" He shouted while pointing at him.

"Fourteen, sir!" He answered as loud as he could.

"What are they feeding you? Well, kid, you'll need that size if you want to keep the corner I'm giving you. Do you think you're tough enough? You're definitely big enough."

"I am, sir. Just give me that corner and *The Eagle* will own that spot."

Chapter Six

"I like a kid with spunk. You got it kid. Go see Tommie over there and get a stack. We'll make arrangements to deliver more to ya later."

All the other kids started to complain and moan. "Aw, man." "That's not fair! I was here before him." "Hey, Mister! I'm as tough as he is."

The man answered them with clenched teeth holding an unlit cigar in his teeth out of the corner of his mouth.

"Quit ya whining, or you'll never get any papers from me. Ya sound like a bunch of babies and I don't hire babies. Got it?"

No one answered as they all clammed up in fear of finding themselves on the outs with this man. Adam got a stack of papers from Tommie as directed and hefted the tied bundle onto his shoulder and started the long walk to his appointed corner. He had to ask a few pedestrians for directions. He eventually found his spot. Adam went straight to the curb and held up a single copy while standing with one foot on the rest of the stack on the sidewalk.

He mimicked what he had seen in the old movies on Turner Classics in our time.

"Get your latest copy of *The Brooklyn Eagle* here!" He yelled.

In a moment a man came up to him.

"I'll take a copy, son." He flipped him a coin which hit him in the chest and fell to the ground at his feet. Adam handed him a paper before he picked up the nickel. Within a half hour all the papers were sold, and he was catching almost every tossed coin with his left hand easily. He sprinted back to the paper for more and by the end of the day had sold 100 copies and brought home a dollar.

A dollar went a long way here. Gasoline was ten cents a gallon. A loaf of bread was seven cents, while a gallon of milk was forty-two cents. The price of the average car was around $550 and you could buy a house in the suburbs for under $2,000. It might as well have been a million for most people since the average weekly pay was only fifteen dollars.

So, things looked cheaper but all the pricing was relative to the economy of the times. Adam was bringing in two to three dollars a day while Jim Barton continued to pay me fifteen a week. Considering that we had just dropped into the Depression we were doing fine by any standard.

CHAPTER SEVEN
A Tough Guy
March 22, 1933

There is something interesting about areas with dense populations. You seem to run into people much more often than you would imagine. I was always surprised at how often I ran into my grand uncle Harry McLaughlin, my Mom's uncle, while I was attending St. Francis College in Brooklyn Heights during the late sixties. He was the second to the youngest of my Grandma's siblings. The point is that he did not live anywhere near my college in Brooklyn which had millions of people walking around town every day. Yet, at least a half a dozen times during my college years, I bumped into him on the streets of Brooklyn near my college.

It was no surprise then, that I had seen my father earlier this month in his car on Court Street and then again today at a speakeasy in the Bay Ridge section of Brooklyn. Jim was checking this club out as a possible venue to dance and entertain until he landed something again on Broadway. That's when I spotted a young Julian Majeski coming out of the office area. He came over to where we were standing and tipped his fedora to the club manager quietly taking his place at his side. He never cracked a smile as his light blue eyes scanned us and assessed that we were not packing any heat. When I was a kid he always told me that he made bathtub gin for the mob. Now, from my first-hand observations I could see that this was a creative understatement. It was obvious that he had other, more substantial job duties with the mob.

I've been saying that nothing happens by accident. The fact that I was bumping into him again told me that he might be the reason I had traveled back in time. I had the sense that I needed to get to know this young man and jumped at the opportunity.

"Nice that you could join us, Mr. Majewski," I said looking directly into his eyes.

I put the emphasis on his last name by using the Polish pronunciation, "Mayevski" to get his attention and it worked.

He had to be using the "W" in his name because I knew that at this point in his life, he had not discovered that it was missing on his birth certificate. When my father was born in 1915, most people were born at home and delivered with the guidance of a midwife. In his case, she was Irish and that was his reasoning why his name was misspelled. He would not discover the error until he had to obtain a copy of his birth certificate to apply for his marriage license in late 1937. His marriage would occur in January of 1938. He said that he did not have the money to have the record corrected. I think he preferred the sound of his name without it. It was like nails on a blackboard to him when he heard others address him as "Mr. Ma-juice-ski."

His demeanor changed as his head snapped quickly with his eyes drilling a mean look into mine. With his thick Brooklyn accent, he answered in a low, threatening tone.

"How do ya know my name old man?"

He stressed "old man" in a way that was not meant to be respectful.

Since I hadn't really thought that he might react badly when I used his name I had to think fast.

Chapter Seven

"Brooklyn's a small place and I heard it somewhere. It stuck in my head since it's almost the same as mine. It was easy to remember."

I extended my hand to shake his.

"My name is Bob Majeski. Pleased to meet you also, young man."

I stayed with the American pronunciation to keep the sound as different as possible. We shook hands and I did my best to give him as close to a vise grip as I could to let him know that there was more to this "old" man than met the eye. He reciprocated with a tight grip, however, it was not as strong as mine which really surprised me. It was now obvious to me that the legendary grip he had when he was my age had not been acquired yet. That would come with the future manual labor he would do during his working career.

When our hands touched, I got that same feeling that I had when I first spotted him in the roadster. I felt a shiver as the hair stood up on the back of my neck. We kept eye contact until I relaxed my grip giving him a chance to break the hold. He returned his hand down to his side and I found it funny to see him flexing his fingers as if he felt the blood circulating, and return feeling to his fingers. My glance returned to his face, and I saw no expression that gave me the sense that he had any idea that this was nothing more than a first-time casual meeting. He was too busy trying to look like his hand didn't hurt.

Jim brought us back to the task at hand.

"If you two Polacks are done getting acquainted, I'd like to get back to business here."

He laughed to show that he was not angry.

Waiting for Einstein

We all continued walking around the club while the manager showed Barton the dance floor which was surrounded with small round cabaret tables.

"We can push the tables closer together and away to make the dance floor bigger if you need it without losing a seat."

"I could dance on a pinhead if I had to. No, son, this is just fine. I'll put on a show that will pack the house. Now, tell me about the band."

The manager informed Barton that he paid band members well to attract better musicians from the big bands which were in town. He obviously had a good ear as he mentioned some of the young men who had played at the club.

"We've had some good guys play here and the word is out that they can make as much money under the table here between their gigs with their bands. Bix played here a few times. Also, Glenn Miller, Benny Goodman, Gene Krupa, Tex Beneke, and a guy named Nelson Riddle. Even Joe Venuti likes to bring his violin at times. I only let the best of the musicians play here. Don't know how long I can get them. They all keep talking about fronting their own bands someday."

We toured the bandstand and even got a glimpse at the kitchen before we ended up in the office to finalize a calendar. Barton and the manager sealed the deal with a shake. There were no paper contracts to leave a trail that any legitimate entertainer wanted to connect them with such places. I found this funny since it seemed like everyone knew where and when any entertainer was performing. The audience was full of public officials from City Hall to law enforcement. There was an unwritten rule to keep such agreements verbal so that the police could say that they did not find any evidence of these personalities connected to illegal venues other than hearsay.

Chapter Seven

As we were leaving, Jim and the manager said goodbyes with a last handshake. Surprisingly, Julius extended his hand.

"By the way, my friends call me Jules even though my name's Julius. Maybe we can meet again, old man. Who knows, maybe we can figure out if we are related somewhere. Your name is close to mine."

There was no edginess in his words this time.

When my Dad introduced himself as Julius, I remembered that at this point in his life, he believed that was his birth name. Family and friends always referred to him by that name and he used it all through grade school and even after his marriage to my Mom. Just as his birth certificate had revealed the misspelling of his last name before his marriage, he also found out that his given name was really Julian.

He questioned his Mother about why everyone called him 'Julius.'

Her answer was simple and direct.

"That's your nickname. Julian is your baptismal name."

Returning to the moment, I took his hand, I answered.

"Oh, I have a feeling that we will see a lot of each other."

However, in my mind I wasn't sure if it would be in this time or only after my birth sixteen years from now. I didn't try to squeeze his hand as hard this time since he seemed to have softened his approach toward me and I wanted him to subconsciously know that I was open to the possibility of meeting again.

I drove Barton's '33 Lincoln KB convertible sedan back to his home on The Island. Sitting behind the wheel of this custom-bodied, Brunn-built, automotive masterpiece was a thrill I never thought I'd ever have. With the light blue body accented by dark royal blue fenders and metal covered side mounts this car stood out in this part of Brooklyn as we cruised back toward his home. It was like driving a freight train onto the open road except the ride was incredibly smooth. The two-and-a-half-ton behemoth's V-12 motor effortlessly pushed the car down the road.

"You're not talking. What's up, Pop?"

Jim had been calling me Pop ever since he heard Adam call me that in his company. It seemed appropriate to him since I was definitely his senior by many years. Jim didn't like silence any more than I did.

"I'm sorry. I guess I was just thinking about that young guy, you know, the Polack."

"It is interesting that your names are almost the same. Be careful. That won't buy you much with a guy like that. I get along with them, but I watch my back. This is a tough bunch, and you don't want to get on their wrong side. There was a time when the Irish mob ran Brooklyn. Later, the Italian mob came over from Manhattan and the rest is history."

"Don't worry about me. I grew up here. I picked my teeth with the bones of guys like that kid when I was younger."

I had to laugh inside at that last phrase since I always used it when I went to St. John's Prep in the Bedford Stuyvesant section of Brooklyn and even later when Henny and I moved to Connecticut in 1973. I still use it but only in jest. Adam's father, my son David, just rolls his eyes when he hears it remembering how I used it to challenge someone with the hope, on my part, that they would back off from any real physical confrontation. It always worked.

Saying you're from Brooklyn, especially in Connecticut, still verified that you were tougher than your stature might imply. Being only five-foot-five, I've had to occasionally remind people that I was more threatening than I might appear. In high school,

Chapter Seven

I only had three fights with bullies and they were all *one punch* affairs.

I also had another rule. As soon as I realized that my verbal warnings were not working, I made sure that I hit first. This worked well and the stunned adversary never struck back, not wanting to know if my second hit would be as bad as my first. I still don't know if I'm really that tough since I never had to go a full round with anyone. I realized that if I was going to survive Brooklyn again, and in the 1930's, I was going to have to dust off my old 'attitude' to keep my grandson and me safe.

I dropped Mr. Barton off at his house, put his car in the garage and drove my little Chevy back to Brooklyn. Adam had a good day also, bringing in another few bucks. We decided to take in a late movie at the Paramount.

CHAPTER EIGHT
Movies

I love movies! I always have. I never knew life without television since I was born in 1949, the same year that commercial television first took off. I had missed the era of the radio dramas which we were now listening to in our apartment on a cathedral dome table top radio that came with the furnishings. This was our entertainment after dinner most nights that we stayed in. Shows like *The Shadow, The Lone Ranger,* and *The Green Hornet* were radio plays in serial form with every episode ending in a cliffhanger so that the listeners would tune in next time. My older siblings told me about this form of entertainment. I grew up watching all the old movies of the 30's and 40's on New York's WPIX, Channel Eleven. I also learned things on television with Miss Frances' *Ding Dong School* and remember the first season of *Captain Kangaroo. Howdy Doody, Andy's Gang, Abbott and Costello,* and *The Three Stooges* provided pure delight for children of my age as well.

Many of the radio shows came to television as well. *The Lone Ranger* led a long list of cowboy heroes and detective dramas as well as sitcoms, which were on every channel. New York television had many hosts for the children's shows who became iconic. Gabby Hayes, Sandy Becker, Officer Joe Bolton, Andy Devine, Buffalo Bob, and Shari Lewis were as familiar to my friends and me as any uncle or aunt. More serious fare, presenting current and past history, was also there in the form of Walter Cronkite's *You are There* and *Victory at Sea,* while Perry

Chapter Eight

Como, Dinah Shore, Nat King Cole, and Lawrence Welk entertained with musical variety shows. My personal favorite was Sid Caesar's *Show of Shows*. This was live television comedy at its best in the '50s, and in my opinion, that was only equaled once, when Carol Burnett had one of the last great comedy/variety shows in the '70s.

There was one particular movie show that really appealed to me and got me hooked on the movies of the '30s and '40s as a kid growing up in the '50s. It was called *Million Dollar Movie*. What was most interesting was how they aired a movie. They would show the same movie four times a day for an entire week. One summer all the kids in my neighborhood watched every airing of *Yankee Doodle Dandy*. James Cagney won an Oscar for his portrayal of George M. Cohan. No kid in the neighborhood wanted to be the only one that had not seen all twenty-eight airings. This was followed by a backyard re-creation presented by all of us for our parents. I don't think any of the kids missed a word of the screenplay.

Adam and I were actually living in the era when Cagney was a rising star in Hollywood. Barton and Cohan were still a force on Broadway. One night I told Adam I was going to take him to the movies. This was going to be the first time that Adam was going to see a black and white movie on the big screen. I remembered the first time when he saw a black and white movie in 2003. He was only five-years-old. I picked *Yankee Doodle Dandy*. I wanted to see if this movie could catch Adam the way it did with all the kids in my age group fifty years early. It was fun to watch his eyes which didn't seem to blink through most of the movie. When it was done, he begged me to let him take the DVD home to show his mom. My daughter-in-law, Karen, later told me that when they finally found time to watch the movie, he gingerly took the disc out of the holder and told her that he had to be careful because "this movie is really old. It's in black and white."

It was only apropos that the first movie we would go to in 1933 was a Cagney flick, *Lady Killer,* with Mae Clark and Margaret Lindsay. The film was preceded by a News Reel. Adam didn't seem surprised by this because he already knew that we were in a time period when there was no television or Internet to get the news other than print, radio, or newsreels.

His livelihood currently was based on selling the news and today the news was not good. On the big screen, moving images showed Adolf Hitler addressing a massive crowd from a balcony in Berlin with the narrator announcing that he was the new Chancellor of Germany. We looked on in true sadness, both of us knowing that this was only the beginning of arguably the darkest period in human history. We had talked extensively about trying to let someone know about the impending doom that we knew was coming with the Nazis, Mussolini, and, of course, Imperial Japan's sneak attack on Pearl Harbor on December 7, 1941.

I can't explain how we knew this, but we were certain that we were not here to try and change world history. Even if we could get to the powers that be, it would be hard, if not impossible, to get anyone to believe us. We doubted that there would be the open-mindedness of a Kitty Barton anywhere in government. I was convinced that this was not the reason we were transported back in time. Believing that nothing happens by accident and there is always a purpose in all the events in our lives, I could add to this that we are constantly learning and growing from everything that comes into our lives or, in some cases, what is thrown in our paths.

Chapter Eight

In my opinion we had traveled back in time for a different reason. Although I was equally sure that we could not possibly alter world events, we just might be able to protect our own future. I still wasn't sure what we were supposed to do, outside of trying to return to our own time. The hope was that opportunities would present themselves and we would recognize them in a timely fashion. Maybe it was something as simple as appreciating our own world in the future when we returned, always hoping that was possible.

The images of the rise of the Nazis in Germany, as they were happening, gave us increased concern and motivation to find a way back. At our biological ages in this time, it was not hard to calculate that Adam would turn twenty-one when World War II broke out. There was no way I wanted him caught up in that epic conflict knowing that he would not hesitate to enlist to help defeat the Nazis. That vision of impending doom was very unsettling for the both of us. Finally, the main feature started.

Unlike films in the modern era, all the credits were run before the movie started. This did not take long since only one or two people were credited with any task in making the film. In 2013, 98% of the credits run at the end of the movie and it takes as long as some short films. The list of people involved is in tiny print to allow for the cluster of hundreds of names to fit on the screen. If you read them closely like I do you'll find the name of the guy who replaced the broken shoelace on the star's left sneaker. In 1933, it looked like only twenty people were needed to make a film. We sat back and enjoyed the short credits quickly getting to the movie.

Cagney was great. It was interesting to see him at the beginning of his career. It was not hard to see the dancer in him as he walked across the set, or had a fist fight with another character, like the best choreographer. Although the storyline was a bit trivial, it was still entertaining and lots of fun. It was a great diversion from our problems as movies were designed to do. After all, most people sitting there were just like us, only they were trying to forget about the hard times of the Great Depression.

We had joined the masses of this decade. During our stay in 1933 we were not alone since 70-80% of the population went to the movies weekly. This became one of our major escapes and what a year it was for films. We came from a time when digital special effects could create the amazing world of *Avatar*, or bring any DC Comic superhero to life. While there was no limitation to the modern filmmaker's imagination, we were impressed with the accomplishments of the pioneers of special effects when we saw *King Kong* and *The Invisible Man*.

The visual effects were cutting edge for the time and to our surprise just as amazing. We discussed the fact that we were truly surprised by the quality of the films and acting as we might have been in our time. We found ourselves watching King Kong climb the Empire State Building and Claude Rains take his wrappings off, revealing his invisibility with the same wonder as all the other movie-goers around us. Hollywood did rely on the imagination of the audience to bridge the gap in their technical skills. It was nice to realize that our imagination had not been blunted by our dependence on digital effects. Adam and I came out of these movies just as satisfied by the filmmakers' storytelling as in our own time.

CHAPTER NINE
Crossing Paths
April 8, 1933

We had just gotten out of a late showing of *The Gold Diggers of 1933* at the Paramount Theater on Flatbush Avenue. Traffic was brutal as it always was at the end of a movie with people going in every direction to find buses, cabs, and in our case, parked cars down the side streets. I had become good at marking where I had parked the Chevy after two embarrassing evenings spent roaming the neighborhood over and over until I realized I was on the wrong side of Flatbush Avenue. Adam did not let me live this down for a while and I was not about to give him more ammunition to harass me.

After we easily found the car this time, I had taken a side street to avoid a traffic jam when I turned into another street. Before I realized it, we were stopped dead due to a cluster of paddy wagons halfway down the block. I turned quickly, shifting the coupe into reverse with the intention of backing out before I got boxed in. I was too late. A huge 1928 Packard screeched to a stop, inches from my rear bumper. He could not move for all the cars rolling in behind him. A sigh of frustration escaped me as I looked at Adam and threw my hands up. To kill some time, I started a conversation with Adam asking him what he thought of the movie.

"For sure, Busby Berkley knows how to make a spectacle."

Before I could throw in my two cents, a young guy in a suit came running down the sidewalk from the direction of the commotion and ran up to the rear of our car. I thought he was going to run between the cars to cross the street. Instead, he reached over the back of the car and grabbed the handle at the top of the trunk lid, turned it, flipped the lid open and with incredible agility jumped into the rumble seat. The car bounced from the force of his entry and settled quickly. I rolled down the back window which was designed for ventilation as well as socializing with passengers in the rumble seat.

Presenting my best Brooklyn tough guy persona, I yelled at the guy.

"Hey, Jerk! Does this look like a cab to you?"

A young, deep voice came out of the darkness.

"Just shut up, buddy. Look straight ahead and if anyone asks, we've been together all night."

"If you don't get your ass out of my car this 'buddy' is going to kick your butt from here to the Brooklyn Bridge."

I turned forward and waited for a response. God, I hope he didn't take me up on that. I knew I could hold my own but I had my doubts that I'd come out on top. I adjusted my mirror to get a glimpse of the unwanted passenger. I could not believe it. Under the shadow of his fedora brim I saw his face.

"Jules?"

What the ... My future Dad had just jumped into my rumble seat.

He leaned forward and squinted into the car and finally recognized me.

"Great! It's old 'Bob' right?"

"I'm really getting tired of being called 'old,' KID," I answered in my best tough and now annoyed Brooklyn drawl.

Our attention was focused on our new companion in the rumble seat and neither of us saw the cop walk up to the

Chapter Nine

passenger door until he tapped the window with his nightstick. We both jumped and Jules put his head down to block his face from view. The stout man in the long, ungainly, dark police uniform spun his clenched hand indicating to Adam to roll the window down. Adam complied quickly.

"Have either of you seen a guy run past here?"

Boy this guy had a thick Irish accent.

"No, Sir." I said shaking my head side to side to reinforce my answer.

"Who's in the back seat?"

He pointed at our new arrival with his nightstick.

"My nephew, Sir."

"Really?" the cop answered with a wry smile. "What's your name, mister?"

"Bob, Robert Majeski, Sir."

Indicating who he wanted an answer from next he pointed his nightstick at my grandson.

"And you, kid?"

"Adam Majeski, Sir."

He looked back to me and continued, "And the guy in the back seat?"

"Like I said, that's my nephew, Julius Majeski."

This time I deliberately pronounced his last name like mine.

The cop stepped toward the back of the car and addressed Jules in the rumble seat with a big grin.

"Is that the story tonight, Jules?"

My young friend returned the smile.

"That's right, Officer O'Connor. I'm just hanging out with family. Aren't you far from your home with all the other Micks up there in the Bronx? What brings you down here so far from your beat? Did you come here for the cleaner air? I heard it really stinks up there this time of year."

Officer O'Connor pointed a short thick finger at Jules.

"Listen, wise guy. They just raided a speakeasy down the block and I'm just here for the night to help me fellow officers. Sometimes there's more bums like you in Brooklyn than they can handle. Someone said they saw a guy that looks just like you running in this direction. How long have you been sittin' there?"

I jumped in.

"He's been with us all night, Officer O'Connor. We just came from the Paramount where we saw *The Gold Diggers*."

I was sure that would give Jules enough to add to his alibi. My Dad was always good at picking up a story line and embellishing as if it was rehearsed. In my teens we could continue a nonsensical story for as long as we wanted before our family realized they were being had.

O'Connor raised an eyebrow. Addressing Jules he asked, "Was it a good show there, Polack? The brogue emphasized "Polack."

"It was a great show. Dick Powell and Ruby Keeler were neva betta."

"Boy, you Poles really stick t'gether. I'll be taking me leave now. When da traffic moves get your arses out of my sight."

As an afterthought he added, "And stay out of me precinct and the Bronx, Jules. We don't need you Brooklyn bums bringing your troubles to our part of town. We've got enough scum of our own t'deal wit. I mean it now, or I'll cuff you and run you in so fast it'll make your head spin."

"And a 'Good Evening' to you, too, Officer O'Connor."

The cop turned and as he got back to the sidewalk Jules added under his breath, "Dumb Mick."

Chapter Nine

Suddenly, a realization came to me. I could not stop myself and asked, "Hey, excuse me, Officer O'Connor. Would you have two boys named Timothy and John?"

He laughed heartily.

"Are we writin' a book now? You might be smarter than you look. It doesn't take a genius to guess that there would be a 'Timothy' or a 'John' in any Irish family. I'll be taking me leave now."

I gave it one last shot.

"And you have a daughter, Irene."

I didn't ask this time. O'Connor spun quickly. He moved quickly coming around to the driver's side this time and glared at me getting up close and in my face.

"That's enough now. If ya think you're goin' to rattle me from me duties because ya know me family you're wrong. If I find ya Polack mug anywhere near me family I'll kick ya fat Polish arse from here to County Cork where the rest of me family will finish ya off. There won't be enough of you left for a proper burial."

He was waving his nightstick in my face the whole time. It looked more like a short thick broomstick. The shiny black sticks you see in the movies were saved for dress parades. This was the everyday working stick and I'm sure it had done some damage more than once at the hands of this Irishman.

"And in respect for me girl, I will now bid you a final good riddance."

During this whole exchange I was reminded how thin peoples' skin was about their nationality since many were first-generation immigrants. It was still evident, even as late as the 1950's, when I was a kid. These were times when you or your family's country of origin was a major part of your identity. And the Irish liked to remind all the other immigrants that their ancestors came over from the old country way before most of others, even when it was obvious, they were off the boat themselves. The one commonality of all the nationalities also came out. Never appear to be threatening a man's family. You will rarely come out on top.

We saw O'Connor climb into the passenger seat of a paddy wagon up ahead and pull away from the front of the speakeasy. As the wagons started to head back to the station house, the traffic finally moved again. It would be so cool telling my Henny that I met her grandfather on the job, if I ever could.

Peering into the rearview mirror I locked eyes with Jules. "Where can I drop you off, Kid?"

"If it's not too far out of your way, 62nd between 2nd and 3rd."

Actually, I knew exactly where it was after years of Sundays visiting his parents, my grandparents' brownstone.

"Bay Ridge, it is then."

Jules sat back and enjoyed the ride. He took off his fedora and put it on his lap so it would not blow away. It was interesting to see his hair flying around as the air whipped over the roof into his face. That was a first for me since I never saw my Dad with hair except in pictures. By the time I came on board he was as bald as I am now.

Meanwhile, Adam wanted to question what he witnessed between me and the officer.

"What was that all about, Pop? You really rattled that guy."

"I guess I did. That wasn't my intention. You know Grandma's maiden name is O'Connor, right?"

"Yes. I know. Why? Do you think she's related to that policeman?"

Chapter Nine

"I'll have to tell you that I'm a little confused right now. Because we keep running into Jules, I thought I figured out that we are here because of him."

I pointed my thumb at the young man in the back trying to keep his hair out of his eyes.

"Now, I don't know again. It could be a coincidence but I'm pretty sure that was your Grandma's grandfather, the guy her family always referred to as "Big Dave" O'Connor. He's the one that came over from Banteer in County Cork, Ireland. If I'm right, then you just met your great-great-grandfather. Isn't Brooklyn a small world? Crazy, huh."

I've already said it. The bigger the city, the smaller it seems when it comes to bumping into people you know. When my wife and I started working on our family trees, we were also surprised to find that our families had crossed paths in death more than once. Amazingly, we found four branches of our ancestral families buried in Holy Cross Cemetery. Locals call it Flatbush Cemetery. In my family tree, Majewskis, McLaughlins, Harkins, and Burns were buried there while Gleesons, Hayes, and Hotters from Henny's side shared other plots. Yes, for all its size, Brooklyn could seem like a small town.

CHAPTER TEN
The Brownstone

Twenty minutes later we pulled up in front of the brownstone that I remembered so well from my early childhood in the '50s. Grandma and Pop Majewski's was a gathering place for all the Majewskis and their kids back then. It was rare when we didn't visit at least once every few Sundays. The house was always teeming with activity with the adults sitting around the dining room table debating current events. Some of the cousins were outside playing stickball in the street while others took turns pumping the foot pedals of the player piano in the parlor. I think my favorite piano roll was actually a song from the time period Adam and I had stumbled into, "Barney Google, with the goo goo-goo-goo-ga-ly eyes, Barney Google had a wife three times his size." I played that every chance I got until it eventually was lost. At least that's what one of the adults said. I think that they just hid the roll. It was always a happy place and I have cherished memories of their home. They sold it in 1958 and moved in with my Aunt Jean and Uncle Frank out on the Island. They generously left the piano for the new owners. My Dad, Jules, said that it hid some rotting floor boards.

All of a sudden, I heard Jules' voice. We felt the back of the car bounce and he was already standing on the curb at the passenger side window. Adam rolled down the window.

"Hey, Bob! Are ya deaf or something? I asked ya if ya want to come in for some coffee. And, my Mom makes the best babka."

"Yeh. Sure, why not?"

Chapter Ten

Jules turned, went around the wrought iron fence and we followed, entering a door under the large brownstone steps that most people used to enter their homes. We followed him into the living room. Unlike other brownstones I had been in, my grandparents used the ground level as their living space which also had a dining area and kitchen. They used the second and third floors for bedrooms and rented the fourth floor for added income.

I leaned toward Adam and said in a low voice, "Well, I'm still not sure what we're supposed to be doing here. This should be interesting. And be warned. If you think that I'm a talker, trust me, I'm an amateur. These guys are Olympic class. Ready to meet your namesake great-great grandfather and his family?"

I knew most of the people behind these doors when they were my aunts and uncles, married and with kids. For all the stress of being stuck in the Depression with no idea how to get back, these surprise experiences were quite enjoyable for me. Each was also a potential piece to the puzzle of why we were here.

Adam and I followed Jules into the front parlor. This was unbelievable. Everything was almost the same as I remembered it, twenty years into the future, just not as worn and faded.

The player piano was in the exact place it was when I would peddle to keep the piano roll at a steady speed in the future. My Pop's chair was in the corner near the front window where my cousins and I would surround him and tickle him as he laughed and gently wrestled with us. And there he was sitting just the way I remembered him only much younger and less rotund. I turned to him and he quickly stood up and extended his hand. He moved a lot faster than I remembered.

With a thick, Polish accent I had forgotten, he asked in a warm deep voice that I had not heard in over fifty years.

"Julius," he pronounced it 'Yulyus,' Who's dis quests dat you bring to our home?"

I reached out my hand to shake his. He had hands as big as a baseball glove and my hand got lost in his strong grip. I knew he worked as a dock worker after he lost all his money when the Stock Market crashed in '29. With seven mouths to feed, not counting Grandma and himself, he had to start all over again working the docks and never trusted banks again. As hard as he worked, it still took what money my Dad made, working for the Mob, to feed the family. His grip was like a vise. It took everything I had not to wince until he released his grip. What goes around comes around.

Jules jumped in. "Pop! Meet my new friend, Bob Majeski and ..... I guess I don't know your kid's name."

Adam introduced himself. "I'm Adam Majeski. I'm Pop's grandson."

He nodded his head in my direction. Adam said this while trying to take in every aspect of this incredibly warm man and his namesake.

Pop Majewski laughed heartily.

"Dat's my name too, boy!"

He grabbed Adam by the shoulders and gave him a greeting that did not surprise me. Adam was totally taken aback. Pop grabbed his shoulders and kissed him on both cheeks and then shook his hand vigorously. Adam winced as his hand was also crushed by his great-great grandfather. The older Adam laughed.

"Glad to meet you, Adam Mayevski."

The patriarch looked at me. "He called you Pop."

Chapter Ten

"That's correct, Sir. All my grandkids do. I asked them to with the hope that I would be as good of a grandfather as mine was."

He had no idea that I was talking about him.

With a hearty laugh, he put his stamp of approval on my tribute.

"Vell, with a name like Mayevski I am sure he must be a vonderful man."

I looked toward the dining room just as my Grandma came out of the kitchen in the back of the house. She was wearing a print dress with an apron that was like so many I saw her wear when I was a kid. She walked into the parlor, drying her hands on the apron as she studied us. She looked at her husband and back to me and back again.

"You could be brothers."

She said this with an even thicker accent than her husband.

"Hi, I'm Clara, velcum to au house. Vouldn't you have some coffee and cake with us? Come to the table, come now, sit."

She indicated a chair on the left side of the dining room table toward the middle.

I studied her quickly before she returned to the kitchen. Her face was smoother and barely had a wrinkle. She had a gentle look that I had never noticed as a kid. It hit me that I never spent much time with her because she was always in the kitchen with the women and girls. The only time she sat down with company was when she had supper on the table and then she would sit at the far end of the table opposite Pop. If she had a waistline I never saw it in later years and it was not evident even now. Was it the way she dressed, or the fact that she had eight kids in seventeen years? I said earlier there were seven mouths to feed and that's because the first-born son, Vincent, had passed away while my Grandma was carrying my Dad. Actually, for those times it was pretty amazing that seven out of eight children survived to adulthood.

Within moments, word spread through the house that Jules had guests and the Majewski siblings barreled down the stairs from their rooms. This family simply loved to socialize, any time, any day, with anyone. Introductions were made over and over as the children threw questions out with everyone talking over each other. This was a trait that stayed with them throughout their lives. Watching them around the table in later years was like watching a tennis match with seven players on the court at the same time. It's an art form that has carried down through the generations. I know it was that way in our own home when our kids, Adam's Dad, David, and our daughters, Tara and Eileen were still at home. Every conversation around our table was an animated affair and each one of them could carry on multiple conversations with each other simultaneously with little effort. These folks, however, were the grand masters of this type of conversational skill.

Jules' brother, Stas, jumped in as he pulled out a chair at the dining room table. "So, your name's Majewski too. That's neat!"

The girls, Jean and Ronnie said almost in unison, looking at my grandson, "You have the same name as our Pop. Wow! How old are you?"

"Fourteen, I'll be fifteen in August."

Jean commented before Ronnie could open her mouth,

"Jeepers, I thought you were seventeen. You're taller than most of my friends. How tall are you?"

"Five feet ten inches."

Both girls just said, "Wow."

Jean added, "You're cute."

Chapter Ten

Adam blushed and looked a little uncomfortable. After all, he knew these were his relatives, great-grand aunts no less. They were pretty and had bright and bubbly personalities.

"Do you live in Brooklyn?" Ronnie squeezed into the chair next to him.

"We live over in Flatbush."

Jean suggested, "Maybe we could take in a movie together."

Jules jumped in, "Hey! Girls! Let the guy get some air already."

They settled down as their Mom brought out a plate with fresh babka. She returned to the kitchen and came back with coffee. The girls jumped up and returned with some juice.

"Hey! Hey! HEY!" A shout came from the doorway.

There stood the youngest, Alphonsus. I calculated that he must be around eight-years-old. I was in a continued state of amazement seeing my relatives as kids. Seeing the short, skinny kid standing in the doorway, no one would ever guess that he would go on to be a star athlete at Power Memorial High School and later be scouted by the New York Knicks and Giants, not the football team but the baseball team. He'd eventually play on their minor league team, West Palm Beach from 1949 to 1951. He never got called up to the majors due to a 'cool bat,' as he called it. However, he did have a 98% fielding average as a shortstop. The sports writers nicknamed him "the Glove" and the "Spider."

Pop Majewski looked toward the boy standing in his pajamas.

"Come in Allie. Meet your brother's new friends."

Two hours later, we left the Majewski home with a warm feeling of belonging. We had been totally accepted and invited to come back whenever we felt like it. Adam had promised to get together for a movie with the girls. Even though they had no clue about how we were related, their total acceptance of us, just for being polite and Polish, was so appreciated since we were far from our own family in 2013. However, it made us realize how much we missed our own families and made us even more homesick.

More importantly, we found another piece to the puzzle and it was significant. The Majewski family had no clue that Jules was working for the Mob. He was a salesman. Really? Jules had given me the eye to keep quiet when the conversation at the table came around to how much he was helping support the family. It was interesting that he never mentioned what he sold and they didn't seem interested enough to ask. They were just happy to have the money that helped put food on the table.

I knew that he was consorting with a dangerous crowd. If he wasn't careful his future could be tenuous at best. I didn't relate my concerns to Adam since I wasn't sure what would happen to us if Jules got hurt or worse, killed. If he died, would we cease to exist, or would we only exist in this present time and not be able to return to the future because we did not exist there? The future wasn't looking so certain now. I was now more convinced than ever that I might be here to get him to change his career path before we left to find Einstein.

CHAPTER ELEVEN
Take Me Out to the Ball Game and Dinner
April 13, 1933

Adam and I talked about our visit with the Majewskis last week.

"You know what's funny, Adam?"

"What?"

He took a huge spoonful of corn flakes. The conversation would be all mine for a few minutes until he could chew what was in his mouth.

"I was the oldest person in the room last night. That sucks. I can't wait to get back to our time."

Adam took a huge swallow.

"What's the difference? You'll still be the oldest when we get back."

"Not when your Grandpa Eggleton's in the room. Anyway, I'm goin' to a Yankee game with Mr. Barton this afternoon *AND* he said there's an extra seat for you if you would like to come. Interested?"

"I'm not sure. I've got a lot of papers to sell."

"I understand. Too bad 'cause it's opening day at Yankee Stadium and I'm pretty sure that Ruth and Gehrig will be playing. Mr. Barton also has great seats."

Adam's face lit up.

"Count me in. I'll sell all my papers and be back in time to leave with you. I know another kid that will sell the Evening

Waiting for Einstein

Edition for me if I let him keep all the money. By the way, who are they playing?"

"Some upstart team from Boston, and it's not the Braves."

The next thing I heard was the apartment door slam. I figured he would find out what time the game was from his papers since he never took the time to ask me.

Oh, what a game it was. Walking into the stadium was magical. I had softened over the years toward the Yankees. After all, I was raised as a Brooklyn Dodgers fan and as a boy I was among the baseball masses that loved to hate the Yankees. Today was different. I was in awe of the 1930's Yankee lineup. They were the reigning Champs having swept the Chicago Cubs 4-0 in the 1932 Series. That was also the series that Ruth made baseball history when, in the 5th inning of the third game, he stepped up at bat, pointed to the center field bleachers. He sent that next pitch 500 feet into the seats, adding to his growing legend with totally-earned credibility.

Jim Barton had box seats behind the Yankee dugout where he could get a good view of the players coming and going and a view of the whole field. He told me laughing heartily, "I like it when I can smell the sweat."

The first inning was almost the game winner. Leadoff hitter Earle Combs struck out when Boston's Ivy Andrews sent two knuckleballs and an incredible curve ball to the catcher keeping the Yankee from reaching first base. Up next, third baseman, Joe Sewell, had a good eye and ended up walking. The Babe strolled out to home plate. His first swing sent the ball down the first base line past Boston's Dale Alexander and Ruth easily made it to first in his own fashion. Sewell advanced to second base.

Chapter Eleven

Lou Gehrig settled into the batter's box. Another knuckleball. Strike one. Curve ball. Strike two. What a swing! The pitcher was feeling cocky after that and sent the third pitch, a fastball, right over the middle of the plate. That turned out to be a bad choice and I'm sure Andrews wished he could take it back as it made its way toward the catcher's mitt. The ball never got there. Gehrig leaned back a little and gave a mighty swing. When I heard the ball hit the bat it sounded like it cracked. It didn't and the ball sailed over the right field into the upper deck for a crushing home run. The stadium went crazy. I sat there not believing that I had just seen Lou Gehrig hit a home run, LIVE, IN color in real time! Holy crap!

I looked at Adam. I would have made a comment but he was too busy screaming "Lou, Lou, Lou!" along with the entire crowd.

The Red Sox would score a run at the top of the second. It would not be until the fourth inning that Yankee shortstop, Frankie Crosetti, would drive Tony Lazzeri in to give the Yankees what would be the eventual game-winning run. Boston threatened with two runs in the eighth. In the end, the Yankees prevailed 4-3. I was numb realizing that I had just seen a live baseball game in 1933 with Ruth and Gehrig. My head was spinning but it was about to get even better.

As the 40,000 in attendance left the ballpark, Babe Ruth's head popped up over the dugout roof. I recognized him immediately. His face was as familiar to me as if I had grown up in this time. Even though he passed away the year before I was born, his image was known to every boy who followed baseball even in the decades after his death. Whatever and whenever anything was happening in baseball there always seemed to be comparisons made to the "Sultan of Swat." His eyes quickly scanned the seats over the dugout until he found Jim sitting with us.

"Hey Jimmy boy! Are we still good for dinner at Sardi's?"

"Sounds good to me, Babe. Is it still an 'all boys' night or are the girls coming?"

"No girls tonight. It's a school night and Claire doesn't want Julia and Dorothy out late. They'll never get up in the morning. So, the evening is all ours. Did you come in the Lincoln or do I call a cab?"

"If you wear your spats I might let your sorry Packard-loving butt in my Lincoln."

"Don't you dare say a bad word about Packard. I'm still alive because of one."

"Please don't start again with how a Packard saved your life back in 1920."

"Well, it did! That Packard saved me when that Mack truck hit me."

"Wasn't it you that sped into a one lane culvert in Connecticut and hit the Mack?"

"I was running late to get to that exhibition game in Springfield."

"That accident was in Wallingford at the Yalesville culvert and if I remember correctly, you had to hitch-hike to the game after your beloved Packard was destroyed."

"What of it?"

"I promise you that we won't have to hitch a ride tonight."

"Is that a comment about my Packard or my driving?"

He had taken the bait.

"Both!"

The friends broke into a hearty laugh.

Chapter Eleven

"Either way, I'll wear my spats for sure since I have to show those ragtag actors you hang out with, how a real gentleman dresses. Let me get showered and I'll meet you at the front gate in twenty minutes. That will still give me time with the kids before we leave."

His head disappeared from sight below the dugout roof.

I addressed Jim, nervous that we might be heading for a night I could not afford.

"I'll get you both to the restaurant. Adam and I will park the car and pick you up when you are done."

Jim looked at me a little confused. "What are you talking about? You and the boy are having dinner with us."

"I'm afraid Sardi's is a little rich for us."

"I never asked you to pay. You're our guests."

"Really?"

"Really! And don't worry about my pocketbook. God has been generous to me in the talent department and has blessed me with lots of appreciative audiences."

As we headed toward the front gates to wait for Ruth, he added, "Oh and by the way, it's Babe's turn to pay. I'm still being nicer to him than he was with me when it was my turn. The last time he brought half of the team to eat at Delmonico's."

Jim punctuated that with a hearty laugh.

Adam looked at me wide-eyed.

"Are we going to dinner with Babe Ruth? Really?"

"It looks that way, Buddy. I can't believe it either. I know they are best friends, but I never imagined that we'd actually get to dine with him."

Then it really hit me.

"Holy sh.., Adam! Babe Ruth is taking us to dinner."

Jim could see the look of shocked wonder on our faces.

"You two better not walk too far with your mouths open like that or people will think you're not right in the head. Adam, what do you say we go find our host?"

"Sounds great to me!"

Adam was on cloud nine.

By the time we got to the main gate, the Babe was already there and surrounded by at least fifty kids, all waiting a turn to shake his hand and get his autograph. His six-foot two-inch frame towered over the bunch. It took almost an hour before the last of his fans left. He never hurried any of them and made sure to ask each kid his name and age before he signed programs, and autographed balls and books. He made each one feel like he, the Babe, wanted to know how he personally liked the game. He apologized for not hitting a home run. He promised to try harder at the next game. It was magical watching him with his fans. What was more amazing than anything was when he was done, he climbed into the back seat of Jim's Lincoln. I adjusted the mirror and caught Adam sitting between these two giants in their respective careers. The glare from his smile almost blinded me.

"So, kid, what's your name and how'd you end up with this old hoofer?"

"I'm Adam, sir. My grandfather works for Mr. Barton. He's driving the car tonight."

He looked at Jim, "You've got a chauffeur now?"

Barton cut in.

"Are you daffy or something? Bob just loves to drive my car. He keeps telling me that someday it's going to be a classic, whatever that is. I'm sure he'll do a better job driving my car than you did driving any homers today."

"Put a sock in it, ya Mick."

Chapter Eleven

The Babe laughed and sat back. Adam just sat speechless. As for me, I was in seventh heaven. Why wouldn't I be? How many people could say that they drove a classic Lincoln with James Barton, Babe Ruth, and his own grandson all in the back seat after attending a Yankees - Red Sox game? I did wonder if Adam and I had died and were in some sort of heaven. However, wasn't heaven what you wanted it to be? If that was true then where were my wife and our families? Okay, it wasn't heaven. It wasn't hell either.

We rolled up to Sardi's on West 44th Street between Broadway and Eighth. The iconic Art Deco letters, identifying the restaurant, dominated the entire front of the building above a canopied entrance. A valet opened the rear door and as Jim exited the car, he welcomed us, "Welcome to Sardi's, Mr. Barton."

Adam exited next.

"Welcome young man."

He figured he must be someone important if he was with Barton. Then Babe stepped onto the sidewalk. He looked back at Adam and wondered who was this kid?

"Hello Mr. Ruth! Welcome to Sardi's."

"Hi, Buddy," Ruth took his hand and shook it vigorously. "How's the family?"

"Fine, Mr. Ruth."

"Is our table ready?"

"It's always ready for you, Mr. Ruth. Just go inside and we'll take care of the car." I came around and handed the keys to the valet. Adam and I were dressed in nice pants that we had recently bought with nice dress shirts. We had yet to buy any more elaborate attire to conserve our money. The maître d' took us aside into a small room and supplied us with jackets and ties that were chosen by fit and color coordination to our slacks from a moderate selection reserved for customers not suitably attired to dine at fine establishments of the times. This was common practice in fine restaurants even as late as the 1960's.

It was a night never to be forgotten. The Babe was the consummate host. Under the pen and ink caricatures by Alex Gard adorning the deep red burgundy walls, we sat with arguably the most important patrons dining that night. The lush atmosphere with the most attentive staff at our beck and call made us feel like we actually belonged for some unknown reason. The Babe made Adam and I feel like we were close friends, as close as he was to Mr. Barton. By the end of the meal, Adam was totally comfortable calling Mr. Ruth, Babe. Ruth never refused an autograph to anyone who came to the table. Eventually the place settled down to dine.

When I'm nervous I lean on my joke telling to calm myself and hopefully disarm my audience. Jim actually started me off.

"Hey Bob, tell Babe that joke about the Irish priest in London. It's pretty funny."

It was my favorite also. That got me started and when there was a pause in the conversation I'd jump in with, "Did you hear the one about the two Irish ditch diggers in front of the house of ill repute?" or "This guy goes into a bar and sees a big glass jar stuffed with ten-dollar bills."

All I can say is that no other table laughed more than ours. My Dad would have been proud. Making people laugh was his favorite pastime.

We were just finishing up dessert when a man approached the table.

"I thought I heard that loud Irish mouth of yours. How are you doing, Jimmy?"

Chapter Eleven

Barton's face lit up. I thought I saw him slightly wince before he looked up.

"Georgie, me boy, what are you doing in town?"

"I'm going across the street to the Majestic to see *Strike Me Pink*. Durante is supposed to be a hoot and I heard it's a good show. Of Course, Lupe is never hard to look at, pretty as a picture, that girl. I guess Tarzan is a lot smarter than he looks. He caught a good one with that kid, as pretty as his movie girlfriend Jane, maybe prettier. And what's up with you? Any new shows in the works?"

As they continued their conversation, I studied George carefully and just as I realized where I saw that face their conversation ended and Barton introduced him as Mr. George M. Cohan. Oh, my God! I had just seen his picture on the cover of *Time Magazine* at the newsstand in front of our apartment building. The article spoke about his classic songs, *You're a Grand Old Flag* and *Over There* which he had written in 1906 and 1917. Those were just two of the many hits he wrote and performed on Broadway. He cut a commanding figure.

"George, I don't think I have to introduce Babe."

They shook hands.

"And this is my friend Bob Majeski and his grandson Adam."

We both stood and took his hand in turn.

I leaned over to Adam who didn't seem to react to the revelation that should have come with the introduction. After all, he had watched Cagney's *Yankee Doodle Dandy* enough times to recognize the name. I had even pointed out Cohan's statue at Broadway and Times Square more than once when we had visited the City to see *Wicked* and *Mary Poppins* in our century. I had worked diligently to expose my children and grandchildren to Broadway and movies over the years. Adam had also been in many school productions himself. It did not take much to kick start his memory.

I looked at Adam and said, "If I remember correctly, you really like Mr. Cohan's songs especially, *Harrigan,* and *Mary.*"

Adams eyes grew to the size of silver dollars. He started shaking his hand vigorously.

"It's awesome to meet you, Mr. Cohan."

George started to laugh, "And it's 'awesome', as you say, to meet you too, young man. May I have my hand back?"

Adam's face turned red as he apologized and released Cohan's hand.

"Well, Jimmy, I need to get going. If I don't get to the theater before the crowds, they'll never let me get to my box before the curtain goes up. The price of fame, I guess."

He didn't wait for a comment and quickly turned and headed for the door.

Now there was a man without any negative self-image issues. I looked at Jim. He looked like he wanted to say something. Barton commented under his breath, "That's if you can get that big head through the door."

During a pause in the conversations while everyone was finally partaking in their desserts, I found the chance to lean toward the Babe and ask the burning question that I had wanted to ask him when I was a kid in the '50s. I was a Brooklyn Dodgers fan and even I knew about that famous event. Heck, when I was playing sandlot baseball with my friends, I think every kid mimicked the Babe's iconic moment. Here I was, just months after "The Called Shot" and I just had to know.

"Babe, please forgive me, but can I ask you a question?"

"Anything, Bob. What's on your mind?"

Chapter Eleven

"That 'Called Shot' with the Chicago Cubs last year in the World Series."

"What about it?"

The Babe smirked knowing exactly what I was going to ask.

"You did point to the outfield knowing you would cream Charlie Root's pitch, right? There's been debate for years . . . er, I mean months."

"So, you are trying to jump the line to get an answer that everyone has been asking me? If I had a nickel for . . . . Okay, what do you want to know?"

"Is it true?"

"Makes for a great story, doesn't it? What idiot would tell the pitcher what he was going to do with the next pitch? He'd have to be daffy."

"So, you didn't call that shot when you pointed out there."

"I didn't say that either. There was a lot of shouting and name calling from the Cubs dugout and the fans. I got a little cocky and maybe I got carried away. Either way, I hit that homer and it all makes for a great story. In a year or two some kid will do something big and it will be forgotten."

"I can assure you that it will be talked about forever. It's the thing that legends are made of."

"That's nice to hear you say that. I hope you're right, but I'm not putting my chips on that yet."

I'm sure he is looking down from wherever and saying. "Hey, the old man was right."

The rest of the dinner went without event. For Adam and I, the whole evening was an event.

After we dropped Ruth off, I drove Jim back to Mineola and switched cars. We sat in the Chevy for a few minutes to let the engine warm up before we drove home. As Adam and I headed back to Brooklyn in our little car we reviewed the events of the evening.

Adam remarked, "Are we dreaming or did we really just have dinner with Babe Ruth and even got to meet George M. Cohan?"

"Don't forget Jim, the man who is making this possible."

"Will we ever be able to tell anyone about any of this when we get back?"

"I don't know, Buddy. We'll just have to wait and see."

CHAPTER TWELVE
Not A Game
April 30, 1933

I had just left Jim Barton off at the front door of a speakeasy in the Bensonhurst section of Brooklyn on 83rd between Bay Parkway and 23rd. When I looked up the block, I heard the *Hallelujah Chorus* in my head as I spotted, not one, but two parking spots together. If you have ever tried to back park a huge '33 Lincoln without power steering you would know why I was thrilled. The spot was big enough that I could drive in nose first and then back into the space nice and tight to the curb. I did this easily and left the wheels a few inches from the curb to keep the wide, white-wall tires from being scuffed.

I'd offered my little Chevy to make the trips into the City which would make my life easier when it came to parking, but Jim liked his Lincoln's ride better. Over the last few weeks, I had driven miles circling blocks for hours because there were no spaces big enough to handle Jim's land yacht. Jim respectfully declined further offers stating that it was all about his *image*.

I was heading back to the club after locking up the car when I heard a ruckus in the alley alongside the club. In the dim light, I saw a guy with his back to the wall and two other guys landing one punch after another to his abdomen. He doubled over, slumped forward and fell to the ground, curled up in a ball.

"Just let your boss know that we don't need his shitty booze in our territory. The next time we won't be so nice."

Without thinking I ran down the alley yelling, "What's going on here!"

I thought they would run off. They just stood there until I was standing next to the man on the ground.

"What's it to you, old man?" one guy said in a threatening tone.

God, I was really getting tired of being called that and I could feel my face flush with anger. That was not good because when I lost my temper, I usually stopped thinking and did stupid things that could get me hurt.

"I don't like guys who don't fight fairly."

"Really? And what are you going to do about it?"

Now the *stupid* in me rose to the surface.

"Hit this guy one more time and find out asshole," I warned.

My mind was already dusting off my old unused tactics that I had to resort to in my high school days in Bedford Stuy during the 1960's. To challenge me, the six-foot thug went to kick the guy on the ground. Surprising myself, I moved faster and, in my best street fighting mode, I kicked the guy squarely in the family jewels. His eyes opened wide followed by a low groan before he went down like a ton of bricks. I think he was surprised that the old man could move that fast or kick that high.

He didn't know that where I came from *sixty* was the new *forty*. Well, at least in my mind it was. His partner headed toward me as I stood between him and their victim who was starting to get back to his feet behind me. I turned quickly and saw his face.

"Jules?"

"Yeah?" he groaned as he finally stood up straight. Now I had real motivation and more anger. No one was going to hurt my Dad!

Chapter Twelve

I looked back to the second mug.

"Are you looking to join your friend, or do you still want to have children someday?"

"You think you can kick my ass, OLD MAN?" he growled.

As he stepped into the light, I got a good look at him. He was no older than Jules. These were kids trying to act like men. Even though I knew he could still be dangerous I didn't feel so threatened. Experience can really be useful when dealing with youth. I continued to stand my ground.

Okay, Bob, sound confident. He can't see your kneecaps jumping in your pants legs.

Slowly but with conviction I replied, "No brag. Just fact."

I've always wanted to say that since I first heard Walter Brennan use it in every episode of *The Guns of Will Sonnett* on television.

He looked like he was measuring me up as we locked stares. I shifted my weight to the balls of my feet, ready to spring into action. I saw a bead of sweat trickle along the side of his face as he sized me up. He must have sensed some primal danger from the crazed look in my eyes because his stance loosened. He bent down and grabbed his partner under the arm and helped him stand up with more groaning.

As they headed down the alley toward the street he turned and said, with exaggerated bravado, "Watch your back, OLD MAN."

"Watch your front, KID."

Man, I had to find a bathroom soon. These were my best pair of pants and I didn't want to soil them.

I turned and saw Jules massaging his bruised abdomen.

"I guess I need ta say thanks."

Waiting for Einstein

"Ya think? Have you given it any thought that this may not be the best way to make a living? They could have killed you."

"They wouldn't a killed me. They needed me to get da message back to my boss. It's just what they do."

"They couldn't have given you a note to bring him?"

Jules just answered with a, "Very funny."

As we walked out of the alley, I added, "I think you guys need to start using the phone."

Jules just laughed followed by some coughing as his ribs were also sore.

"Let me buy you a drink. I think we need to talk."

We entered the club and before I could get the head waiter's attention Jules led me to a table in the back corner just as the bandleader was introducing Barton. Jim ran out onto the dance floor and took a bow. Turning to the bandstand, he said, in his signature deep gravel voice, "Maestro!"

The bandleader raised his hands and the band broke out into a quick jazzy version of *Makin' Whoopee*. I wanted to watch the show, but I had to focus on Jules while I still had his attention. I didn't know when I might lose contact with him. I was becoming more convinced that Adam and I were back in time because of him.

Why wouldn't I think that after we kept crossing paths? All kinds of issues popped into my head. Would we just stay in 1933 having been born in our currently pretended birth years of 1869 and 1919? This time travel was full of questions with no answers. I decided that I was not going to test any hypothesis and became more determined than ever to get Jules to give up this job and live to see me born.

I turned to Jules as he was wiping his mouth with the back of his hand as he noticed a bit of blood on the cuff of his sleeve.

Chapter Twelve

"It's on your left."

He picked up a napkin and dipped the corner in a water glass. He started to clean the right corner of his mouth.

"Your other left."

His face was clean again with no outward evidence that he had just been beaten up.

"Good, you got it."

He put the napkin down and flagged a waiter.

"Frankie, a scotch and water."

He turned toward me.

"I owe you a drink, Bob. What'll ya have?"

"I'll have the same."

I went with that since there were not many choices during Prohibition. I rarely drink hard liquor and, depending on the speakeasy, the booze could be really good or what many called rotgut. It was this infusion of bad tasting liquor that brought about the invention of the cocktail with any and all flavor additives to make it palatable. In my time, when I want alcohol, I usually drink Guinness stout but I could not find it anywhere here.

I looked at Jules, still amazed at how good looking he was with his full head of hair, his slim body and those light blue eyes. I was pretty sure that he had no problem finding a date based on a few scattered memories I heard him recall about his life before he met my Mom. From what I could see, any girl would have been proud to be on his arm.

Then, he did something I had never seen him do in my lifetime. He had stopped this ugly habit the year I was born, in 1949. He took out a pack of Lucky Strike cigarettes. He tapped the pack just the right way against two fingers on his left hand and just one cigarette poked out. He pulled it out of the pack with his lips. Before I knew it, he had somehow struck a wooden match, held it at the end of that coffin nail and took a drag until the tip glowed. He looked up and politely blew the smoke toward the ceiling. It didn't help the situation. I had already been having an issue with the smoke that filled the room. I started to cough. I hate cigarette smoking. I was so glad when the laws stopped allowing smoking in public facilities, restaurants, and most places where people gathered in my time. I kind of forgot myself and lost it. I snatched it out of his mouth.

I raised my voice. "Here I'm trying to get you to find a safer trade and you're already killing yourself with these?!"

I pointed the cigarette at him and then threw it to the floor and ground it out with my foot.

"Are you crazy? What'd ya do dat for?"

"Smoking will kill you. Do you know what smoking does to your lungs?"

I lost it and continued without thinking.

"Do you have any idea how many people I've pronounced dead from complications from years of smoking?"

Uh, Oh! I stopped my rant.

Jules looked at me with a confused look.

"What are ya talking about? Are ya a doctor or something? I thought ya were some kinda roustabout for Barton? Why would ya be pronouncing people dead?"

"Ignore what I said about that - not about the bad stuff about smoking. It will kill you. It's not cool. You look stupid with that thing in your mouth. I wish you'd stop it but I'm pretty sure you won't for a while. Just don't do it when you're with me. Okay? I don't want to breath any more cigarette smoke than I have to around here. That can be my reward for saving your ass."

Chapter Twelve

Somehow, my strong reaction to his smoking was enough of a deflection and my comment about pronouncing people dead got lost in the conversation. He didn't light up again. I changed the subject quickly.

"Jules, did that beating pound any sense into your thick Polish head?"

It was kind of neat being able to speak to my Dad like this. I was getting used to it even while remembering the many lectures that I received from him during my teen years in the '60s.

"Your family can't afford to lose your income. You can't work if you're handicapped or worse, dead."

"Ya think I don't know that, Bob?"

There was a touch of annoyance in his voice.

"I'd love ta get out of this business. We need the money. My Pop doesn't make enough at the docks to feed the family. They need whatever I can bring in."

"Don't you know anyone that can get you a real job?"

"Don't ya get it? Many of my friends' Dads are on da soup lines and many of us had ta quit school to help feed the families. One paycheck can't feed the family. Times are not good, if ya haven't noticed."

I could hear the frustration of a generation in his voice. I knew his frustration first hand. In the mid-seventies, I held down three jobs at one time, sometimes working seven days a week, to keep a roof over our heads. It was nothing really exceptional. I just did what anybody would do for his family. I guess every generation has its challenges. You could step up to the plate and work your way out or let it beat you. The Majewskis always worked their way out.

"I hear you, Jules. You must find a safer way to help out. Your kids will thank you someday."

He looked confused.

"I don't have any kids. Are ya daffy or something?"

He looked at me like I had two heads.

"I know that, but you could have a family of your own someday, if you don't get yourself killed first. Don't you want to have kids that carry on the family name?"

"Yeh. Sure. Someday. I haven't had much time for girls, at least, not the kind I can bring home to my Mom."

"Of course, you can't. The girls working at the joints you hang out at are not marrying material. That's why you have to get a regular job where you can meet people that actually go out in the daylight. You'll also get to see what they really look like without all the dim lighting and heavy make-up."

"I hear what ya're saying but I can make more money that my family sorely needs working with these guys."

"Must I remind you that dead people don't draw a salary?"

"Will ya get offa' my case! What are ya, my fairy godfatha' or sumthin?"

"No. I'm just an old man who sees a kid from a nice family that can enjoy a longer life if he can get his head out of his butt."

He had no answer for me. You could tell by the expression on his face that he knew I was right. He simply turned to face the dance floor just as Barton was finishing a second dance routine to the tune, *I Found a Million Dollar Baby in a 5 and 10 Cent Store*.

The conversation was over. Jim's dance had gracefully ended with him proudly strutting off the dance floor with an imaginary girl on his arm. The audience jumped up yelling *Bravo* and *Encore*. Barton jumped back on the floor and looked at the band leader. With the wave of his baton, the musicians broke into a rendition of *If You Knew Susie*. This up-tempo and lively tune

Chapter Twelve

allowed Jim to break into a mind-blowing tap dance routine. I was stunned as he pulled out all the stops with this dance. Jim was truly the master.

Driving home I verbalized my amazement with his dancing skills.

"I appreciate your praise, Bob. You would change your mind if you ever get to see Bill 'Bojangles' Robinson. He's the best."

"I doubt that."

"Trust me. Bill's the best."

With a big grin, he added, "BUT I'm the best white dancer you'll ever see."

I silently added in my mind as I turned the Lincoln onto Kings Highway.

"No brag. Just fact."

CHAPTER THIRTEEN
Dinner at Eight
May 5, 1933

Adam and I talked daily over breakfast. We recapped the events of the previous day if I got in late the night before. We didn't share our worries about what the future might hold for us. We both prayed that we would get back there soon with Einstein's help. If we talked too openly about it, we might succumb to our fears.

These were different times from where we came from. Adam was almost completely on his own. He peddled his papers on his corner every morning and afternoon. He had been challenged a few times by some jealous rivals. His size was intimidating and he used it to convince them that he was as tough as he was tall. The fact was that he was not a fighter. He was just like me. I had schooled him on the power of the bluff which was serving him well. He had never had to really fight anyone yet.

"So, what are your plans for today?"

I poured milk from a glass bottle into my bowl of Wheaties which was already being called 'The Breakfast of Champions.' However, there was no picture of a sports figure on the box yet. That would not start until next year, 1934, when Lou Gehrig would be the first with his picture, not on the front, but the back of the box. God, I have so much useless information in my head.

"Selling my papers first. Then, I thought I'd catch a movie at the Paramount before the afternoon edition comes out. How about you, Pop?"

"I'm free until supper time. Do you know what's playing?"

Chapter Thirteen

"*King Kong.* Are you interested in going?"

"Sure thing. I've never seen "Kong" on the big screen. I've seen it more times than I can count on television. I'll meet you at the theatre for the one o'clock showing. Is there any way you can get a friend to cover your corner for the afternoon edition?"

"Tommy Mulligan, upstairs, still hasn't got a steady corner and has agreed to cover my corner when I need a day off. He'll keep the profit again. I'm good with that if you are. Why do you ask?"

"We've been asked to dine with the Bartons and the Ruths. Jim actually asked if you could attend."

"Why do you think he wants me there?" Adam looked perplexed. "I know he doesn't mind when I'm around. This is the first time he has asked that I come to something."

"It may have something to do with the fact that Babe is bringing his daughters, Julia and Dorothy. He probably wants them to have someone closer to their age there. I think Julia is near seventeen and Dorothy around twelve. Jim told me that Babe was impressed with you when he first met you."

"You would think that he would want his girls hanging around with some other rich kids. I'm just a paperboy."

"Don't you dare forget where you are from and who you are. Babe may not know you're an honor student back at Cheshire High or that you've been doing plays and singing in the chorus for most of your school years but he recognizes that you're different than other boys around here. Your education shows. That's what he wants his girls to see. Just because you're here doesn't negate your upbringing and talents. You're a class act and don't ever forget it."

I had been concerned for some time now that Adam might start thinking less of himself as the tough streetwise kid he had to make believe he was. The reality was that he was one of the gentlest souls I had ever known. As early as middle school he had been a part of programs in school that befriended handicapped students. Although he did try sports his heart was more interested in music and acting in school and town plays. No grandfather could be prouder of a grandson. When he made comments like he just did it made me more determined than ever to figure out how to get us back to our own time.

I pulled the Lincoln up to the front of Delmonico's at 2 South William Street in downtown Manhattan. Jim had offered to pick up the Babe, Claire, and the girls on the way to the restaurant. We actually could carry eight people since this custom motor car had jump seats for added passengers like a limo. Babe simply declined and said they would meet us there.

I ran around the front of the car to get the door before Kitty could get out unassisted. As always, she was dressed impeccably. I could not get used to seeing her like this. She had chosen a sleeveless floor length evening gown in what she described as nude angel skin satin. The high neckline and openings for the arms were trimmed in a rope made of the same material. Brown cire satin and crepe flowers accented her narrow waist. With her perfect makeup and a stylish marcelled hairstyle, she could stand toe-to-toe with any starlet on the cover of *New Movie* magazine.

Kitty had taken Adam and I out shopping last week, expressing her concern that we did not have decent clothes for dining out with them. Kitty took us to Brooks Brothers on the corner of Madison Avenue and 44th Street. She introduced us to Jim's personal tailor and after many measurements our suits were chosen with Kitty's critical eye as to what looked best on each of us. She chose a medium blue classic three button suit with a matching vest for me and a double-breasted pin stripe one for

Chapter Thirteen

Adam. We had raided our coffee can of our savings but when it came time to pay I almost fainted when the clerk stated the price.

Kitty waved to him with a gentle flick of the hand. "Put it on my tab. Have them delivered to my home in two days. If there is an issue with the fit, we will bring them back for a final tailoring."

"Kitty, I can't let you pay for these. You've already been too generous. We'll pay. Just ask them if we can pay over the next few weeks and vouch for us. I will pay in full within the month."

"You'll do no such thing. You are a member of our household and this is our pleasure. End of discussion."

Needless to say, they fit perfect. No more loaner jackets and ties. This was going to be an event dripping with class.

I opened the door and held my hand out for Kitty until she got her footing in her high heels on the wide running board. She made a quip softly so Jim could not hear it.

"Slow down, Bob. You're not a kid *yet*."

We both laughed. Not letting her get the last word I added, "I'm just practicing for the time you get old and I'm not."

She actually punched me hard in the arm.

"I'll never be as old as you geezer." She laughed.

"What are you two up to?" Jim observed as he stepped onto the sidewalk.

"Just reminding Bob that he is no spring chicken, dear."

Before I surrendered her arm to Jim for them to lead us into the iconic eatery, I leaned in and added, "Not yet, anyway."

Kitty got the last word with a simple, "*Touché.*"

This was a game we would play when our ages were chronologically correct in the future. Nothing was different even now. Kitty, as I now called her, always got the last word. I would never win this friendly game that we fell into as naturally as if we had always played it. My losing streak was now extended back another thirty years from those times and I was fine with that. Jim was a lucky man to have a woman this smart and pretty at the same time. I was just as lucky in my life and felt a pang in my heart as I realized how much I missed my wife.

Every great experience I've had in my life was with my wife. Here I was experiencing something that, as far as I knew, no one had ever done and she was not at my side. I kept wondering how she would react if she met the Bartons, Ruths, or Cohan. I was sure that they would love her. Kitty did in later years. She had met more than a few of my dates over the years while dining at my house. When she met Henny, she reacted differently than with the others.

At the end of the first dinner with Henny where she was present, she took me aside. "This one's a keeper, Bobby."

I already knew that as well.

We were led to a table that I noticed had seating for ten. I wondered who the extra chairs were for. We did not have to wait long to learn.

CHAPTER FOURTEEN
Jim and Kitty's Friends

The Ruths soon entered just as we were getting seated. I jumped up to greet them shaking the Bambino's hand.

"My honor as always."

"I'm just a ball player, Bob. Nothing more. Nice to see you again."

He looked past me where Adam was standing as well.

"Nice to see you again, young man."

Adam looked stunned and a bit silly with his mouth wide open as if he could not speak.

"The pleasure is all mine, Mr. Ruth."

Ruth turned back to me. "That's a fine young man you're raising there."

"I'm proud of him. A man could not ask for a better grandson."

I looked around for Claire and the girls. They were still at the coat check where their coats and wraps were being handed to a girl behind a dutch-door with the top half open behind her. Rows of a variety of patrons' coats could be seen behind her in the large closet.

The Ruth family approached the table. Like Kitty, Claire was in a floor length outfit. Instead of a dress, she was wearing a long black crepe skirt matched with a shiny rich-looking white satin blouse with full length draped sleeves. She'd have fun trying to keep them clean, I thought. No reaching over the table for the bread for her. The blouse was finished off with a little bow at the high neckline and a row of satin covered buttons down the left side. She looked like one of those art deco models on the cover of *Vogue*. She mirrored Kitty's grace and beauty easily.

The girls were standing at her side as she greeted us.

"You must be Bob. Babe said you would be here. I'm Claire, Babe's wife."

"Pleased to meet you."

I gently shook her hand.

Looking at my grandson at my side she added, "And you must be Adam. Babe can't stop talking about you, young man."

All Adam could say was, "Really?"

Adam beamed with a broad smile realizing that he had impressed the Babe in some way.

"Really. You impressed him greatly when he first met you. He even mentioned you by name, which he never does since he rarely remembers someone's name. That's not easy to get him to do. I told him I had to meet this amazing young man. May I introduce you to our daughters?"

She did not wait for an answer and gently pushed the girls forward. "I'd like you to meet Julia."

She indicated the girl on her left with a head nod.

"And this is Dorothy," she said this almost as an afterthought.

She nodded to the shorter girl on her right.

Both girls were attired in what could only be described as party dresses by modern day standards. In 1933, girls were dressed in styles that in 2013 would be considered girly or fancy. Julia wore a pink dress that was more appropriate to her age. The dress had short one-quarter-length sleeves. The cut accentuated her youthfully narrow waist with a dark pink bow that almost spanned her midriff side to side. Dorothy was in a short red dress that was high-waisted with a big white collar and

Chapter Fourteen

puffy short sleeves. A row of white buttons ran down the front, from the collar to the thin white ribbon which accented the high waist.

Julia's dress ended at the knees in a length more appropriate for a young woman. Dorothy's dress stopped a few inches above their knees and looked a bit juvenile even for her age. Her outfit was nowhere as fashionable as her sister's. Julia's hair was also cut and styled in long waves while Dorothy sported curly hair that stopped just short of her shoulders. Bows accented their hair.

Adam stepped forward and greeted them.

"Pleased to meet you Julia, Dorothy."

He bowed at the waist. Where did he get that from? Maybe he was just got caught up in the elegance of the setting. The girls almost simultaneously took the hems of their skirts and dipped into curtsies. Girls still did that in polite society. Claire turned and directed the girls to their seats and had Adam take the seat between them. I looked at him and gave him a "You're on your own" look that guys give each other. I added the grandfatherly, "Be good!" look, even though I knew it would not be an issue.

Jim looked over my shoulder and exclaimed, "If these guys ever show up on time, I'll eat my hat. Here, they finally come. Over here, Jimmy."

I turned to where he was looking and my jaw fell to the floor as James Cagney and a woman, who must have been his wife Willie, came toward us at a quick pace. I knew that her full name was Frances Willard Cagney and she got the nickname based on her middle name. Kitty had told me that around 1964. Kitty and Willie would remain friends long after their husbands had passed away.

Waiting for Einstein

Kitty showed me a letter in 1984 from Willie which she let me read. In the correspondence, Willie related her concern about her husband's health. She felt that he should not make the movie, *Terrible Joe Moran*, because the shoot would take too much out of him. He was more frail than he wanted to admit and Willie worried that this project could kill him. He did the movie in a wheelchair and after he died in 1986, she wrote Kitty telling her that the movie was the beginning of the end for him health-wise.

But here he was as Adam and I had just seen him in the movie, *The Lady Killer* just a few weeks ago. He had that signature walk of a dancer which he always proudly said he was. He was still slender with a lean athletic body. I tried to forget what I knew would happen in the future. After all, that would be fifty years from now.

Willie equaled the five-foot-seven-inch Cagney with her heels. She was dressed elegantly in a long black satin gown and easily matched Kitty and Claire with her natural beauty. I was starting to feel under-dressed even in my new suit. I would have felt better in a tux if it hadn't been for the fact that Babe and the two Jims also wore suits. My attention returned to her husband.

All my mind could say was, "Wow! we're going to have dinner with James Cagney. Wait. What was I thinking? We're having dinner with James Barton, Babe Ruth AND James Cagney! Holy S***!"

I looked at Adam and he looked like he had just been hit with a stun gun as he stared up at Cagney. He recognized him immediately and pushed his chair back knocking it into my hip which prevented it from falling over. At five-foot-ten-inches, he seemed to tower over the actor.

Cagney looked at Barton.

Chapter Fourteen

"And who's this young lad? A footballer, I hope."

Cagney looked up at Adam and held his hand out to him with his legendary grin. Adam hesitated for a moment before realizing that he was being offered a handshake.

He stammered a bit and could not hide his excitement.

"I'm a huge fan Mr. Cagney. I can't believe I'm meeting you in person. I think your movies are great."

I hoped that Adam could keep his wits and not bring up movies Cagney had not made yet. He did not disappoint me.

"I really enjoyed *The Lady Killer*."

"I'm glad you liked it my boy. It was great fun, wasn't it?"

"Oh yes, sir. My Pop and I really enjoyed it."

Cagney looked at me.

"Can I assume that you're the boy's Grandpere?"

"Guilty as charged and proud of it."

"As you should be, sir."

He spoke to Adam. "How old are you kid?"

"Fourteen, Mr. Cagney."

Cagney looked back at me.

"What are you feeding the boy?"

I heard this over and over. My shortness only brought attention to the fact as well.

He waved his hand and looked up at Adam.

"Don't tell me, boy. It's too late for me anyway."

He laughed loudly and slapped Adam on the back.

"Why don't we take our seats and get this dinner going. Hey, Barton! Stop courting the ladies and let's order something. I'm famished."

With Cagney's rapid-fire speech this exchange took only seconds.

Babe put out his hand to Jimmy.

"If it isn't 'One Punch Cagney."

"Well, I do have to keep this face pretty for the cameras, Slugger." Cagney's movie characters, more often than not, punched or slapped an adversary only once to show he was not to be messed with. Not very different than what I did in school, I might add. Life imitating art?

They embraced in a warm handshake of mutual admiration.

Everyone took a seat and an unforgettable night was about to begin. I looked around the table not believing what I was seeing. Barton took the first seat on the far side of the table with Babe and Claire to his left. Kitty sat opposite her husband. She liked facing him when they dined. The Cagneys sat to her right. This organized the couples nicely for the lively conversation that was sure to follow. Adam was flanked by the girls to Claire's left and across from me.

What a night! Barton told stories about his latest work on Broadway and even in the speakeasies. He also retold the story of how he introduced Babe to Claire.

"She was part of the chorus in one of my shows. It was *Dew Drop Inn* and we were on tour before we hit Broadway with it. She was a shy sweet kid from Athens, Georgia and Kitty and I took her under our wing to keep her safe among all the stage door Johnnies. We took her to a Yankees/Washington Senators game down in D.C. and Babe came over to our box after the game. He reminded us about a party he was throwing that night. He took one look at Claire and invited her as well. It wasn't long before he asked her if he could call on her. The rest is history. Claire gently jerked on the pole and set the hook deep and landed this big 'lunk.' It's the best thing that ever happened to him since he discovered he could play baseball."

Chapter Fourteen

During our friendship in the '60s, Kitty told me that Jim was always proud of his friendship with Ruth and his involvement in getting him together with Claire. Ruth had been in a loveless marriage before and was separated at the time he met Claire. She was different. She was this bright and beautiful Southern lady unlike any woman he had known. His first wife later died in 1929 and he married Claire afterwards. Many credited her with keeping Babe focused and true to the image of the hero kids could admire. He became more of the family man he is best remembered for with less drinking and carousing that had accented his time "BC," before Claire. The Yankee management and his friends were happy with the results. The baseball icon was in good hands.

As I listened to Jim tell this story I could not help but remember what Katie related to me years later. Shortly before the Babe died in 1948, the biographic movie *The Babe Ruth Story* was released with William Bendix playing the Bambino. Ruth attended the premier. Katie told me that when Jim saw the movie, his friendship, as well as his part in getting the Ruths together was never shown or even mentioned. This hurt Jim a lot since Ruth supposedly had been consulted during the making of the movie. He never found out how these omissions could be allowed by such a close friend as Ruth. The Babe died shortly after but not before he and Claire told Jim that the studio ignored all their complaints about the story's inaccuracies. The Ruth family would hate the end result then and even to this day as I was told years later.

This has always bothered me since Katie told me the true story in the '60s and now, as I witnessed the depth and the strength of their friendship, I was certain that this was a classic case of the Hollywood moguls determined to edit and tell the story the way it would sell best and make money. It was always about money.

My experience in hospice, as a registered nurse, also made me equally certain that at that late stage in Ruth's life, with the cancer taking its toll, that he most likely did not have the energy or drive to fight the movie makers. After all, Ruth passed away just two months later. Watching the boys together, there was no doubt in my mind that these guys had as solid a friendship as anyone could find. Jim's hurt was understandable, but he had to know that their friendship was as strong as the Rock of Gibraltar.

Cagney took his turn and regaled the party with stories about backlot Hollywood. Then, he told some stories about the early days of vaudeville and his early run-ins at different theaters with Barton and others. Oh, how I wish I had a tape recorder or smartphone to capture this night. I hoped that Adam was getting a chance to hear some of this because he might never get this opportunity again. It sure looked like the girls were monopolizing his attention. Actually, Julia was dominating the conversation. Dorothy sat quietly, looking dreamily at Adam. I was trying to listen to their conversation when I saw a man stagger toward our table.

Just as Cagney was regaling us with another anecdote about Hollywood life, this interloper reached out and tugged on his shoulder.

"You don'd look tho big and duff as you do in da movies. You're a fwaud."

It was obvious by the slurring of his words that he was well over his alcohol limit. Jim, Babe, and I were already pushing our chairs back to confront the drunk when the Sardi's staff swooped in and the offender was politely but firmly escorted toward the

Chapter Fourteen

front door. I heard the *maître d'* telling him that he would never be dining there again.

Cagney defused the tension.

"That happens more often than you would think. It never amounts to much but there are a few guys that will have to suffer with their wives' cooking for a long time."

That was followed by that high Irish laugh he was famous for. The meal continued without interruption until near closing. It was good for business to have a table full of celebrities, so we were never rushed to turn over the table. I saw more than one patron looking at me and Adam wondering who we were and what might be our claim to fame.

As we drove the Barton's home, I commented to them.

"It's an understatement to say that you have the most incredible friends. I have never been that entertained for free in my life."

"I have to agree, Bob. Kitty and I are blessed to have friends like them. Did you like Jimmy's stories about Vaudeville? He loved the stage so much that in his early days he even took a job dressed as one of the chorus girls in a show just to get a gig and be in the footlights. That's kind of funny since Hollywood likes to cast him as the tough streetwise gangster now. I think that was a good move since I don't think he's pretty anyway."

Jim laughed at his own comment.

"I can't thank you enough for including us this evening."

"Think nothing of it. We enjoy your company as much as you seem to enjoy ours," Kitty interjected.

"Adam, I hope the girls were not a bother to you. I got the impression that the three of you were having a good time."

"Julia and Dorothy were nice to me and seemed to want to know all about me. I don't know why. I'm just a paperboy."

Kitty made a comment that only made sense to Adam and me.

"Oh, I think we know that's not true. You're a fine young man and it shows through clearly. Babe picked up on it the first time he met you. Never sell yourself short, young man. I think you are destined for great things."

Adam beamed and blushed a little under her praise.

"Thank you, Mrs. Barton. I appreciate that. I hope you're right."

"I'm certain of it."

"Ditto for me too, kid," added Jim.

CHAPTER FIFTEEN
The Task at Hand
May 18, 1933

Although our life was what most people might call "enchanted," rubbing shoulders with celebrities and occasionally dining at fine restaurants, we were still very homesick. Adam was missing his family and friends and I was missing my wife as well as my daughters, Tara and Eileen's families. Worst of all, we were missing family events and lots of birthdays. Today was my granddaughter, Emma's ninth birthday. Well, it wasn't really, since she would not be born for another seventy-two years in 2005. However, Adam and I were sure that they must be celebrating it back in our time.

All we could hope was that it had to be an extremely important reason to have been transported back in time to this specific year. I still can't explain why I felt this but I was more convinced than ever that we had traveled back in time because of my Dad. Today would confirm that I was on the right track.

Adam had left for the *Brooklyn Eagle* loading dock while I was free for the morning. Jim had asked me to pick him up at five. He had a show at the Cotton Club that started at seven. We both felt that would be plenty of time to drive into the City since most of the rush hour traffic would be heading away from the City while we were driving in. I had decided to take the Williamsburg Bridge. The Triborough Bridge, which would have been my first choice would not open until 1936 and my second pick, the Queens Midtown Tunnel, would not be a viable choice until 1940. It was still a challenge remembering which bridges and tunnels were not around yet and not mentioning them when I was with anyone.

It was only a few weeks ago that I had slipped up. Jim was telling me stories about vaudeville that he knew entertained me. I was not concentrating and started heading toward the Hunters Point section of Queens to catch the Tunnel.

Jim looked up and realized we were not in Brooklyn. "Where the hell are you going, Bob?"

It hit me that I was heading for the-not-built-yet tunnel.

"I'm sorry, Jim. I wasn't even thinking. I was lost in your story."

"If you're not going to pay attention to the road, I'll stop."

"No, don't. I'm good. Finish what you were saying."

I navigated the Lincoln into the next side street and around the block finally heading in the right direction to catch the Brooklyn Bridge into Manhattan. Jim shook his head but seemed to accept my explanation.

We finally pulled up to the Club, and before he headed in, he asked if I wanted to see the show. I could not believe myself when I replied that if it was alright, I'd like to go back to my apartment in Brooklyn and check out how Adam was doing. I was surprised because just a few weeks earlier I would have never passed up a chance to see Jim dance. My focus was now getting back on track as to how we were going to get back. Einstein's return to America seemed like ages away and I was clueless where to start. I needed his genius which I was sorely lacking in. But the effort had to be obvious to Adam since I did not want him to give up any hope of returning to our time.

Chapter Fifteen

Two cars pulled out just halfway down the block from our apartment leaving a huge spot that allowed me to park the Lincoln easily. Kids swarmed all over the car since cars like this were not common in these parts.

"Hey, Mister! Are you a millionaire or sumptin'?" one kid yelled.

"Sorry kid. I'm just a driver. This is my boss's car."

I tossed him a dime.

"Can you make sure the other kids don't leave too many smudges on the shine?"

He looked at the dime like I had just given him a fortune. Without answering me, he turned around and got between the car and the other kids.

"Okay, ya bums. Take it easy. Y'all get a turn. Line up and I'll let ya get a closer look, but don't touch da merchandise."

I obviously had picked the leader of the pack. They got in line and one-by-one he let them stand on the running board and look into the car. I headed down the block to my place knowing the car was in good hands.

When I got to the apartment, the door was ajar. I kept telling Adam to check that the door was closed when he left or returned. Henny always reminded me to do the same when we left our room at motels, and I finally had gotten the hint over time that it was a good idea. This door tended to not latch properly at times. I walked in and was surprised to see Adam sitting at the kitchen table with Jules who looked obviously nervous and worried.

"What are you doing here and how do you know where we live?"

"Second question first, Pops. I know people. If you're not trying to hide, like youse guys, it's easy to find someone. First question. I may need your help. You seem to know stuff."

"Okay, but do me a favor. Don't call me Pops. That's reserved for my grandson and in some ways, it creeps me out when you say it. Don't ask me why. Just don't do it. Alright?"

"Understood. Now here's da rub."

I pulled out a chair to listen. Majewskis never have a short version in any conversation.

"I've been given a huge honor. The mob wants me to take an oath to da Family and den I am a member for life. They rarely let anyone who is not 'Eye-talian do this. And..."

I cut him off.

"You can't do this!" I said, raising my voice.

"If you take that oath, there is nothing they can't ask of you and that includes murder. After that, if you refuse anything that they want you to do, that oath gives them the right, in their minds, to punish you and that can include *your murder*."

"How do you know this stuff? Were you a part of the mob or sometin'?"

"I have friends, too. We share information when we find it out. It helps keep us in the know and out of trouble."

"Who are these guys?"

"You've never heard of them."

"Who are dey? Maybe I know them."

"Not likely. One group I use a lot calls themselves 'Google.'"

"You mean like 'Barney Google', the cartoon guy?" he said, scrunching up his eyebrows and shaking his head slowly as if to clear the fog.

I had to think fast.

"Kind of. But they refer to the fact that they have 'eyes' on stuff, googly eyes on information."

Chapter Fifteen

I looked over to Adam who rolled his eyes and slapped his forehead while he waited to hear what horse crap I was going to sling next.

"I've lived in Brooklyn my whole life and I've never heard of dese 'Google' guys. What gang are dey with?"

"They're not with a gang. It's just a group of people who collect and share information."

"Are there many groups like this?"

I could not resist the entertainment factor for Adam. I pushed my luck and added.

"There are a lot but I mostly go to the 'Googles' and sometimes 'Yahoos.'"

At this point, Adam could not control himself and started to laugh.

Jules looked at him and was clearly annoyed. He looked back at me.

"Are you pullin' my leg, old man? The only 'Yahoos' I know of are all jerks and dhey're all from outa' town. That's why we call them 'Yahoos'."

I had to get him off this subject.

"What difference does it make who I get the info from? The information is good and I have more."

"Go on," he said with a languid wave of his hand.

"The other part of this is, if you don't accept the offer to take the oath, they will be okay with that and you can refuse to do the nasty stuff that family members have to. Most likely they will never ask you because you're not a family member. But they will keep you on the payroll because you're obviously a good worker."

"How do I know dhat what you're sayin' is true?"

"I got it straight from the horse's mouth. I overheard one of Lucky Luciano's pals tell it to some guy. They didn't know I was listening."

Well, technically I had heard it from one of Lucky's associates. I saw an interview with one of his henchmen on the History Channel. That counts. Right?

"You know some of the Luciano Gang?! Are you a Fed or something?"

"Focus! Forget where I got the information. It's all good. Get that into that thick skull. You have to come up with a better plan for your future. I've already told you that if you keep hanging with these guys you could end up as a casualty and then you'd be of no help to anyone. I have some connections. Let me see what I can find for you. I'm sure your Pop would want you to change jobs if he knew what you were doing."

"Leave my Pop outta 'dis."

"Look, you came here for my advice and I'm giving it to you. Sorry it's not what you wanted to hear but it's the best you're going to get from me or anyone else. So wise up. You're starting to piss me off."

Adam never heard me talk like this but sometimes 'Brooklyn Speak' was the only way to get the message through to this young Polack. The wisdom of his later years was yet to come. He was still a kid and hadn't learned anything worthwhile as far as I was concerned. Tonight, he was still an eighteen-year-old knucklehead with much to learn.

Jules sat back and as he played with a fork that was on the table he relented.

"You're right. I know it. It's just so hard to leave the money I get for doing half the work my Pop does down on the docks. He makes a lot less den me."

Chapter Fifteen

"But he sleeps like a log at night and doesn't have to worry about being shot unloading the ships at the dock. He knows he'll be there for his family. Wouldn't you like that feeling?"

He simply nodded his head. He had no more argument left in him. He knew I was right. He pushed back his chair and held out his hand. I took it and we shook.

"As soon as I hear of something I'll leave a message at your house. Until then, keep your nose clean and watch your back. Understood?"

"Sure thing, Bob. Thanks."

He shut the door and this time it latched properly.

I looked at Adam.

"Now why can't you remember to do that."

We both laughed.

CHAPTER SIXTEEN
The Girls
May 26, 1933

I dropped Adam off in front of the apartment house at 345 West 88th Street which was the home of none other than Babe Ruth. I was surprised at the plain exterior of the building with its simple brick work and lack of architectural ornamentation. This was a far cry from the Babe's previous residence at the Ansonia Hotel on Broadway which almost looked like a Victorian Castle. His wife had told me, the last time we met, that they had opted to use her apartment after they got married because she had fourteen rooms to his seven.

I couldn't help but think that their place had more rooms than my house in 2013. It took up one entire floor of the building. They needed all that space because, in addition to the four of them, Claire's two brothers and their mother also lived with them. Claire had told me with pride that her brothers were World War I Vets and had not settled down yet to start their own families. I accepted her explanation, knowing that in this time period that Post Traumatic Stress Disorder had not been identified nor was it treated in almost any form. The common medical wisdom was that eventually the patient would get over it after returning home and leading a non-combat normal life. I knew little to nothing of her brothers' history and could only surmise that they were still close to the home fires due to the comfort they found from staying with loving family. Meanwhile,

Chapter Sixteen

many vets filled 'mental hospitals' for decades with little progress.

I grew up in a post-World War II, Korea, and the Vietnam War era and realized we were still learning what the horror of war did to men and boys that we sent overseas. Somehow, we are still learning how to help our troops coming home from war, even in the 21st Century. Maybe the only answer was to try and eliminate the need for war. My sixties mind, both that of a man in his sixties and one who lived through that decade, never stops hoping.

I parked the Chevy and caught up with Adam just as he was ringing the doorbell at the Ruth's apartment. Claire answered the door with a broad smile.

"Welcome, gentlemen. Adam, the girls are waiting for you in the living room. Bob, Jim did tell you that you were going out to dinner with us, didn't he?"

I turned like a men's wear model holding my suit jacket open to show the fine silk lining.

"Jim did tell me that was Babe's plan. So, I dressed to impress. I don't want to embarrass you."

"You look the refined gentleman. Babe looks great in suits as well. We've made reservations at the *Top of the Sixes*. Paul Whiteman's band is always great. I just love his recording of *Willow Weep for Me*. I hope you like to dance because I feel like dancing tonight. You do dance, don't you Bob?"

"I have to admit that I'm not up to date on the latest dances."

I was thinking that I never learned dances from the '30s. I do remember that my parents were supposed to be the best at a dance called the Peabody, but I didn't know if it was invented yet. I went for it.

"Do you know the Peabody?"

"Do I know the "Peabody?!" she answered with a tone that suggested that that was a stupid question.

"Jimmie taught it to me after I saw him do it in his movie *Taxi* last year. Do you know it?"

"No."

"Well, I guess I'll have to teach you, won't I? Babe loves to dance but gets tired before me. When he runs out of steam, you'd better be ready. I will warn you that he is a tough act to follow. He's a great dancer."

Babe had walked in on the end of her comment but knew what she was up to.

"I hope the old ticker is up for some dancing, Bob. When Claire wants to dance there's no excuse you can come up with that she can't hit out of the park."

He laughed heartily then added, "I'm good for five or six. I'm counting on you to pinch hit for me when I need a rest."

"You do remember how old I am. But I'll do my best if Claire leads."

"Don't worry about that. She always does with me and I'm sure she will lead you in the dance as well."

I wasn't totally comfortable with the idea of dancing with another woman since my wife has truly been my only dance partner for the last forty plus years. I was pretty sure that when I got back to our time and if I ever had to explain the situation she would understand. After all, I was old enough to be Claire's father and how do you say no to Babe Ruth?

Babe came out of the kitchen carrying a cup of coffee. He started to place it on a credenza when I noticed some baseball cards scattered on the top of the cabinet. I am not a collector of baseball cards but have seen enough Antiques Road Shows on PBS to know which cards had real value. I had a heart attack

Chapter Sixteen

seeing a Goudy yellow Ruth card among the random selection scattered about. Most had multiple coffee ring stains on them leading me to think that they were more appreciated as "coasters" than anything of value. I did not want to think about how many hundreds of thousands of future dollars were being stained beyond value to preserve a forgettable piece of furniture. He placed the cup down adding a new stain to the collection.

Babe helped Claire with her black, satin wrap which matched her long evening dress. I was glad I had opted for my best suit. By this time, I had saved enough to buy a second suit without Kitty's generosity. I was getting used to the fact that men dressed up a lot in this era. Henny would be laughing at how often I had to wear a suit. I'm basically a T-shirt and jeans kind-of-guy, "lost in the '60s", or is it "lost in the future past"? She'd waged many a battle just to get me to wear a shirt with a collar and here I was attired, more often now, the way I dressed for weddings and wakes back in our time.

I made one last pass back to the living room to check on Adam and the girls. They had already set up the board game called *The Landlord Game*.

"Hello girls. My you both look very pretty tonight."

Julia was wearing a smart, white dress with pink lace and satin accents. Dorothy's was more like a plain party dress and again more juvenile. Were they trying to impress Adam?

Adam looked up at me and remarked, "This looks a little more complicated but it reminds of...."

I cut him off.

"It's the latest version of one that we had a few years ago. Read the rules. I'm not sure that they changed although the real estate names might be different."

Adam glanced down at the board.

"These sound like New York streets and neighborhoods. What were they before?"

"I'm pretty sure that they were based on Chicago landmarks originally. Whatever, the goal should still be the same. Whoever builds a monopoly first should win. You girls had better be on your toes. Don't let him buy up too much property and don't let him sweet talk you into any trades that you'll regret later."

Dorothy spoke up first. "We won't, Mr. Majeski."

"Daddy taught us that winning is always more fun. Sorry, Adam," said Julia.

Adam laughed.

"Okay, girls. The gloves are off. I'll be the banker, okay? I'll start counting out the money."

I turned back toward the foyer, grabbed my hat and headed out the door with the Ruths. I still could not wrap my head around all of this. I was going out for dinner and dancing with the Babe and Claire. We were going to the *Top of The Sixes* to hear Paul Whiteman and his orchestra. I was going to hear the 'King of Jazz' live. No scratchy eighty-year-old record here but the real deal.

Meanwhile, Adam was staying with Julia and Dorothy. Their grandmother and uncles would also be home so I knew that the kids were in good hands. Wait till I tell Kitty about all this. She'd laugh her head off knowing that when we got back to our time we could never tell anyone unless we wanted to get locked up in a psych ward.

CHAPTER SEVENTEEN
666 Fifth Avenue

We took the elevator up to the top floor and stepped out into the incredible art deco embellished foyer of the famed *Top of the Sixes*. You could hear Whiteman's orchestra weaving their magic around the Irving Berlin tune *Blue Skies*. The *maître d* immediately recognized the Ruths. He looked at me as if to say, "This guy is a power player, who?"

Before he questioned my presence, Babe put his hand on my shoulder and introduced me to him.

"Er, kid . . ."

"Francis," whispered Claire.

"Yes, Francis, this is Bob, a good friend of mine. Treat him as you would me."

A huge grin appeared and he bowed at the waist.

"Welcome, Bob. Any friend of Mr. Ruth's is always an honored guest at our establishment."

Turning to Babe, he said, "Your table is ready. I'll take you there personally. I saved you the best, as always."

He led us through well-spaced tables that allowed elegantly gowned women to easily pass to be escorted to the large dance floor. I was impressed, but not surprised, that our table was dead center directly across from the bandstand and right on the edge of the dance floor. After all, the Ruths were a big deal and as with everywhere we seemed to go we were seated in full view to boost the facility's reputation as the place to be. I didn't look directly at those who already watched our arrival. I didn't want to see faces all screwed up trying to figure out who I was and then realize that I was no one famous.

A waiter came to our table and took our drink orders. You would never know that Prohibition was still in force. I ordered a rye and ginger not knowing what cocktails might be around yet that were common in my time. This was a safe guess and the waiter never blinked when I ordered. As we listened to the waiter's presentation of the specials for the night, the band left the stage for a break. Babe ordered a twenty-four-ounce New York steak while Claire chose the Atlantic salmon. I could not pass up the venison medallions.

Our conversation was lively, centering around the music of the day. I was disappointed that Babe and Claire were not impressed by my knowledge of the bands, singers and songs of the times. Why would they be? After all, why would they, since they thought of me as a contemporary citizen of their times. My Dad, during the 1960s, would have been proud knowing that he had taught me so well.

I was surprised that we were interrupted only twice by patrons requesting autographs from the Babe for their kids. Anyone who knew Babe would know that he could never say 'no' if it was for a kid. I had to wonder if they really had any little ones at home. I found out that this was really a rare event for the Ruths since Babe preferred small local restaurants like *Conte's* in the Village and *House of Chang* near their home to avoid the autograph seekers and enjoy a little privacy.

Paul Whiteman and his musicians returned to the stage, just as we finished our main course. Whiteman turned toward the tables focusing directly on our table.

"Good evening, ladies and gentlemen! I hope that you are ready to dance off some of the splendid meals that you have just

Chapter Seventeen

enjoyed because my boys and I are here to make music. I have also heard from a reliable source that there is someone here who just loves our rendition of *Willow Weep for Me*. I have brought Irene Taylor to reprise her vocal refrain just as she sang it on our hit record."

He looked straight at Claire and added, "For your pleasure, Madame."

Turning to the band, he raised his baton and the violins laced into the slow opening tempo soon covered by the brass section. When Ms. Taylor started to sing the intro, I could not believe how sweet she sang with a wonderful hint of the swing sound that would not follow for another few years.

This was followed by applause as the band went right into *It's Only a Paper Moon*. Miss Taylor did another great rendition with the vocals.

"Our next number features Phil Dewey and the Pickens Sisters. Join us on the dance floor while we play Cole Porter's great song *Night and Day*. Claire grabbed Babe and pulled him up to dance. It was something to see that big guy glide across the floor into the crowd. What a tragedy that people did not dance like this in my time.

Before Claire and Babe could leave the floor Whiteman made another announcement.

"I have a special treat tonight and I know one young man who is going to be thrilled."

He tipped his baton toward a couple in front of the bandstand.

"Welcome Joe Venuti and his jazz violin to the *Top of the Sixes*."

My jaw dropped. Venuti was undeniably my Dad's favorite jazz musician and here I was seeing him perform in person. He went right into his rendition of *The Blue Room* which I knew note-for-note since my father played that seventy-eight RPM record more times than I could count.

All of a sudden, the dance floor seemed to respond to something as people moved off to the sides to allow room as an elegant couple glided around the floor in what could only be called the perfect Peabody. Their shoulders never moved as their feet seemed to barely touch the floor circling the room. Claire and Babe stood aside with everyone else as the tuxedoed gent and his beautifully gowned partner garnered the attention and admiration of the entire room. Even the waiters and bartenders stopped to watch.

As they came closer to where I was standing with the Ruth's I could not believe my eyes. Jules, my future Dad, went by leading a drop-dead gorgeous girl, in a royal blue satin gown, around the floor to the music of Joe Venuti and Paul Whiteman. When the song ended, Whiteman motioned for Venuti to take a bow and then pointed his baton toward the young couple in the middle of the dance floor. The young woman held the hem of her gown up slightly as she performed a perfect curtsey while Jules bowed at the waist.

"Let's hear it for the best Peabody dancers in New York. Jules and Patricia!"

The crowd erupted into applause and then filled the dance floor as the orchestra broke into Jerome Kern's *Let's Begin*.

I stood stunned at the edge of the dance floor until I saw Jules and his partner making their way directly to me through the dancing couples. He walked right up to me with the biggest grin I had ever seen him make.

"How'd ya like dem apples, Pops?"

Chapter Seventeen

I looked at him in a perfectly-cut tuxedo. He was the picture of gentry that in my time someone might have said, "Women want to be with him and men want to be him." There was no hint of his ethnic and working-class background. His date was truly a stunner. Her satin gown brought out the electric blue of her eyes that was further enhanced by her flawless makeup framed by shiny dark brown wavy hair that was almost black.

"You both were fantastic out there. Somehow, I knew you might be a good dancer but that was incredible. I have to ask. What are you doing here? How did you get a gig like this?"

"We're here by popular demand, Bob. We won a dance contest a few months ago. Whiteman happened to be there and now he pays us to dance every weekend. We even get a table in the back row and meals. Great gig, huh? I could ask the same of you."

"I'm here with some friends."

Then I gave him a sly grin. I stepped to the side to give him a full view of the Ruths who had just returned to our table. His jaw dropped and his eyes almost popped out of his sockets as he immediately recognized the Babe.

Babe had looked up just as Jules reached out with his hand.

"It's an honor to meet you, Mr. Ruth."

I quickly jumped in.

"Babe, this is a good friend of mine, Jules Majewski. He lives over in Bay Ridge."

Ruth stood up and shook his hand vigorously.

"Wow. I finally get to meet the best Peabody dancer in New York City."

Jules was stunned at this remark. Here was the best baseball player alive being honored to meet him, a guy from Brooklyn. For the first time in my life, I saw my father almost speechless.

"Trust me Mr. Ruth, the honor is all mine."

Ruth waved to the *maître d'* who quickly came over.

"How may I help you Mr. Ruth?"

"Please bring two chairs for our guests. And please take their drink orders."

He looked at the young couple.

"You will join us for drinks, please."

"Yes, yes. Of course, it would be an honor."

"Stop with the 'honor' stuff, Kid. I'm just a ball player but you're a great dancer. Now let's have a drink and enjoy the night."

Jules pulled out a chair for his date and as he took his own seat Ruth added, "And who might this lovely lady be?"

"Pat, Patricia Dugan, Sir."

"It's Babe, Okay, Jules and Pat?"

"Right. 'Babe' it is." They answered in unison with grins as big as any teens could make. The tough mob guy was gone and for a moment Jules was just a star-struck kid.

"And this is my wife, Claire."

Hands went across the table as everyone accepted their introductions. It was another night for the books. Seeing my Dad in his prime commanding the dance floor every time he stepped out with Pat topped my having dinner with Babe. For an eighteen-year-old, Jules held his own in the conversation and had everyone laughing at his jokes. He had that talent as an older man but I had no idea when it started. Now my guess was that he could probably tell a joke better than anyone all the way back to grammar school.

Claire kept to her promise and taught me how to Peabody. I couldn't wait to get back to my time and show Henny my new dancing skill. As I danced with Claire, I again realized how much

Chapter Seventeen

I missed my wife. I had no idea when, if she knew I was gone. If she was aware, then I know she had to be even more worried about us since it must seem like we dropped off the face of the earth. The whole family must be beside themselves. All I could do for now was live in the moment and continue to wait for history to catch up so that we could get Einstein's help. I had to believe that he could figure out a way to get us back home.

I shook my head and returned to the moment. I was amazed by the level of dancing skills that I saw all evening. This generation of Americans socialized differently from later ones. These were times when almost all forms of entertainment were live. Even radio was mostly live. Television was not invented yet and this was, in my mind, what may have killed dining and dancing. Television made it possible to be entertained without ever leaving the comfort of your home, or your couch. Henny and I caught the tail end of this genre in the late '60s when we frequented our favorite dinner/dance venue at *The Riverboat* in the basement of the Empire State Building. Now, here I was at the height of this way of life, dancing with Claire Ruth to the band that was piloted by the self-proclaimed *King of Jazz*. Wow!

We broke up the party when the club closed at 3 A.M. and headed back to the Ruth's so I could pick up Adam. When we entered the apartment, we found that the girls had gone to bed and Adam was sleeping on the couch.

"We have a spare bedroom for guests," said Claire as she pulled a blanket over Adam.

"You take that room Bob and we'll see you for breakfast in the morning. It's too late to drive back to Brooklyn now."

I admitted that I was tired and let her lead me to the room and turned in for the night.

CHAPTER EIGHTEEN
A Real Jerk
June 9, 1933

After our evening with the Ruths, we fell back into a routine and waited out the calendar. We got up early in the morning so Adam could have breakfast and get to his corner to catch his bundle of the morning edition of the *Brooklyn Eagle* as they were tossed from the delivery truck. Later, I'd take the Chevy to Mineola to be available for anything that Jim or Kitty Barton needed of me.

This routine was disrupted two weeks later. It was 9 A.M. and I was just heading out when Adam stumbled into the apartment. His jacket was torn at the shoulder. His left eye was almost swollen shut and his upper lip was purple and bleeding. There was a cut on his right ear. That had left a big blood stain on his shirt before it stopped bleeding sometime before he got back home.

I helped him to a chair in the kitchen. I didn't say anything. He was doing everything he could not to cry in front of me. I figured that he would tell me what happened in good time. Until then, I went into my wound care nurse mode and got a bowl of warm water and some clean cloths and tended to his wounds. I knew the injuries would not look as bad as the amount of blood might indicate. Head wounds usually bleed like crazy since there is such a large blood supply to this most important part of the body. I was proud of him because while I did my job he never cried or complained. However, I was also concerned because he

Chapter Eighteen

normally would never be this quiet. He said nothing while I dressed his wounds.

Finally, he opened up and told me how one of the other newsies, who was jealous of his increasing sales, had gotten some of his friends together to gang up on him. Even though Adam was a head taller than any of these kids he was simply outnumbered. He did state proudly that none of them got away unscathed. He wondered how they would explain the black eyes and cuts to their parents. I reminded him that some of these boys probably had no parents. Many had come to the city alone because their families could not afford to feed them back home. I reminded Adam that even though we were doing well by 1933 standards, there were many more faring far worse during these hard times. It took some prodding, but Adam reluctantly gave up the name of the ring leader. I think he was afraid that I might try to exact some revenge and he was right.

I sought out my father and asked for help from his mob connections. After all, he told me that he could find anyone when he sought us out and showed up in our kitchen. They were a bit slower than an internet search in our time but not by much. Within twenty-four hours I had the names and address of the boy and his father. More importantly, he told me about the father's situation and whereabouts.

I planned on taking care of this on my own. Jules insisted that he come with me when I confronted the boy's father. I told him it wasn't his fight. Jules reminded me that he still owed me for saving him that night in the alley. He was not going to be dissuaded. I watched the brownstone where the boy lived for two days before I made my move.

The boy's father was at least six feet tall and weighed in around 220 pounds. He was muscular but some of it had settled around a bit of a beer gut. Conversely, I was five-foot-five-and-one-half-inches-tall and about 170 pounds. Years ago, I had noticed that people under five-and-a-half-feet-tall always counted quarter inches while those over that mark rounded up to the nearest inch. All my life there had always been this mismatch when I was either confronted or defending myself. Not to brag, in time I got good at leveling the playing field by learning some street fighting techniques that saved me more than once. In reality, I had never lost a fight and I surely was not going to end that streak, technically, before I was even born.

That afternoon when Art Kearney, Sr. came home from his job unloading trucks at the docks, I was well prepared to confront him. I climbed the stairs of the Kearney home and twisted the bell in the center of the large oak double doors. As I had hoped, Art, Sr. answered the door.

"Can I help you?" he sneered looking down at me. It was obvious that he was the bullying type just like our surveillance had uncovered. No wonder his son was the way he was.

"Is your son the Art Kearney that's the newsie for the *Eagle*?"

I never blinked and looked him straight in the eye while I asked.

"And if he is, what's it to you, old man?"

Man, how that got my dander up. It was just the right thing for him to say to help get my adrenaline to the level I would need for what I knew I had to do. I tightened my grip on the baseball bat that I hid behind my right leg.

"Well, it seems that your boy decided that he wanted my grandson's corner for himself and got some of his friends together and took it by force. Six against one from my calculations."

"And you got a problem with dat, OLD MAN?"

Chapter Eighteen

He let the last two words drip off his lips slowly. I thought that the adrenaline was going to start spurting out of my ears.

"Not really. But you do."

Before he could comprehend what that might imply, I pulled the bat from behind my leg and, with all that strength that had been building up in me, I swung it forward and up, adding the grip of my left hand, and caught him squarely between the legs where the sun doesn't shine. His eyes bugged out in shock as he fell to his knees. He could not catch his breath and this gave me the opportunity to finish my speech.

I held the fat end of the bat to his nose.

"If you or any of your family or friends so much as look cross-eyed at my grandson again, it will be you that pays for it every time just like now. And that's 'no brag, just fact.' Do I make myself clear?"

He didn't answer.

"Do I make myself clear?!" I calmly but emphatically repeated.

I still don't think he had breath to verbally answer and simply nodded his head, "Yes."

Now, I'm not stupid. I know that the element of surprise only leveled the field for the moment. It only tilted it in my favor for a while. He could easily do the same thing to me. I played my insurance card. After all, I didn't want to get killed before I was born or before I got Adam back home.

"Oh, and before you get any stupid ideas to get back at us, I'd like you to meet my good friend from our local alcohol distributor. They were the ones who gave me your name and address. I don't think they would take it as a sign of respect if you came looking for me or my grandson."

I stepped aside so that he could get a good view of Jules standing at the base of the stairs leaning against the cast iron railing. He gave Kearney a wave.

"How are you doing, sir? Lovely evening."

My Dad was a well-known face at the neighborhood speakeasies and he had told me that he had crossed paths with Art, Sr. enough times that the man had to know him and his affiliation with the mob. His presence confirmed that I was under their protection.

Before I turned, I made one last statement.

"You know, I could have easily broken your arm. But I'm not the kind of person to take away a man's ability to feed his family. These are hard enough times without you and I making them harder for each other. Have a good evening. I'm sure you'll be having a heart-to-heart talk with your son tonight. And by the way, we'll just keep it between us that you just got your ass kicked by, what did you call me, oh yeah, an old man. No need for the guys down at the docks to know about that."

I turned and left him kneeling there. I did not look back when I heard the thud as he fell back into his foyer.

CHAPTER NINETEEN
Another Kind of Jerk
June 12, 1933

At breakfast I announced to Adam that maybe it was time to get out of the newspaper business and try something new. I told him he needed a few days to recover to hunt for a job. Looking like you went a few rounds with Jack Dempsey, was not the way to make a good first impression. I'd keep my eyes open for any opportunities on my way out to the Island. I told him to rest and recuperate until then.

Two days later, I was driving down Jamaica Avenue through Woodhaven. I normally did not take this route, but word had spread that there was construction on Kings Highway which was backed up for miles. I could not remember the last time I had been in this neighborhood. It had to be in my junior year of high school in the fall of 1964. I was on the track team at St John's Prep and hung out with a few of my teammates regularly after a meet. The common thread with this group was that we all commuted from Nassau County into Brooklyn to attend the Prep in Bedford Stuyvesant.

Since we had a longer trip home than others on the team, we had come up with ways to break up the trip. Our favorite stop was in Woodhaven. My friend, Al Popp had grandparents who lived here on the corner of 85th and Jamaica Ave. They had an apartment over their ice cream parlor cleverly called "Popp's." On one occasion they invited Al, our mutual friend, Kevin McCormack and me to sleep over on a Friday night after track practice since we would have to turn around the next morning for a cross country track meet at Prospect Park in Brooklyn.

There are many memories in life that get tucked away to enjoy later. That night was one of them for me. Grandma Popp had made a great meal although I can't remember what it was but like any teenagers, I am sure that we left no scraps. It was the dessert that I remember like it was yesterday.

We waited until 10 P.M. when the ice cream parlor had been closed for an hour. With the Popps' blessing, Al, Kevin and I went down the back stairs to the darkened eatery. We only turned on the lights behind the white marble counter so that people walking by outside would not think that the parlor was open for business.

I don't think that this place had been remodeled since it was built around the turn of the century. All the cabinets and showcases were made of black walnut. The counter and any top shelves were crafted from white Carrera marble. The wall behind the counter sported an immense beveled-glass mirror with beautifully etched designs in the corners. Classic heavy wire framed ice cream parlor chairs and tables with marble tops mounted on ornate black cast iron pedestals were arrayed across the shop floor. Small hexagon white and black tiles covered the floor. The Popps' place was a time capsule of 1890's decor and was a cherished tradition for the local patrons in the nineteen sixties when I first visited it. Over dinner I commented on the high quality of the bar and fixtures in the shop downstairs.

Mr. Popp told us that before he converted it into an ice cream parlor it had been a liquor bar.

"Then Prohibition was instituted in 1920. Mrs. Popp came up with the idea to switch to ice cream and confections and the rest was history. We started making so much money, more than we

Chapter Nineteen

made when it was a saloon that we never changed back after Prohibition ended in 1933. The clients were a lot nicer, too. That's why the rich furnishings. It was originally meant for the drinking class."

We lived an 'ice cream lover's' fantasy that night when we were allowed to go down to make whatever we wanted. We spent the next ten minutes switching places behind the counter while digging the scoopers into our chosen flavors. These mounting scoops were topped with fresh whipped cream, cherries, and in my case, coconut shreds. Today I'd gain three pounds just looking at a sundae like that. Back then I could lose all that weight the next day during a two-and-a-half-mile cross country race.

What a great experience in a life peppered with so many wonderful events. Everyone has them but most people do not recognize them until much later and sometimes never at all. I have the wonderful clarity to be able to appreciate how special these moments are while I'm living them. Every detail is captured and catalogued to revisit and enjoy all over again in the telling or simply with quiet reflection. I have never taken this gift for granted and my memory bank never gets overcrowded with these wonderful thoughts.

As I passed the corner at 85th Street, I saw a "Help Wanted" sign in the window of Popp's Ice Cream Parlor. I was floored. The interlocking of my life in the future with what I was experiencing now was simply crazy. There were so many questions running through my brain as I spent more time in the '30s. Was my roaming around in this time period having an influence on my life in the future, or was it the reverse? Do we all crisscross with places and people through multiple lives, and what is the reason or purpose if this is true?

Waiting for Einstein

I just had to accept the fact that maybe our life is not full of coincidences. Maybe these are purposeful encounters that help us move along through the continuum of time. I really could not wait to talk to Einstein about this, if and when we ever got together. I hoped that we would since the one thing missing from all these events so far was the answer to how Adam and I could get back.

I found a parking space quickly and approached Popp's to see if there was a phone number or instructions on how to apply. It was too early for the shoppe to be open. As I was reading the "Help Wanted" sign looking for information, an attractive woman in a house dress with a heavy white bib apron that reached the hem of her dress looked around the sign and unlocked the door.

"Can I help you?"

"Actually, you can. My grandson is looking for a job and I spotted your sign."

She introduced herself as Margaret Popp. "You can call me Marge."

Wow. I remembered her when I would have described her as a kind old lady. The funny thing is that she, like everyone I seemed to be running into from my future, was definitely younger than me by a lot. I have to think that she may have still been younger than my current age even when I first met her in 1964. She invited me in and offered me a seat at one of the small tables. She brought over two cups of coffee and asked me about my grandson. I was truthful about Adam's encounter with other newsies and his current appearance due to the post-fight bruising. She must have been impressed with openness and honesty and assumed that, if the apple doesn't fall far from the tree, Adam must be a nice kid as well.

Chapter Nineteen

I left her after she promised to hold the position open until she could do a face-to-face interview with Adam later in the week.

"I'm sure my husband Andy will want to meet him as well."

Knowing how Adam seemed to impress everyone that he met, I was confident that he could get the job. I sure hoped so. It's not that we needed the money. My job with the Bartons had more than taken care of any money issues. I needed Adam to stay busy. That job with the *Eagle* seemed like a good idea but I hadn't considered how the times made it more dangerous than when I had a paper route in the late '50s out in the suburbs of Long Island. Working at an ice cream parlor just seemed like a much safer alternative and I knew that the Popps were good people.

There was a good possibility that my father, Jules, had probably quit high school to help my grandfather support the family. In this society it was expected that the oldest boy start working as young as possible if the family needed him. Since I never heard my father talk about his schooling, I had surmised that he had not spent much time if any in high school. If he had graduated from high school, his life would have been quite different because back then graduating from 12th grade was the equivalent of graduating from college in the 1960s.

In the twenty-first century, a high school diploma might get you a job in a fast-food eatery. With the same diploma in 1913, my Grandpa Kennedy was able to start in the banking business working for J.P. Morgan at one of his banks in the Wall Street district. When the market crashed in 1929, J.P. personally made sure that my grandfather was set up in a good job after the banking office he worked in closed. Raymond Kennedy would work for the Keystone Paint Company as their CFO and office manager until he retired in the mid-sixties. One fact has always been true. It's always good to have friends in high places, this was especially true during the Depression.

As expected, after prompting Adam to wear a tie and jacket, he interviewed, and with no surprise to me, was offered the job on the spot. He was now going to be a "soda jerk." Knowing the Popps and the fact that this was not the tough neighborhood that Adam had been frequenting made me feel better. It would be interesting to see what Adam's take-away would be from this experience working at a soda fountain. He definitely got 'street smarts' from his last job. I did worry that he would change too much and that it would be noticeable when we got back to our time. After all, we are a product of our personal influences, environment, and experiences. At Adam's age, he was growing and changing on a daily basis. What would he be like by October when Einstein finally settled in New Jersey? Time would tell.

CHAPTER TWENTY
"Just Fact"
July 10, 1933

I was sitting across the table from Jules at a luncheonette around the corner from our apartment. He was telling me the latest Brooklyn 'street news' that you could not find in the *Eagle*. It seemed that the latest buzz was that there was this old guy that had made quite a name for himself with the young thugs and local bullies. The recommendation by his victims was simple.

"Don't mess with his friends and definitely don't think of doing anything to his grandson."

Jules continued, "And when he says *No brag, just fact,* you'd better protect your jewels because you won't have time to turn and run. He's as quick as a rattlesnake."

At first, I thought this was funny that an 'old man' could get this kind of notoriety. Then I thought it wasn't so funny when I realized that the 'old man' he was referring to was me. And how would anyone in Brooklyn know how fast a rattlesnake strikes? I had another thought based on the storyline of the *Guns of Will Sonnett* that worried me. What if there was somebody out there that now saw me as a challenge? Wouldn't it be a feather in his cap to be the one to take down this new 'street legend'? I relayed my concerns to Jules.

"We took care of that when we visited Kearney. I have repaid my debt to you. I'm here to tell you that the mob protection that we pretended you had to Kearney is real. When I told my boss how you saved my skin that time in the alley, he felt the least he could do was protect your *dupa* as well. The other part of the news that I can tell you is this. If there is anyone stupid enough to try and hurt you, his knees won't be working so well after that. That's the best insurance policy in Brooklyn. You have nothing to worry about. We got your back."

So now my Dad had me connected to the mob as well.

"I don't know what to say. This is really a load off my mind for me and Adam. But you know I'm still worried about you. The life expectancy of a mobster is not much better than a front-line soldier during war. I can't tell you why you are so important to us but you are."

It was really interesting to realize that I was trying to protect my future existence by getting my Dad into a safer lifestyle while he was providing me protection provided by the same mob connections. I also could not tell him how much I loved him and had missed him in my life since he had died in 1988.

"Now that we have assured my safety, how do I convince you that a career change might be a good thing? I know that you are helping your Pop with feeding the family but that all goes away if you're wounded, or worse, dead."

"Bob, ya have said dhat to me more dhan once. I get it and ya worry too much. I'm good. Nothin' is going to happen to me."

"Don't you ever think about your future? Maybe meeting a girl, settling down, having kids? At your age I had already met my future wife. Are you serious about that Dugan girl you're dancing with?"

"Nah. She's a good kid but we're just friends. I've known her all my life. She's more like a sista' than a girlfriend."

I already knew that she was not going to be the one, since my Mom, Dorothea Kennedy and he would not meet until 1937. My job was to set him on a path to stay alive long enough to get to that point in his life without me. I could not hang around and

Chapter Twenty

hold his hand for another four years. I had to get Adam back home as soon as possible.

Jules sat there looking pensive, and then asked me a question.

"You never mention your wife to me. Is she still alive?"

I had prepared myself for any questions like this and had rehearsed a plausible answer. It just surprised me that no one had asked me until now.

"You know Jules, things are not much different here than they are in the midwest and on the west coast. Some people leave their families to find work when they can't find any at home. I have a great wife of forty-one years back in Connecticut. Adam's family is back there also. We came down here to find work. Since my family came from Brooklyn and the Island, I know my way around here and felt I had a better chance to find some employment. I was right."

"I'd say, wit' hangin' out with Babe Ruth and all those famous people in the City. Seems like ya've hit the jackpot."

"It will only be the jackpot when the economy gets better and I can be back with my wife and Adam, with Karen, David, Colin, his Mom and Dad and little brother."

"Well, I really like ya, Bob. I think ya have style and, God knows, ya know how to take care of ya'self. I hope ya get to go home soon. I'll miss ya but I won't miss ya nagging me about gettin' out of the bootleggin' business."

"The only thing I'm going to say on that subject is that I want you to always remember that you have a responsibility to the next generation as well as your own."

"What is ya problem? Ya're always worried about some imaginary kids that I don't even have yet. I don't even know if I'll ever have kids. This is a tough world and I'm not sure I want to bring any more kids into it. No one knows how long this Depression is going to last."

"Sometimes I don't think I know you. Your family is the most optimistic group of people I have ever met."

Jules looked at me deeply. I had to stop talking.

"How do you know anything about my family? You only met them once. Don't tell me what my family is like." He mumbled lowly. "No matter how right you are."

"Okay, I'll back off. Just keep your options open. Alright?"

We shook hands on it. That was the best I could hope for at this point. However, I still felt that my future was on a shaky foundation until my father got his act together. I'd have to keep an eye on him without him knowing it. Meanwhile, Adam and I had to hunker down and continue to live life until Einstein arrived.

CHAPTER TWENTY-ONE
Meeting Winnie May
July 15, 1933

Life fell into a new routine. I'd drop Adam off at Popp's on my way out to the Island to work for the Bartons. If I had to take Jim and Kitty somewhere then Adam jumped on the BMT elevated train to return to the apartment. Other days I'd pick him up on the way home if he worked until closing. On occasion, Adam was invited to the Ruths to keep the girls company while Babe and Claire went out on the town. He was the only boy the Ruths trusted with the girls.

Jim continued to hang out with his famous friends. He collected them like some people collect seashells or postcards from around the world. Inadvertently, he exposed me to people and places that historians from my time could only dream of meeting. There could be no better example of this than an event that Adam and I got to witness due to Jim's influence in a society that caters to celebrity just as much as it does in the twenty first century.

It was on Saturday, July 15th to be exact, when we had to get up at 3 A.M. Adam had asked for the day off and because of the significance of the event, Mrs. Popp gladly gave him the time off. He had exceeded her expectations over the past months and had been looking for a way to reward him when he asked her. What made it even better was that she promised him the day off with pay.

Waiting for Einstein

We had a tight schedule to keep and I wanted to leave plenty of time to get out to Mineola, pick up Jim, and double back to Brooklyn. I had quickly learned the traffic patterns for all times of the day and every day of the week. It's a New York thing but we all talk traffic and the guy that knows the fastest way between two points in and around New York City always wins.

Even though we had no idea how big a crowd would be there, we knew that Jim's celebrity would give us a front seat for this historic event. Due to the early hour of the morning, I covered the seventeen miles out to the Bartons in record time. I almost dragged Jim out of his house by his heels and threw him into my little Chevy. Adam had jumped into the rumble seat as Jim took the passenger seat next to me. There was no time to warm up the Lincoln. My little Chevy coupe was quick enough to negotiate any traffic and would be easier to park when we got there. Adam had barely slid down into the rumble seat as his head snapped back as I popped the clutch, quickly made a huge U-turn on Jericho Turnpike to race back toward the city line and Brooklyn. I had removed my collection of political and sports pins a while ago so that was a problem avoided with any of my passengers not in the know.

"Wow! This little puppy can fly!" Jim commented.

This was the first time that he had been in my car. I drove a little more aggressively than when I was ferrying him to his shows where the Lincoln would have been impossible to find parking.

"Let's just say that she is tweaked a little."

I had to leave it at that. The reality was that there was a 1939 Chevy six under the hood with 20 more horsepower than a '33 six. Not to mention the '46 ½ ton Chevy truck transmission, '41 Chevy high-ratio rear end and hydraulic brakes that were

Chapter Twenty-One

necessary to stop her since she could easily hit seventy miles per hour when needed. These refinements were all compliments of my mentor, Guy Roese, and had come in handy while negotiating traffic in our time and especially now in 1933.

I won't deny that I ran a few traffic lights and cut off a few trolley cars along Flatbush Avenue as we approached Floyd Bennett Field across from Dead Horse Bay. We actually pulled up to an area behind the hangars by twenty-five minutes to five. I had checked out the airport two days earlier so I knew the best place to get closer to the action. I had found the hangar where the *Winnie Mae* was. I was sure that she would be kept close after being pulled out for publicity photos and interviews before she would eventually taxi down the runway for takeoff. My planning paid off. A short, brisk walk around the hangar found us standing between the building and the *Winnie Mae* where less than a dozen airport personnel were milling about watching the event.

We continued under the nose of the C5 Vega monoplane. God, that plane was prettier in real life than any photo could capture. I reached up and touched the engine cover with its beautiful blue accents, trimmed in black lines that converged into one single line going all the way back to the tail. I knew that I would never get to do that again. The security staff at Smithsonian Air and Space Museum in Washington, D.C. would never let that happen where the plane sits on the second floor in my century.

Winnie Mae was in big block letters on the fuselage near the tail section. A huge black NR-105-W dominated the underside of the left wing. On the other side of the plane, a large crowd gathered around this guy in a leather jacket with a patch over his left eye.

Waiting for Einstein

I leaned over to Adam and almost had to yell in his ear for him to hear me.

"That's Wiley Post, the famous aviator."

"I know, Pop," he yelled back. "I haven't been living under a rock. I've read lots of papers in the last few months and he's been in the Pathe Newsreels at the movies often enough."

Jim walked up behind the aviator and put his hand on his shoulder. Wiley turned and recognized Jim immediately.

"Hey, Jimbo, I was wondering if you'd show up. I know you love a good show and I promise you this one will be a hit."

In his gravelly voice Jim laughed and replied, "There's no doubt in my mind, my boy. The only question is how fast are you going to do it?"

"I recommend you start camping out here in a week. I can't pinpoint it better than that. I plan to land here in eight days or less. I just have to figure out a way to stay awake."

Wiley turned back to the reporters and the crowd. Jim looked at Adam and me.

"I wish I had an answer for that problem. It's a pilot's worst nightmare to fall asleep at the stick."

Adam gave us the look he always gave me when we were playing computer games at home.

"Why doesn't he just hold something heavy, like a wrench in his hand and if he falls asleep it will fall to the floor. The sound will wake him up."

Jim and I looked at each other. Jim looked at Adam.

"Don't tell us, tell him."

Jim tapped Wiley on the shoulder and he turned around again. "The kid has an idea. You might want to hear this."

Wiley stepped toward my grandson and Adam spoke loudly into his ear relaying his idea.

Chapter Twenty-One

"Not a bad idea, kid but that motor is pretty loud. I wouldn't hear anything drop."

Adam thought quickly and answered.

"Why don't you tie it on a short cord to your wrist so it can't reach the floor. It will tug on your arm and wake you if you drift off and drop it."

Post beamed a huge smile. He yelled to his mechanic.

"I need some cord and a big wrench, Fred."

He turned to Adam.

"Thanks, kid. I'll let you know how it worked when I get back."

He shook Adam's hand and turned back to the crowd.

Shortly after all this and lots of handshakes with dignitaries and 'Good Lucks' all around, Wiley climbed onto the front wheel cover to a footstep in the fuselage and ascended to the top of the plane. After giving a final wave to the crowd, he climbed into the cockpit. By ten minutes after five A.M., Wiley took off for his record-breaking solo flight around the world.

July 22, 1933
Witnessing History

Seven days, eighteen hours and forty-nine minutes later, his wheels touched down on the landing strip. He taxied the *Winnie Mae* slowly through the huge crowd which closed in on the plane when the propeller sputtered to a stop. The three of us were there again to shake his hand after he popped out of the top of the plane and climbed down the nose, onto the landing gear to alight onto the tarmac. We had been pushed by the sea of people right under the left wing of the *Winnie Mae*.

He spotted my grandson and recognized him immediately.

"We weren't introduced properly by that no-good Irishman. What's your name, kid?"

"Adam, sir."

"Adam what?"

"Adam Majeski, sir."

"A Polack! Thank you Master Majeski, it wasn't very technical but your idea worked just fine and weighed a lot less than a co-pilot. I used the heavy wrench like you suggested and when I fell asleep it fell from my hand and jerked my arm waking me every time. You may have saved my life more than once. Thanks again, kid."

He turned toward the crowd again and was swept away in a sea of well-wishers.

When I was young, I had always been fascinated with the look and design of the *Winnie Mae*. I even made a model of the plane in the late '50s. Was my interest in the plane a subconscious awareness of my experience in the past, or was my involvement in this event now the trigger for wanting to build the model in the future? The longer we spent in the past, the more blurred experiences became between the future and the past.

Maybe all my current experiences were the trigger for wanting to obtain my '33 Chevy for most of my driving career in the future. If nothing else, 1933 was a pretty good year to visit the New York City area. God knows that I was looking forward to the outcome of the current baseball season I had been following since April. In pro hockey, the N.Y. Rangers had already won the Stanley Cup. These events were the kind of things that helped the common man get through the hard times of the Depression, and they were helping Adam and me keep our sanity as the calendar slowly crept along toward October.

CHAPTER TWENTY-TWO
World Events

No matter where and when you are living, you are affected by, and should be concerned with, world events. In our little world, I was bemoaning the fact that we had missed another birthday party for my granddaughter Julia, which was the twenty fifth of July. We had already missed three in May for Ian, Kevin, and Emma. Would my grandchildren ever talk to me after this? Either way, stuck in the times we were living in, that was such a small issue. I'd figure out a way to make it up to them when we got back.

In our new-old world, times were still bad for many people during the Depression but through my connections, Adam and I were living as good of a life as anyone could hope at this point in history. Conversely, I could not ignore that things were just getting dramatically worse for many people around the world.

Adam and I would watch the newsreels at the movies and watch the reports of the darkening cloud of the Nazi takeover of the German government. It was obvious to us, how life was changing there, especially for the Jewish population, because of our knowledge of what was really happening. We knew, from history, what was not being reported yet. The concentration camps that were being built for Jews and most of the hierarchy of every religion and race had already been planned, built and were soon to be populated by hundreds of thousands of poor souls deemed 'enemies of the people.'

Waiting for Einstein

I mentioned earlier how Adam and I had wrestled with the idea of whether we should risk exposing our time travel experience and try to warn our government. We had decided that even if we could get to Roosevelt or any of his lower-level government officials, our story would be a hard sell and we could end up locked up in a mental hospital without the freedom of movement to find Einstein and get back to our time.

I also felt that we were not here to change world history. Maybe these things cannot be tampered with because the human race has to experience them to become better over the years and centuries, something like tempering steel by constantly heating, hammering, cooling, and reheating. I could not help but think that events that followed the coming World War, followed by the fifties all the way into the 21st Century would prove that many of the future world leaders, including our own, had learned little and were still too eager to use their armies to solve political issues. It has always been frustrating for me to see that some people still believed that imposing the miseries of war on the general population was justified by whatever political, ideological or fiscal dominance they were trying to achieve.

The reports coming out of Germany were telling the stories of university professors, political opponents and, of course, the majority of Jews being rounded up and sent to work camps. These were called concentration camps by the world and later it would be revealed that they were really death camps when the Nazis started using them for mass murdering those who they considered ethnically un-pure or enemies of the state.

My eyes would tear up when these newsreels came on the screen. I sat there knowing that these were not even the worst of times in Europe. I had read that some historians felt that there were not really two World Wars but simply one with a nine year

Chapter Twenty-Two

pause in the middle. World War I resolved nothing and all the problems that caused that war just festered, allowing the Nazis to gain control with the finale not coming until the end of World War II. The frustrations Adam and I felt were maddening at times and were part of the reason that we truly regretted our time-traveling experience. Obviously, missing our family was the primary fact. All the generosity of the Bartons and Ruths could not change our feelings.

There was also the fact that there were so many people throughout our country whose lives were barely hanging by a thin financial thread. There were many more whose threads had already broken. Foreclosures were a daily occurrence in the City and across the country. It was common to see furniture and personal items piled at the curb with the women of the displaced family guarding their things while the men of the family scrambled for alternative living arrangements and a place for their belongings. Sometimes this was not possible and these people would turn to trying to sell their furniture to pedestrians for any amount of money, rather than abandon it to be taken away for free by junk men and rummagers. Kitty had definitely saved Adam and me from a potentially miserable life in the thirties.

Hollywood and the arts were bucking this trend and flourishing since the public looked to the movies to escape their day-to-day hardships. In the past, I had equated those images on the silver screen as 1930s reality. Now I knew they did not mirror the concerns and misery of the average American of the times. This trip definitely was an eye opener and I was going to be viewing classic movies on TCM quite differently when Adam and I got back home to our time.

It was becoming obvious that we really did not belong here. I had to get my Dad back on a better track and complete the mission I was only guessing to be the reason for stumbling back in time. And then we had to get back home as soon as possible.

CHAPTER TWENTY-THREE
Katie Revisited
August, 15, 1933
Adam's Birthday

Last February, in 2013, my wife took me out to dinner and a movie for my birthday. It was a wonderful evening, as always, since Henny and I have always enjoyed each other's company since we started dating back in 1967. I was feeling good about turning sixty-five since I was still in good health. I was on no maintenance drugs, unlike many people my age. All my blood level results were in normal range due to a recent diet that had trimmed twelve pounds off my medium frame.

If you had asked me forty years ago where I would be at this time in my life, I would have correctly guessed still married but probably an old man by most standards, not being able to do many of the things I could as a youth. That had not been the case and I was thrilled that I could still keep up with my grandchildren. Actually, when kayaking during the summers at the lake, it was the kids trying to keep up with me. However, I will admit that I would be the one trying to keep up with them soon enough.

During dinner, I shared my thoughts with Adam, as our conversation turned into a bit of what you could call a 'life review.' I mentioned that one of the best things about my life was the people who I had come to know and love and how they all had a part in shaping the person I had become. Obviously, Henny was first on that list. Without her, I'd probably be some lonely bachelor living over a garage full of old cars, no children, no grandchildren, with none of the achievements of any value that I had experienced in my life.

We had been together since we were teenagers, and Henny had met many of the people that I was naming as influences in my life. When I mentioned Katie Barton, we both agreed that she was probably the most colorful character in our lives. She was a wonderful storyteller and, boy, did she have stories to tell. Having been a Ziegfeld Follies Girl, she told tales as only someone who was a veteran of the Golden Age of stage in New York City could. Her parents were performers and as they say, greasepaint was in her veins. When they performed on stage, she was backstage and as I have mentioned before, that's when she first met the love of her life and now my boss and friend, Jim.

Here I was in 1933, and spending time with Katie, known at this time as Kitty, in the prime of her life. This is a gift I could never have imagined. During my time here, I had spent many an afternoon and evening in the Bartons' company. She was as charming and as down to earth as she was when I knew her thirty years later. The difference was that she was obviously younger, and physically at the most attractive period in her life. The casual and formal dresses in her extensive closet hung perfectly on her.

Heads turned whenever we entered an event or restaurant. Many eyes were on Jim due to his celebrity but then eyes went to Kitty because of her confident beauty and sense of style. Then it hit me. It was her love for Jim that made her glow. I could see that the happiness she felt at being at Jim's side made her more beautiful than her actual physical attributes. It was wonderful to see her so happy since I had met her shortly after Jim's fatal heart attack in 1962. It wasn't till now that I realized that back in 1963

Chapter Twenty-Three

I had only met a part of the whole person that I now knew as Kitty Barton. This was the complete Kitty.

In 1933, she was with her soulmate and I was experiencing the different aura that she gave off while she accompanied Jim to galas, opening nights, and dinners. To be in her presence at this point in her life was to experience her true happiness. It was the same way I felt when I was with my Henny. Jim completed Kitty and I'm sure she completed him as Henny and I do each other. It was also this realization that made me even more homesick and wanting to get back to her more than ever.

To say that Kitty enriched the lives she touched was an understatement. She was the consummate life of the party. Even in the 1960s, when she would get herself invited to my parents' house for Sunday dinner, she could turn a bowl of mashed potatoes into a party event. My teen years and later were richer by far because of "Katie."

I have to say that some of my favorite times with the Bartons in 1933 is when they are with their best friends, Jimmy and Willie Cagney. Stories fly back and forth across the table. They always start with their shared experiences in Vaudeville. Then, Jim Barton will tell current stories of backstage Broadway while Jimmy Cagney regaled us with tales of Hollywood. It's heaven for a guy like me to be in their company because of my love of stage and film. Kitty's quick and generous laughter is the soundtrack for every magical night just as it was when she was at my folks' house for Sunday dinners. She is and was the heart of every party she attended.

With the help of the Bartons, I was able to surprise Adam for his birthday. When we arrived at the *Top of the Sixes,* we were directed to a table near the dance floor where Adam was greeted with a loud, "Happy Birthday!" by Jim and Kitty. He was overwhelmed. Their kindness filled the huge void left by not being with his family.

My father and Patricia Dugan were reprising their Peabody, wowing the crowd as they did every Saturday night. I wanted Adam to see my Dad, his great grandfather, in his prime as a dancer. He was not disappointed. Pat and my Dad danced around gliding across the dance floor as smoothly as skaters at an ice dancing competition, except they were not on skates. The audience was mesmerized by their perfect dance hold and Adam was awestruck by the level of their talent.

"Pop, this is the best present you could have given me short of getting us back home."

"I knew that you would appreciate seeing this. My Dad in the future would have been thrilled to know that his great grandson had seen him dance. It was something that he was always proud of. That being said, there are some more surprises to come. Happy Birthday, Adam."

A couple walked up to our table which still had six empty seats.

Kitty stood up and gestured for Adam to stand as well.

"Jack, I'd like you to meet Master Adam Majeski, a huge fan of yours. It's his fifteenth birthday today."

Jack Dempsey, one of the greatest boxers in history, reached across the table and shook Adam's hand. "Happy Birthday, Adam. Pleased to meet you."

Adam was almost speechless and could only manage a terse, "Thank you, Sir."

I didn't try to even introduce myself to Dempsey since I did not want to interfere with Adam's special moment. I felt confident that Kitty and I had given Adam a birthday that he would remember for a long time.

Chapter Twenty-Three

This particular evening the Bartons and Jack Dempsey and his new wife, Hannah were hosting special guests.

The Whiteman Orchestra was weaving tune after tune as patrons danced the night away. Hannah was famous for introducing the 1930 hit song, *Cheerful Little Earful*, in the musical revue *Sweet and Low*. It was no surprise that Hannah sang when the orchestra went into a rendition of the song while we were seated. Soon after that the guests of honor showed up with their dates. I knew who they were immediately because the sports pages and Jim's conversations had kept me up to date about their cycling success since March.

Alfred Letourneur, the French cyclist and his teammate from Belgium, Gerard Debaets, were led to our table by the *maître d'*. Jim and Jack jumped up as did I to shake their hands. Kitty and Hannah remained seated as they were introduced. The cyclists' dates were sport groupies of the day and sedately hung on their arms until the men pulled out their chairs for them to sit. These two men were mega stars in 1933 when 'six-day bicycle races' at Velodromes all over the world were packing the seats.

These races called "sixes" were one of the top money makers for Madison Square Garden in 1933. These two athletes had been the toast of the town since they had won the 54th International Six Day Race at the Garden in March. Races were run on indoor banked, wooden, board tracks and while these cyclists pedaled around day and night for six days, spectators came and went while the Velodrome owners raked up the ticket sales. The Garden was said to bring in $250,000 in one week during one of these events.

These were the Greg LeMonds of their day, except I'm not sure that the cyclists of the 21st century could do what these guys did. There were no restrictions on drug use either. Unlike modern times, there were no growth hormones available but stimulant use was rampant with the athletes trying to fight off fatigue for six days while they tag teamed the event to continue around the track for a straight 144 hours. Professional cyclists were welcome celebrities at any table in the City and Barton and Dempsey made sure that they were seen with them.

Years later, around 1964, Katie took me into the finished basement of her house and proudly showed me a bicycle hanging from the ceiling against the wall. There was a pair of cycling shoes tied together by the laces hanging over the center bar.

"Alfred Letourneur gave Jim the bike and even the shoes he wore when he won the Sixes in 1933. Jim was his biggest fan and we traveled the world to see him race here and all over Europe."

I remembered seeing a rekindled excitement in her eyes as she described the spectacle of a past generation. I asked her what the 'Sixes' were. I had no clue. She described the event so accurately that when I actually got to go to one of these six-day bicycle races, in 1933, it was as if I had been to one already. I now knew that the excitement I witnessed in 1965 with Katie's retelling of their following the 'Sixes' was probably more exciting because it was also a time when Jim was by her side, her favorite place in the world.

It's pretty obvious that my life was enriched by the older Katie in my youth as the younger Kitty was now enriching my life in my later years living in the past. You can see how hard it is to sometimes keep track of my past and present as they become more entangled.

It was a night Adam would appreciate for all it was worth.

CHAPTER TWENTY-FOUR
The World Series
October 3, 1933

Anyone who knows me well knows that I'm not a serious sports fan. I root for the Yankees just to drive my son-in-law, Scott, crazy because he eats, drinks and breathes the Red Sox. It drives him mad when I brag about Yankees accomplishments when he knows I really don't care. I was a Brooklyn Dodgers fan as a kid and when they moved to L.A., in 1958, I lost all love for the sport vowing never to be interested again until they return to Brooklyn. I'm still waiting. My son David, regularly tells me to let it go.

Cars, movies, theater, and music are my guilty pleasures. Now couple Adam and my situation with the World Series. Which is going to keep my attention? It is enough to say that all my attention was on preparing to find Einstein as soon as possible when he finally hit Princeton.

But this was 1933. That changed everything, and the Series this year was like no other. Each game was a real pitching duel between the New York Giants and the Washington Senators. Yup, that's the Giants like in New York, not San Francisco. These were the golden years of baseball for New York. It was the home of no less than three major league teams. Boston had the Braves and Red Sox but we had the Yankees over in the Bronx, the Dodgers in Brooklyn, and the Giants at the Polo Grounds in Manhattan. I guess for sports fans this was baseball heaven, at least for New Yorkers. I was not surprised that hating the

Waiting for Einstein

Yankees was as much a national pastime in 1933 as it is in our century. Many people across the country were happy to see that the Yanks did not make it to the World Series but they had to be frustrated to find another New York team in their place.

The opening game was at the Polo Grounds and Adam and I had tickets up in the nosebleed section. I have to concede that while we were stuck here, we might as well see more history as it was being made. My Dad's younger brother, Allie, an all-round athlete, had a chance to play basketball for the New York Knicks but opted to play in the minor leagues with the Giants in the late forties. He was a shortstop for West Palm Beach, the Giants' farm team. I felt that was enough of an excuse to support them in this series without challenging my loyalty to the Dodgers.

There was no tagging along with Barton to sit with celebrities near the dugout because he did not go as a sign of respect for his buddy, Babe. I'm sure he was listening to the radio at home though.

No sooner did we find a seat when I heard a whistle that I had not heard in at least thirty-five years. It had to be my Dad, Jules. For as long as I could remember, he could make this distinctive whistle that had a pitch like no other I ever heard. It also had the volume others could only attain with two fingers in their mouth. My sisters, brother, and I were conditioned like puppies to run toward that sound when we were separated and he needed to gather his children. I realized that even at the ripe age of eighteen he had already mastered that call. I turned sharply and spied him six rows up waving his arms over his head for us to find him. When he saw that I had spotted him he pointed to empty seats next to him.

"Hey, Pop. There's Jules."

Chapter Twenty-Four

"I see him and it looks like he wants us to sit with him. Let's go."

We climbed the stairs and took the seats next to him. He reached over and we shook hands.

"How's it goin' Bob?" Wow, his accent was thick.

"Good, and you?"

Before he could answer, the loudspeakers blared with the announcement to stand for the National Anthem. Afterward, we took our seats but when I looked over at Jules he looked worried. As a batter walked up to home plate you could hear the umpire shout, "Play Baaaalllllll!!!"

"You don't look good, Jules. Something on your mind?"

"It's like ya can see right through me, Bob. Yeah, there's a lot on my mind. I actually followed ya here because I need to talk to ya 'bout somethin'."

He leaned over and spoke low in my ear so people above and below us could not hear him.

"My boss wants me to go on a job."

"What kind of a job?"

"We're supposed to be hitting a rival's booze warehouse. It's revenge for hijacking some of our booze from ships coming in from Canada last week with a ton of whiskey. Anastasia, the boss was not happy. And when he's not happy, people die. I don't want to be a part of that. I just want to help support my family. I've never wanted to kill anyone."

Jules actually looked scared for the first time since we had become confidantes. He was more pensive than I had ever seen him. No smiling. Why wouldn't he be? Albert Anastasia was one of the most ruthless mob bosses of the twentieth century. He was the leader of a group called Murder, Inc. which was responsible for hundreds of mob hits.

Waiting for Einstein

Growing up in the Greater New York City area, in the fifties and sixties, everyone, adults and kids alike, knew about the mob and all the killings. The *New York Post* and *Newsday* regularly published front page pictures of mob hits showing a body on the street or in a restaurant lying in a pool of blood. Even in black and white these images were pretty gruesome and there was no censorship. Any kid from the 1920's to the early sixties could walk up to any newsstand and see the graphic images on the front page of contemporary papers.

I remember clearly seeing the picture of Anastasia's lifeless body on the floor of a barbershop somewhere in the City. He was lying behind one of those rotating white enameled chairs that tilt back, just like in the shop my Dad would take me to for a haircut. That image was burned into my brain. It was the fall of 1957 and the trees were turning into different shades of red, yellow, and orange. I was eight-years-old and in fourth grade. Mom sent me out to buy her a pack of cigarettes. I bicycled a few blocks up to the United Cigar Store on Jericho Turnpike in our town, New Hyde Park. I entered the store and went straight to the counter and slapped down a quarter.

"Chesterfields, please."

Since I was a regular, the old man behind the counter didn't blink as he scooped up the coin and threw a pack of cigarettes on the counter. I grabbed them, squeezing them enough to get a whiff of tobacco and stuffed them in my pocket. I knew that it would take a while after I got them home before the smell that I hated would leave the fabric of my pants until the next trip to the store tomorrow. I turned to leave the store.

That's when I saw the papers on a low, long bench spread out with the pictures of a lifeless body on the shop floor on one of the front pages of a newspaper. I worried about going to the barbers

Chapter Twenty-Four

for weeks after that. Like most kids, I eventually stored it away and forgot about it till now. In the 1930s his assassination was unthinkable. Anastasia was no one to challenge in any way.

I was glad that Jules was finally getting it about the consequences of working for the mob. I was worried, however, that it might be too late if they were already tapping him for a job like this. This is how the mob sucked you in. They get you to do a serious crime that, if caught, could get you jail time or even the electric chair. Then, they own you by promising you protection, telling you that they have the prosecutors and judges in their back pockets. The payback is that you now must do whatever they tell you, even murder. If you don't want to go down that rabbit hole, they give you the final push by implying that terrible things could happen to your family without their protection. They own you for life. This was a roundabout way of getting my Dad to become a soldier since he had turned down their invitation months ago. They really liked him because he was such a hard worker but that had become a two-edged sword.

I was really scared for him and was more convinced than ever that this was why I was here. I looked at Adam.

"Hey, Buddy, Jules and I have some business to deal with that's pretty important. Are you okay with staying for the game and getting home on your own if we don't get back before the end of the game? It's really kinda important."

Adam could see the concern in my eyes.

"Hey, old man, down in front. There's a game going on here!" yelled a fan behind us. Jules scowled him into silence with a menacing glare and grabbed me by the elbow. I looked to Adam to get his assurance as Jules tugged me away.

"Sure thing, Pop. I'm good. Do what you have to do. I'll meet you at the apartment. I'm okay."

Waiting for Einstein

"Thanks, Buddy. You can let me know how it turned out when I get home."

I thought about my son, David, and how every time I had Adam and Colin, I had to promise him I would never leave them out of my sight. If he only knew what was going on here in 1933, he'd have me arrested. This fell woefully short of "helicopter parenting" that was the norm in the 2000's. However, I'm not sure that it was a bad thing, giving Adam space to develop and get streetwise. Adam was up to the task and every day that passed he made me prouder of him than the day before. He could now take care of himself and had an air of confidence that was becoming more evident day by day. He had become a citizen of one of the toughest venues in America during the hardest of times. Would it be noticeable to family and friends when we returned home? Hopefully, we could get the chance to find out.

Jules and I headed out of the ballpark. We found a coffee shop and reviewed his situation over cups of the worst coffee I had ever tasted. I had to take the lead with this and I had to get all the details. I hoped to determine where my part was and how I could save my father from doing something that would destroy the soul of the man that I would come to love in my lifetime.

I was finally getting answers. I don't know the genealogy of the mob families well, but I knew some of the big names. Jules started to tell me the plans for the next night. He never mentioned the names of the mugs that he hung out with before but tonight he did.

He had previously mentioned that Anastasia was not happy and had ordered the hit on the warehouse. Albert Anastasia, as an underboss in the Vincent Mangano Family, was responsible for running the famed Brooklyn-based Murder, Inc. Through further conversation, I found out that the other guy who was in

Chapter Twenty-Four

the Chevy roadster, the first time I saw my Dad months ago on Court Street, was none other than Paul Castellano, the brother-in-law of another mobster future Hall of Famer, Carlo Gambino.

My blood ran cold when I heard this. I knew that in the future only Gambino would die of natural causes, if that's how you classified a heart attack. My Dad's buddy would take over running the Family after Gambino died. Eventually, he would join all the others mentioned above by being planted in an early grave after being murdered. I had to get Jules out of this somehow. The death rate among the Mafia soldiers was even higher since these bosses killed them regularly to make a point with their rival bosses. Just like in chess, pawns are readily sacrificed to gain a position on the board that could win the game in the end.

There also wasn't supposed to be any exchange of pawns on this job but where there are men with guns, things sometimes happen. Jules told me that "Big Paul" Castellano, a few of his cousins and he were going to raid the warehouse down on the docks just below Atlantic Avenue around 1 A.M. They'd ambush the guards, smash the shipment and get out clean. That was a simple plan.

"On this job, no one is supposed to get hurt. It was simply tit for tat, 'I lost ten grand in booze and now it's your turn.'"

What I didn't like was that everyone, including my Dad, would be heavily armed. Up to this point, Jules confessed, he had never carried a piece.

"I don't like this plan because it sounds like there is no plan. Has anyone checked out the location for escape routes, or even places to take cover? These guys think this is just fun and games, but it's dangerous and someone is going to get hurt or worse."

Waiting for Einstein

"I know that already! Why do you think I came to ya? Ya seem to know the right thing to do. Can ya come up with a plan?"

"What about a note from your doctor?"

"That's not funny."

"I've got to think it through, but I might have a way to save your ass. I just can't tell you all the details since I haven't worked them out yet. I'll get back to you. Until then, just do whatever they tell you. You just go along with everything, and I promise that I will get you out of this mess somehow. Trust me."

I already had a plan but if I told him I didn't think he would like it.

"I trust you, Bob. Just don't take too long. If I do anything that looks like I'm stalling they might see a rat."

"I won't let you down. You are going to owe me big time. You have to get a legit job, even if it pays less. There are people counting on you. It would kill your Mom and Pop if anything happened to you. Your sisters and brothers need you and in ways I cannot explain, Adam and I need you as well. If I don't have your word, I'm out of here and you can figure this out on your own. I don't need the grief if you are not going to give me that commitment."

This was a huge bluff because, if he didn't agree, I had just taken myself out of the equation making it harder to explain why I would want to be around him. I had underestimated how scared he was. All that exterior toughness was gone and the eighteen-year-old kid came to the surface.

"I'll do whatever ya want. If you can get me outta dhis mess, I'll go legit. I swear to God," he almost pleaded.

"I'm holding you to that, Jules. I just don't want to hear any complaints about my solution or how many hours you are going to have to work to make the same money later on. Welcome to

Chapter Twenty-Four

the world of the working stiff. At least you'll have a chance to live to be an old man."

That reminded me that, like with Jim and Kitty Barton, I knew how long he was going to live if I got him through this. I was thirty-nine-years-old when he died in 1988. I cried more than any other time in my life when I lost him. I remember that the sobs seemed to come from deep in my soul. I had never cried like that before or since.

My plan was to get my father to at least live until he was elderly. God, how I hate that term. And here I was using it to describe my Dad in his later years, when I flinched when it was used to describe me. I did wonder if our adventures together in 1933 were going to flavor our closeness in the future. Was the relationship we enjoyed in my youth purely based on a father and son relationship or something more that started in 1933? An interesting thought, but right now I had to concentrate on the immediate problem.

I already had the nucleus of an idea. My plan was simple and could achieve the result I was hoping to attain. That is, if I didn't get him or myself killed in the process. Jules stood up and as he did his sports jacket opened just enough for me to see that he was now carrying a gun in a shoulder holster hidden under his jacket. Seeing that made me realize the danger that was all around us. The clock was ticking and there was no time to waste.

I realized that this plan had another major complication. There was another potential victim if it all went south, Adam. If I didn't survive this, what would happen to Adam? Would he be stuck here? Would he find Einstein on his own and get home or would his future life be erased if I died along with my Dad? Most of these scenarios left Adam stranded here alone. I really had to make sure that my plan was as close to foolproof as possible.

There also had to be a contingency plan with escape options so that I could increase our chances of survival and eliminate stranding Adam without his grandfather and worse, the entire family. Either way there was little margin for error. Adam would have to know what I was up to and we had to have contingency plans in place in case things went sideways.

.

CHAPTER TWENTY-FIVE
Giants 6 - Senators 1
October 5, 1933

My focus was totally on figuring out a plan to get my father out of this mess. Every idea I came up with was fraught with a level of danger. Adam was not happy with any of this. We agreed that there was a risk he could be stranded without me in the past. I could only hope that he would seek out Einstein if I didn't survive.

I did tell Kitty about what I was up to because I felt that she would willingly take care of Adam if everything unraveled. She assured me she would take him under her wing and that she would even help him find and meet Einstein.

"Let's not worry about the details until you hammer out your plans. Adam and I can coordinate a backup scenario. Let's keep this close to the vest for now. He doesn't have to get crazy with anxiety this early."

Kitty was beyond a great friend.

I gave Adam a ticket to the second game of the Series. He reported to me later that the Giants had won. The Senators were winning with one run until the sixth inning when New York scored six runs. That ended up being the final score and the teams left the field heading to Washington for the third game to be played the next day. Adam was surprised that in these early days of baseball there were no off days between games. The entire Series would be played in seven games, in seven consecutive days, if it went that long.

Waiting for Einstein

Of course, I remembered my Uncle Al telling me about that Series because he attended the two games played at the Polo Grounds. I stuck to my conviction that I was not here to tamper with history, other than what I had identified as my true purpose for being here. That eliminated placing any bets on a sure thing.

When I finally got to lay out my plans in front of Adam, he surprised me by supporting it. He also recognized all the risks involved.

"Pop, what if . . . ?"

I decided to repeat my plans but listened to any suggestions he had. He brought another set of eyes to my overall plan and helped clean it up. That truly increased the chances of success for all involved.

This refined planning went for an hour or more. We also agreed that if things went badly, Adam would seek out Kitty and let her know what happened. I told Adam that Kitty had already assured me that she would help him in every way possible. We eventually felt that we had all our bases covered as best as we could.

Adam had to work at Popp's Ice Cream Parlor and I had my work cut out for me finalizing the details of when and where I could put my plan into action that night. I also had to prepare the little Chevy so that it could not lead anyone back to me. I needed the '33 to blend with all the hundreds of '33 Chevys rolling all around Brooklyn.

Although the little Chevy coupe might be unique in 2013, in 1933 they were everywhere and even in the same colors. However, there were no others running around with Connecticut plates in Brooklyn with an older trunk sporting the distinctive political plates I had put on the back.

Chapter Twenty-Five

I had explained the 'Remember Pearl Harbor' license plate topper to a few curious pedestrians as a message to citizens not to forget our sailors serving far from home out in the Pacific. It was interesting to find that few knew where Pearl Harbor or even Hawaii was. Many never heard that it was a territory of the U.S. Of course, the meaning for later generations would be obvious post-December 7, 1941, that 'day that will live in infamy.' There would be a similar impact for his generation later as Adam would experience annual memorials to the events of September 11, 2001 in our time. What a great world it would be if we didn't have to remember anything but birthdays.

I took the trunk off the back and folded the rack up against the body. I had gotten a set of New York plates from a shady character down a dark alley. These guys actually do hang out in alleys. With all the telltale markers off my car, I would have to sit and wait until I could go into action. Jim Barton gave me the evening off without asking why, allowing me all the time I needed to review my plan and get rolling.

I set myself up at Goldie and Leo's Luncheonette on King's Highway. This was across the street from a garage that Jules told me was the gathering point before the gang would head out to a warehouse at the docks where another mob was storing their illegal whiskey.

I took a seat at the narrow lunch counter that faced the street. I had eaten there many times in the 1960's and always ordered the best pastrami sandwiches ever made. I had to take small bites around the edges and work my way toward the middle because it was just too thick. In the future, that garage across the street would become my Dad's Ultramatic Rusco Window store. I worked for him many weekends, affording me the chance to enjoy Goldie's amazing sandwiches thirty years into the future.

Waiting for Einstein

It was interesting to watch this young Jewish couple in 1933, as they worked the counter and grill. They maneuvered around each other while cooking and serving customers keeping up a steady conversation, answering questions from each other with another question. Their voices were not as husky as they were in later years but their unspoken love for each other was just as evident.

As I nibbled around the thick sandwich, I took in the conversational sparring that was classic Brooklyn Jewish lingo.

"So, Leo! Did you call the refrigerator repairman?"

"What! You think I didn't call him?"

"So, is he coming to fix it?"

"What! You think he's coming all this way not to?"

"So, is he coming tomorrow?"

This finally required a 'yes' or 'no' answer."

"What? Yesterday?"

I almost choked on the last bite I had taken. Three young men, obviously thugs, and looking dangerous came in and sat at the counter. There was no one in the place since it was near closing time. I felt intimidated as two took stools to my left and the other sat to my right. There were plenty of empty booths.

"How's da sandwich, Old Man?"

I thought I felt sweat instantaneously start to drip from my pits. That's not possible, is it?

"Goldie makes the best pastrami sandwich in Brooklyn. You won't be disappointed. You should order it."

I talk even more when I'm nervous.

"Thanks, but we just came in to check out da scenery. Ya know, new faces and all."

The guy to my left added. "Say, youz look like a new face! Where youz from?"

Chapter Twenty-Five

"Flatbush. A buddy of mine had told me about this place and, wouldn't ya know it, I'm drivin' back from my job on da Island and I spot it, and just a day afta I first hear about it. What are the odds?"

"Jeez, I don't need your life story. Just wanted to make sure that your movin' on after youz finish dat."

I could not sit at the counter any longer. It was 5 P.M. and Goldie had finished putting all the condiments away after topping them off. All the paper napkin holders were refilled, and the counters cleaned with a wipe rag soaked in bleach. I was impressed with her dedication to cleanliness but not surprised. This was one of the benefits of eating kosher. As I heard the lock close behind me, I moved to an alley a block down the street. From there I still had a clear view of the building without being seen.

Throughout the evening, cars arrived from every direction. Most were obviously mob soldiers like Jules because they drove less expensive cars like Ford, Durant, Chevy, Willys-Knight, and Plymouth. Jules had pulled in around 6 P.M. parking his roadster around the corner after putting on the side curtains. These were leatherette with clear vinyl panels sewn in, that hooked and snapped onto the open sides of roadsters that did not have rollup windows. I have a feeling that he did this more to obscure his image than because of the crisp night air.

Around 10 P.M. a huge, black V-16 Cadillac limo pulled into the open warehouse doors and two suits ran out and closed the big doors behind it. This had to be the Boss coming in to give last minute instructions and directives on what he expected. It wasn't until 11 P.M. that the doors were reopened and the Cadillac slowly exited turning right heading away from the direction where the upcoming raid was going to happen. The bosses always liked to have sound alibis when anything went down. Knowing how well connected these guys were, it wouldn't surprise me if he was planning to have drinks with a police commissioner or DA.

Thirty minutes later a few guys came out, got into three different four-door sedans and lined them up at the curb loosely spaced. They picked a blue '30 Buick 7-passenger sedan, a green '29 Nash and a beige '32 Plymouth, both four-doors. I was sure that these cars were not chosen for their size as much as they were chosen for their speed. One was as fast as the other. The Buick was a Straight 8, while the Nash was a Twin-Ignition 6, and the Plymouth, only had a 4 Cylinder but with amazing gearing. Each could hit seventy miles per hour if need be. I had friends that had almost an identical Buick and Plymouth back in the late sixties and I was impressed with their speed and handling. I had a '29 Nash back in 1972 that I could get up to sixty in short order, even going uphill. If my plan was going to work, I would need every ounce of horsepower in my little modified Chevy to outrun them.

Back in the 1950s, Guy Roese had modified the Chevy to make it his 'distance' car for Vintage Chevrolet Club of America's events which were far from home. As I mentioned before, he had beefed up the horsepower, transmission, and improved the brakes making for a peppy little 'sleeper.' For the uninitiated, that's a car that looks stock but has a lot more speed and power than it had out of the factory. This little coupe was fast and agile enough to compete with the cars I saw lined up. It would be great though if they didn't want to start a chase. I guess, I'd find out soon enough.

Jules told me that they would be heading out at midnight. By then, the streets would have less traffic for them to make their

Chapter Twenty-Five

getaway and put some distance between themselves and the crime scene. These considerations also worked well if my plan was to succeed since I would also need the same advantages for escape.

    I adjusted the choke and started my car to make sure that it would be warmed up and respond quickly when I needed quick acceleration without any hesitation. As it warmed up, I pushed the choke in and the engine was ready to roar. When you're being chased, there is no time for that slightest hiccup. There was no margin for error tonight. I had to hit all my planned marks to make this work without killing my Dad and getting caught in the process.

    I had to get it right for so many reasons. Every possibility ran through my head. If I killed Jules by accident, did all his descendants disappear, or was everyone safe? What if everyone in the future disappeared? Would Adam and I be the only survivors because we were not there for some kind of purge of Jules' descendants in the future? If I got caught or killed, it would surely derail our possible return to the future together and the chance of finding Einstein when he finally arrived in America. How would Adam explain my absence if he could get back on his own? There seemed to be endless possibilities for disaster when messing with the past. Would my Dad find his way out of this without me anyway, or was I always the key to his survival? Simply stated, it all came down to my gut feeling, that this was what I was brought here for. There could be no mistakes and I had to get it right or else.

    I moved my car into position a block and a half west of the mob's gathering point and waited. Nervously, I kept tapping the gas pedal to make sure that it responded upon touch. Yesterday, I had adjusted all the linkage from the gas pedal to the carburetor to eliminate any play that could cause unwanted hesitation. I adjusted the gas mixture to maximize power and acceleration.

    I kept running my plan through my brain over and over for any flaws. The only weakness was that Jules was clueless as to what I was up to and if he was not where he told me he would be, I had no fallback plan in place and would have to make it up as I went along. When he asked for my help, he told me that he would not be a driver. I had no idea what I was going to do at the time but had told him to make sure that he wore his light grey fedora and got into the car on the street side and not the curb. When he promised he would, I started to run different plans through my head until I ended up with the one I was going to attempt now. I knew from my youth that my Dad only wore dark colored fedoras at night. My hope was that his friends stuck to that fashion rule for themselves and I would be able to spot him easier with his inappropriate hat color.

    I was getting nervous as I waited for the mobsters to saddle up for their raid at the docks. Eventually, I saw a group of men exit the building heading toward the line of cars double-parked and idling. I spotted Jules in a light-colored hat and was glad to see him start to go around a car to the passenger's side. I jumped on the gas and raced toward the line of cars ahead. I aimed my car as close as I could to the parked cars to try and get Jules to jump out of the way. My hope was that I would somehow make it look like I shook him up just enough that he might see the opportunity for what it was and tell the others to go on without him and he'd catch up with them. He needed to think on his feet and I was hoping he would use the incident to get out of going on the job.

    I raced toward him as he stood in the street with his back to me. What probably took seconds felt like hours as I held my foot

Chapter Twenty-Five

hard down on the gas pedal. Jules hadn't seen me yet. As I got closer, I realized I'd have to swerve into the next lane if he didn't see me soon. I looked ahead to my left and all of a sudden, I saw a huge Packard sedan heading toward me cutting off any chance to avoid Jules.

I looked forward and held my hand on the horn as I barreled toward my Dad. At the last second, he saw my headlights. At last, he jumped onto the running board of the Buick. I heard a bang as the side view mirror, clamped on the passenger door, hit something and snap off. Pieces of the shattered mirror flew through the open window and a small shard stuck in my right cheek. In my rear-view mirror I saw Jules spin around on the running board, grabbing his left forearm before he fell into the street.

His fellow mobsters ran to him and one actually pulled out a handgun and fired a shot in my direction as I raced away. I hoped he missed since it would be hard to hide a bullet hole in the car. I continued to speed down Eastern Parkway until I turned right and followed the escape route I had planned out.

After an hour of weaving in and out of the side streets, I arrived at the garage where I had hidden the trunk and other trappings which distinguished my car from all the other Chevys around the area. I replaced the New York plates with my Connecticut plates and the topper about Pearl Harbor. Lastly, I removed the broken stem of the mirror that must have hit Jules. I was also happy to find all the pieces from the mirror on the seat, not just the one that I removed from my cheek. I tossed them in the trash.

Like most facial wounds, it bled like crazy. When I finally cleaned it up, the wound was quite small. I was sure it would not draw any undue attention. I was sure that I could pass it off as a shaving nick if asked. My obvious concern was about Jules and how badly I had hurt him. The plan only worked if I had injured him enough to be left behind, but not enough to cripple him. Only time would tell. Other than that, my plan went as well as I ever could have expected. It was past two in the morning before I got back to our apartment.

When I entered, Adam almost knocked me over and hugged me so hard I could barely breathe.

"I'm okay, Buddy, and so is your great grandfather."

"Pop, I've been on pins and needles all night."

He stood back and looked me up and down.

"What happened to your cheek? Are you sure that you're okay?"

"Never better. It's just a nick. Jules may not be doing as well. I guess we will find out soon enough. He knows where to find us. I don't know about you but I'm exhausted. What do you say to getting some shut eye?"

CHAPTER TWENTY-SIX
October 6, 1933

I slept until ten A.M., got up, brushed my teeth and sat nervously at the kitchen table wondering what had happened to Jules. I prayed that he was okay. I had no idea if he knew it was me. Stupid, he wasn't. I just wondered how soon it would be before he sought me out to find out what my part was in all this. Adam walked in from brushing his teeth. He grabbed a box of Wheaties off the counter and placed it on the table. He retrieved a bowl and spoon from the kitchen cabinet and sat down.

"You said that Jules was okay. Did he get out of going on that raid?"

My mind was already on something else.

"I don't care what you tell your Dad when we get back about all this, but you can never tell him that I have left you alone so many times."

Adam laughed.

"You sound more afraid of my Dad than all those guys you have terrified since we got here."

"There's no comparison. He's my son and I can't go kicking him when he starts in on me like the guys that cross me here. Let's just agree that if he asks, you were always in my sight. Okay?"

"Okay, Pop. Whatever."

Adam chuckled.

My mind was still processing all the events from last night.

Waiting for Einstein

"Hopefully, I had completed the task that I believe we were sent here to do. I just pray that Jules appreciates the effort as well. I'm sure we will find out soon enough."

"Well, my guess is he will be coming by any time now. I have to get to work so I'll see you when I get home."

"I love you, Pop."

"Back at ya."

I looked at Adam and changed my mind, deciding to leave later. Listening to the fourth game of the World Series with Adam would be a great way to take my mind off Jules until he showed up. I kept turning the tuning dial on the Cathedral Dome Brunswick radio until I found what sounded like a baseball game. I didn't have to worry about tuning into another game. At this time of the year, there would be only one.

It really was interesting to listen to a game with no visuals. The sports announcer painted a picture for you instead. The listener filled in the images and colors as they imagined them.

It was a great game. The Giants' manager was first baseman Bill Terry. His homer in the fourth inning put the Giants on the board with a run. The Senators answered in the sixth with a run to tie the game. The rest of the game was a monumental pitching duel between the Giants' Carl Hubbell and the Senators' Monte Weaver. Can you imagine a game today when both teams would keep their pitchers in the game for eleven innings? There would have been three relief pitchers on each side before the last inning. As it was, the game ended when the Senators could not answer the run the Giants scored at the top of the eleventh and the Giants won 2-1. They were just one game away from winning the Series.

Chapter Twenty-Six

There was a knock at the door. When I opened the door a crack, Jules pushed past me, almost knocking me over. His left arm was in a sling and there was a bruise over his left eye.

"What the hell were you thinking? Do you know how close you came to killing me? Right now, my boss has his goons combing Brooklyn looking for some crazy guy in a little Chevy for trying to kill me. He thinks it was a hit job."

"I have no idea what you are talking about. What happened to your arm?"

I pointed to his sling.

"Don't act dumb with me, Old Man. That was you who tried to run me down last night. I'd know that weird little Chevy of yours any day. The paint looks like it's sixty years old. Luckily the guys in my gang don't know cars like I do."

"I still don't know . . . ."

"Drop it, Bob. I know it was you. I saw the hubcap on the side mount just before you hit me."

Holy Smoke! I didn't think anyone had noticed that. How could they? That style hubcap wouldn't show up for the first time until the '34 Chevys came out next month, in November. When Guy Roese upgraded the brakes to hydraulics, the newer brake drums were bigger than the original '33s. The wheel hubs from a '34 were bigger and the lug pattern matched up perfectly. Also, the wheels were seventeen-inch versus eighteen-inch and the hubcaps were a different design and bigger. Jules obviously noticed them but never said anything. I could only hope that no one else did either.

"So, cut the crap," he said angrily.

"Okay! It was me but I wasn't trying to kill you. You have to know that, Jules."

He started to laugh, came forward and raised his right arm and pulled his left arm out of its sling to give me a hug. He winced as he held me tight.

"Ya're a genius! Crazy, but still a genius. And that was some great driving. Ya did give me one hell of a bruise on my arm. It was enough for me to convince the guys that my arm might be broken. I played it up real good, when I figured out what ya were trying to do. That was your plan, right?"

"Well, I was trying to hurt you enough so that you could get out of last night's job and maybe enough for you to change careers. Don't you ever look before you enter a street? You had to hear me coming. I had that little Chevy motor wound up. When you didn't turn around that was when I finally had to hit the horn. I was boxed in at the last minute by that Packard. Are you okay?"

He waved his arms in the air and then rolled up his sleeve to show a humongous bruise on his left bicep that went from his shoulder to his elbow.

"Looks pretty bad, huh? Sore as hell. The Doc says it's all muscle damage. I should be fine in a month. It might take longer for the bruising to go away. He says that it's pretty deep and will keep comin' up for a while. Lots of bleeding down deep or sumptin' like that."

"Well, I'm glad you're not mad at me. There weren't a lot of options and I couldn't let you know what I was up to. This way you don't have to lie to your boss. I can't believe you spotted the different hubcaps."

"One of d'udder guys said da car had New York plates. When I asked him if the car had a trunk strapped on the back, he just said it was a coupe and he didn't think it had a trunk. At first, I thought maybe it was not you. Then, I realized you'd never be

Chapter Twenty-Six

dumb enough to keep that trunk on the car. Not with all dat stuff on it."

"You're right about that. I left nothing identifiable on the car and even got some stolen plates. Everything is changed back, except for my missing mirror."

I laughed as I added, "You owe me a mirror."

"Good luck wit dat, Old Man. Your plan almost cost me an arm AND a leg. Why don't we call it even."

He laughed and hugged me again.

We then shook hands and I said, "Done."

"The biggest problem is the Boss's bloodhounds. They're scouring the neighborhood looking for some guy in a two-tone green Chevy coupe. It's only a matter of time before they figure out that it's you. You're just lucky that there's a ton of these cars all over the city. I'm goin' to be hanging out with these guys for a while until I convince them that I have a bum arm and have to retire. Until then, I'll keep my ear to da pavement and if I think they're getting' close I'll give ya a heads up."

"I appreciate that. We just need another week to get our gear together since we were planning to head back home anyway."

"I hope ya're not leaving on my account. I owe ya my life."

"All I want from you is to keep your nose clean. Your kids and grandchildren will thank you. I'm sure of it."

"What is it with ya pressuring me to get married and have some little brats. Ya act like ya life depended on it or sometin'."

He chuckled at the thought.

"Let's just say I see a lot of potential in you. You'll make a fine Dad someday if you put your mind to it. Promise me that you'll stay straight and get a legit kind of job."

Jules promised and left, returning his arm into the sling as he went down the hall.

CHAPTER TWENTY-SEVEN
October 7, 1933

Adam and I just wanted to zone out for a day after the stress of the previous night. Neither of us were totally focused on the previous two games of the Series, as we were always running around trying to make sure that all our bases were covered in the plan to save Jules. It seemed that every prior waking moment was devoted to that mission. It wasn't until I turned on the radio, while we were having breakfast, that I realized that there was going to be a fifth game at Griffith Stadium in D.C.

Neither one of us had to work today. Adam had already given Popp's his two weeks' notice and worked his last day yesterday after he had trained his replacement, a man in his late twenties with three kids. Hard times for a man who worked on Wall Street in 1929, as he told Adam. Even though it was a huge drop in social status, he was glad to get this job. The timing was perfect because after the shop closed, he had plenty of time to get down to the docks to unload ships on the night shift, 11 P.M. until 7 A.M. He sounded like a determined young man, and I knew his pain.

In the 1970's when inflation was in double digits and Nixon froze wages, the only way to feed a young family was to have multiple jobs. I managed a small CVS in downtown Hartford, Monday through Friday, 7 A.M. to 5 P.M. Then I went to a large mall where I worked as a sales clerk and taught drawing classes at an Arts and Crafts store from 6 P.M. until 10:30 P.M. On

Chapter Twenty-Seven

weekends, I roofed houses. Depression or high inflation seemed to have a similar effect on the middle class.

Kitty knew our plans and we would be saying our goodbyes the following day.

Both of us simply wanted to veg out for the day before we finalized plans for the next task of our journey. What better way than to sit by the radio with some snacks and cheer on our home town boys. Since the game was starting around 2:30 P.M. I ran down to the deli to get something to munch while Adam made the beds and straightened out the kitchen.

We moved the radio into the living room and got comfy on the couch preparing for a great game. We would not be disappointed.

The game started out slow. General Crowder was pitching for Washington. The Giants were first up. JoJo Moore got a single. Up next, Critz flied out to right field. Bill Terry singled and Moore went all the way to third. Mel Ott struck out. Kiddo Davis forced Terry out at second.

Hal Schumacher pitched for N.Y. Buddy Myer got a piece of the ball but flied out to right field. Goose Goslin singled. Manush lined one to center and a double play. End of the first inning. It looked like this could be a pitching duel. The stakes were high. The Senators need this game to stay alive; otherwise, the Giants would win the Series.

I've been told that real baseball fans want to see a no-hitter. For Adam and me, lots of hits and home runs make for a great game. The second inning was more to our liking. We had gotten comfortable with some mustard and a half dozen soft pretzels. Coupled with some homemade lemonade I learned to make from scratch, we settled in to listen to the commentators report the action as it happened.

Waiting for Einstein

Crowder was back on the mound for Washington and first at bat was Travis Jackson who singled to left field. This must have flustered General because he walked the next batter, Gus Mancuso. Runners on first and second. Blondy Ryan hit a fly enabling Jackson and Mancuso to get to third and second. You could hear the crowd going wild, almost drowning out the announcer. We figured it was not because the overall crowd was happy since this was not the home team.

The pitcher, Hal Schumacher, singled to right and as he ran toward first, Jackson and Mancuso ran like hell and made it home! Giants drew first blood. There was no further scoring that inning. Schumacher was stranded.

The Senators failed to answer as Ossie Bluege, Luke Sewell, and Crowder all grounded out on great pitches from Schumacher. Giants-2, Senators-0. That's where the score stayed through the third, fourth, and fifth innings as the pitching duel settled in.

Leading for the Giants, Kiddo Davis, slammed a double out into deep left. Jackson sacrificed Davis to third. Mancuso delivered a double, driving Davis in for the score!

Adam jumped off the seat and danced around the living room. I heard myself screaming as well. The walls reverberated with celebration up and down Flatbush Avenue. While we rejoiced, Crowder was replaced on the mound by Jack Russell. After a warm up, he handily dispatched Ryan and Schumacher, stranding Mancuso on second. The damage was done. Giants-3, Senators-0.

The Senators were about to show everyone that they deserved to be there. Schumacher seemed to easily dispatch the first two at bat, Buddy Myer and Goose Goslin. Two outs and one to go. Heinie Manush stepped up to the plate. He singled to right field.

Chapter Twenty-Seven

Joe Cronin singled to left, getting Heinie in scoring range on third. Fred Schulte tapped the plate as a puff of dust came out from the sides. It's like he is daring Schumacher to send the ball over the center of the plate. Schumacher wound up, the throw, the swing. It ended with that horrible sound for a pitcher as the bat and ball met with a loud crack which sent the ball into the stands for a home run!

I thought Adam was going to cry as he yelled, "Oh, my God, NO!"

I knew that the Giants would go on to win the World Series, but I could not remember in how many games. That made the game almost as exciting for me as it was for Adam. The difference was that by the end of this game I would know if it was today or one of the next two. I didn't worry either way and did not share this with Adam. It was payback for obviously "yes-ing" me to death when I had told him to read the buttons over the windshield of the Chevy. One over the driver's seat clearly said, "N.Y. GIANTS-1933 World Series Champions." I laughed to myself thinking of his reaction when I would point out the button the next time we were in the car.

Pieces of Adam's fingernails were piling up on the floor as he leaned toward the radio to hear every play. Schumacher was replaced by Dolf Luque in relief. He got Sewell to ground out to end the inning. It was a tie game.

"Adam, why don't you chew on the pretzels instead of your nails. They're easier to digest," I laughed.

"Not funny, Pop. This is nerve racking."

"But fun, right?"

"I guess."

Top of the seventh, Moore grounded out, Critz did the same and Terry flied out.

In the bottom half, Dolf Luque convincingly struck out Russell, Myer, and Goslin in that order, 1-2-3. Adam wiped the sweat beads from his brow.

In the eighth and ninth both teams had hits but neither scored. We are going into extra innings. Adam was exhausted.

"I'm not sure I can take much more."

"You'll live. That is the one thing I am sure of. Let's listen. The Giants are at bat."

Jack Russell got Critz to fly out to left field. One out.

Terry grounded to second and was out at first. Two outs.

The legendary outfielder and hitter, Mel Ott, stepped up to the plate. He shortly was triumphantly running the bases after sending Russell's pitch into the stands for a home run!

Adam and I both jumped from the couch and started hugging and jumping all over the room. I think I heard a similar pounding on the ceiling above us. There were also cheers all along the street below. There is a magic that only can be experienced by listening to a baseball game on the radio. Your imagination fills in the picture maybe better than any television of the future ever could.

Davis was up next and grounded out to end the Giant's at bat.

As the radio commentator gave some color from his vantage point, I added to Adam's anxiety.

"This could be for the whole enchilada. Let's settle down. We don't want to miss a word."

Washington's Goose Goslin stepped to the plate and in short order grounded out. One down. Next up, Manush lined out to second. One more out to go!

Washington refused to die. Cronin singled to left field putting the tying run on. I only hear squeaks from Adam. Dolf walked Schulte on four pitches. Now Washington has the game-winning

Chapter Twenty-Seven

runner on first. The manager didn't take him out of the game like they would do sixty to seventy years later. Dolf pulls it together and shakes off the walk and strikes Kuhel out with just three pitches. Game over.

People ran out onto Flatbush Avenue with pots and pans banging together as we heard the announcer say that the Giants had won the World Series, the first time since 1922 and the fourth time in franchise history. Adam fell back on the couch physically and emotionally spent.

"I never want to do that again. God that was fun."

We laughed as we bit into our big pretzels. Too late for Adam's fingernails, they were gone.

There was celebration all over the City. For us, it was time to address all the things we had to do before heading to New Jersey besides planning the trip itself. Today was Thursday and we would have to say our goodbyes tomorrow because I wanted to hit the road by Saturday. Weekend traffic would be easier to deal with than weekday traffic. I had picked up some more free road maps at the gas stations that had them. The best I found were from Texaco and Shell. They would merge eventually in the next century. Sadly, the Texaco name would disappear at that time. In 1933, they were two entirely separate and huge companies which dominated the oil industry along with Mobil. I spread the maps out on the table to make sure that the bridges, tunnels, and roads that I would normally use on such a trip in the next century, were already built by 1933.

I remember the first time I heard about the Outerbridge Crossing from Staten Island to New Jersey. On the radio the traffic reporter would just say, "the Outer Bridge." At least that was what I thought until I saw it on a map. It turns out that it was indeed the most "outer bridge" to New Jersey. It was named the Outerbridge Crossing.

I googled it years later and found out that it was named after the first president of the New York Port Authority, Eugenius Outerbridge. I assumed that they called it a "crossing" rather than "bridge" to avoid a tongue twister, the Outerbridge Bridge. Anyway, it was already there, having opened in 1928, the same day as the Goethals Bridge, which also connected Staten Island to Jersey.

My plan was simple. We'd take the Holland Tunnel and, depending on traffic, we'd take one of these bridges to New Jersey and head down to Princeton.

Adam and I planned to do the rounds on Friday to say our goodbyes and leave Saturday morning open if we fell behind. I phoned ahead to make sure Kitty would be home in the morning. I was not looking forward to this, since Kitty and Jim had been incredibly generous and always treated us like friends. They saved us from a homeless fate and they earned a "thank you" and a "goodbye." Kitty also needed more attention since she was the only person in 1933 who knew that we were time travelers. It was her faith in us that made life possible during this Depression year.

CHAPTER TWENTY-EIGHT
Goodbye Kitty, For Now
October 8, 1933

It was hard to believe that almost eight months had passed since Adam and I had visited Kitty for the first time. I pulled the little Chevy into a parking spot alongside Barton's Place which had been reserved for me over the last months. The Chevy spent many nights until early mornings in this spot while I drove Jim and Kitty to shows, dinners, sporting events, and speakeasies all over the five boroughs of New York and Nassau County.

It was hard to believe that I had the chance to drive his incredible Lincoln. Oh, and what friends they had! We had socialized with Claire and Babe Ruth as well as James Cagney and his wife, Willie. Meanwhile, Adam had been a regular at the Ruth's apartment, entertaining Julia and Dorothy. Like me, Adam would return to our time, knowing he would never see his friends again. Dorothy, who was twelve-years-old now, would pass away in 1989 at the age of sixty-eight in Durham, Connecticut, not even twenty miles from our homes, in 2013. I knew that sixteen-year-old Julia would amazingly still be alive and healthy, well into our time. She had regularly popped up on the Internet with accompanying videos of her throwing out a baseball at major league games. She was ninety-seven in our time.

One evening Adam had asked me if it would ever be possible to see her again in the twenty-first century. It didn't take us long to decide that, assuming Julia's health was as good as I had seen

Waiting for Einstein

in a television interview, that it would not be a good thing for Adam to show up saying "Hi!" His looking the same as the last time she saw him in 1933 could give her a heart attack.

We played it out in conversation what that meeting would be like. Julia would see him and say, "You look so familiar, young man."

"Well, I should. We played 'The Landlord Game' enough times with your sister Dorothy back in the day."

Julia would then recognize Adam, realize who he was and realize that he looked unchanged without aging, as she last saw him over eighty years before. She'd clutch her chest and we would have to live with the guilt that he had just killed his friend at ninety-seven. So, no, visiting Julia was not an option when we got back.

I went to the door of the Barton house and rang the bell. Unlike our first visit back in March, I walked in and found a seat in the living room until Kitty appeared from a room down the hall past Jim's office. She was fashionably dressed in what was frequently advertised as an afternoon dress of beige organza. She wore matching open-toed heels. Makeup and hair done perfectly for the period. It always surprised me how dressed up she was compared to the woman I would later know in another era who dressed more for comfort than for style. She had told me a few months ago that she had to look her best for Jim, after all, he was a star and stars' wives also had a part to play. Except she was not playing a part. She lived for Jim and loved him deeply.

When I tried to remember my relationship with Katie when I was a teen, I could not remember a time that I thought I had any previous relationship with her prior to that time. Surely, not thirty years earlier before I was born. Nothing of what I was

Chapter Twenty-Eight

living now in the thirties was ever recalled by me. Yet, I always had a strong affinity for her. I cannot remember a dinner when she didn't tell a story or anecdote about Jim. Even in death, he was the center of her world and I absorbed all the stories with relish. She always had me wishing that I had met him. Who would have thought that I would have gotten my wish over fifty years later, or eighty years in the past?

Kitty had come to know me as well now as she had in the future. She took a look at my obvious sad face as I stood when she entered the room.

"It's time for you to go, isn't it?"

"I'm afraid so, Kitty. I must get back to Henny and the family and I have to get Adam back as well. I really wish this time travel thing was like jumping on a train and taking a planned vacation or something. I would love to come back with Henny to see you again. I know I told you that you were around when we started dating. She loved your company and stories as much as I did. You always got her laughing. My whole family would enjoy the warmth and kindness Jim and you have shown us as well. They've heard so much about you both through me."

I had added Jim to the conversation when I realized she might wonder why he was not mentioned in our future relationship. Her next comment assured me that I had dodged the issue.

"Well, it sounds like we made quite an impression on you in our old age."

I really was having a hard time keeping my emotions together. I could tell she was using her humor to do the same. I was the one going back to my time. Kitty and Jim would not be there. She still had more than half her life ahead of her. My eyes welled up and I just hugged her.

Waiting for Einstein

"I'm going to miss you, Kitty. You saved our lives and I will never forget that. You're my Ziegfeld Angel."

We broke the hug and she slapped me on the chest.

"You're a sentimental old fool, Bob Majeski. I'm no angel and Jim would be the first to tell you that. I just did what any decent person would have done under the circumstances. And I will tell you that this has been the hardest secret to keep in my life but, oh, so much fun as well. I do appreciate that."

"I do, too. Let's just say goodbye for now, until we meet again."

We hugged one more time, she kissed me on the cheek.

"I do hope your journey is successful. If not, I hope you know that you can come back at any time. We won't give your job away."

"Please tell Jim I had to get back to Connecticut for a family emergency and thank him for all the wonderful times and his generosity. And tell him not to scratch 'my' Lincoln."

We both laughed at that ridiculous claim. Then she looked at Adam. He went to shake her hand but she quickly pulled him into a gentle hug and patted his back.

"I'm going to miss your smile and gentleness, Master Adam. I think you are destined for greatness. Do me a favor."

"Name it."

"Take care of that geezer of a Grandpa, okay?"

"I'll take care of him."

"You'd best be on your way."

I saw her eyes well up as we both turned from each other, and I left the house.

I drove back to Brooklyn lost in my thoughts. I reviewed all my meetings with "Katie" when I was a teen and adult. She had to know who I was if this was really happening. Being older is

Chapter Twenty-Eight

interesting. Sometimes an event, a song, an aroma or whatever will trigger a memory so remote and faint that you say to yourself, "Now where did that come from?"

This happened as I turned onto Fulton Street. I recalled the first time that I met Katie. My parents had become friends with her, dining often at *The Dublin Pub*. That's the name given to 'Barton's Place' after she had rented it out, after Jim passed away. The clientele was pretty much the same so she could still walk over to spend time with her friends. Eventually, she became close with my parents. My Dad was a natural born entertainer and Katie liked him. One dinner at my folks' home with my Mom's mashed potatoes sealed the deal and they became fast friends. It wasn't Sunday if Katie wasn't sitting across the table from me.

She had asked my Dad to do her a favor by hanging a few poster-sized enlargements of Jim made from movie and stage stills that she had. On one occasion, my Dad asked if I would like to come. I had not been to her home yet and I was dying to see it. I was only fourteen and excited to be entering the home of a Broadway and Hollywood star. When we arrived, Katie greeted us at the door. We followed her into the living room.

Katie, as I knew her then, gave me a hug.

"I've been wondering when you would come around again. You sure took your time getting here."

"I've never been here before." I looked at her like she might be losing it. She had to know this was my first time at her house.

My Dad cut in.

"I called you ten minutes ago that I'd be here. Did you want me to get a speeding ticket?"

"I wasn't talking about you. I was speaking to your delightful son."

Waiting for Einstein

She looked at me like we had some secret connection.

No comment followed. My Dad just looked at me and shrugged.

Katie gave me a little nod with a wry smile. I had no clue what that was about.

"We'll snack first before I work you to death. I have your tea for you Julie, and correct me if I'm wrong Bobby, your favorite dessert," she added with a giggle.

On the table was a serving dish with a pyramid stack of Entenmann's Crumb Cake cut in neat squares.

"How'd you know? It is my favorite."

"Call it woman's intuition."

She giggled again and for the rest of the visit I would catch her watching me closely out of the corner of her eye. I was never creeped out by it for some reason and just found it odd that she seemed so interested in me. From that day forward our friendship grew to the status of best friends. I was never a kid bothered by generational divides. I enjoyed the company of people any age and loved the stories.

As I continued to drive around looking for a parking spot, this buried memory made so much sense having lived through this time travel experience. Could she have been testing me to see if I remembered her somehow? She could not know the complexity of time travel. I had no memory of this time travel visit since I had not lived it yet. However, she had.

She had to have recognized me and based on what I had told her she must have been waiting for the time when I would show up again in her life. I wonder what she thought when my parents introduced themselves and said the family name was Majeski? Did she connect the dots? Is that why she invited us into her home? Was she curious to see if I was the same Bob Majeski that

Chapter Twenty-Eight

she met in 1933? She had to know and that was the way I have decided to remember that meeting for the remainder of my life.

I hoped that she understood why I did not tell her about Jim's heart attack. She never showed me any disappointment in anything I said or did and never tried to bring up the subject. I must assume that she was okay with my decision. And I was glad that she never told me about my future. I never would have wanted to know about all the wonderful and sad things that would come along in my life as well. One of the last times I saw her was at my Dad's funeral. In retrospect, I think we did right by each other in 1933, the 1960's and beyond. That's what friends do.

I had an even tougher job to do, say goodbye to my Dad. Again.

CHAPTER TWENTY-NINE
Goodbye Jules, For Now
October 8, 1933

I finally found a parking space two blocks from the apartment. Adam was already back from the Ruth's. His eyes were red and a bit puffy. He seemed to look away not letting me see the distressed look on his face. Had he been crying?

"How'd it go? Are you okay?"

"I'm fine. It was a lot harder than I expected but I'm fine. Julia was more upset than Dorothy and they made me promise to visit. I hope that Einstein can help us because that's a promise that I really don't want to keep no matter how much I have become friends with the girls. I really miss my family and we need to get back before I grow anymore."

"On that note, we have a dinner date at the Majewski house. Nothing fancy, just casual. I just want to say goodbye to the family one last time."

A half hour later we pulled up to the old brownstone in Bay Ridge that I knew so well as the family gathering place for my Polish side in the 1950s. I pulled into a large parking spot a few doors down and easily pulled in nose first without any difficulty. That's as big a deal now as it was in our own time. In moments, we were knocking on the door under the large stairs that led up to the family room. Jean answered. She was already five-foot-seven and close to her adult height as a young teen. She greeted us with her typical flamboyant style that she would have for her

Chapter Twenty-Nine

entire life. She grabbed Adam's arm and practically threw him into the hallway.

Everyone was there. The oldest, Blanche, then Jules, Jean, Stas, Ronnie, and Allie. Pop Majewski was sitting at the head of the table already as we were ushered into the dining room. Jean was the self-anointed hostess, another position she would hold throughout her life. I actually loved this about her but I know it drove my Mom crazy in later years. My Dad loved Jean's craziness as well, but feigned annoyance for the sake of my Mom. I remembered at a big family event someone asking my Dad who the lady was that was going around all the tables to make sure everyone was happy. He was sitting with my Mom and gave one of his classic answers, "Oh, that's my wife's sister through marriage."

That always got a rise out of my Mom.

Grandma came out of the kitchen in her dark print dress with the apron that covered most of the bodice and skirt. The apron was a contrasting light-colored print material that was held in place by slipping the bib part over her head and also tied around the waist with sashes making a big droopy bow in the back. It had pockets in the skirt portion and there were flour dust handprints on either side from her swatting her hands on it before she went to her next task in the kitchen.

After greetings were made around the table, we were all seated. Adam was directed to sit in the middle of the girls on one side. They were all chatting away asking him what Connecticut was like and if he was going to miss Brooklyn and city life. It was obvious to me that they were flirting a bit and were hoping he might make the trip down on occasion to visit. If they only knew that they were hitting on their future grand-nephew.

Waiting for Einstein

There was plenty of conversation as the platters of *pierogies* and *golomkies* were brought out. Next arrived side plates of vegetables and a small plate with roast beef. I started to pass the meat around but Jules leaned his head toward mine and whispered.

"That's for you and Adam. Just accept it."

I knew what was going on. The best dish was reserved for the guests. They didn't have enough for everyone, but this was how they put their best foot forward. The kids knew not to reach for it and went about finishing their meals.

With the meal over and the table cleared for dessert, the girls scurried around to finish their tasks so that they could get back to Adam. The original Pop Majewski, sat back contentedly and listened to the conversation among Jules, Stas, Allie, Adam, and me.

"Pop's pretty happy that I'm changing careers. I have a funny feeling he knew more than he let on. I guess we have you to thank for that."

"You're welcome."

Pop Majewski was a real treasure for so many generations of the family. Little was known about his past in Poland since he rarely spoke about it. All anyone could say was that he was the kindest and most gentle man anyone knew. He was a man of few words. I had a theory that had proved itself when I had visited the family now and as a kid in the fifties. He spoke little because he had raised a family of monumental talkers. This, I think, was genetically passed down to my generation and even to the next. Lord help the person that tried to get a word in if any Majewskis were having a conversation among themselves.

"I thank you with all my heart. You saved my boy," he said in his thick Polish accent.

Chapter Twenty-Nine

"Think nothing of it. I was glad to do it and let's just say I have a vested interest in his well-being. I'm glad you approve. That means more to me than you can imagine."

He just smiled and nodded. Conversation over.

Blanche and her Mom brought out the desserts. There was an apple pie, *Faworki,* or Angel Wings, and *Sernik,* a Polish style cheesecake with a fruit topping. Jean brought out the coffee while Ronnie passed around the plates, forks, coffee cups, and saucers.

After all the girls were seated, it was fun to watch Adam as the conversations flew around the table. His head went back and forth like someone watching ping pong. Majewskis are famous for having three or more conversations going simultaneously. Jean would hear a comment at the other end of the table by Allie and put her two cents in and return to her conversation with Blanche. I'm a talker as well, but with this crowd I just sat and listened, not unlike with my older siblings, Martha, Linda, and Raymond.

Pop and Grandma pretty much listened as I did, so I'm not sure which side of the family this ability came from, the Majewski or the Bernatowicz side. My own personal memory was that it may have come from Grandma's side since they were all women and I do remember my grand aunts talking a lot when they were together.

Pop asked me to pass the sugar which I did. As I watched him put three heaping teaspoons into his coffee, I watched Jules' face set into a deep scowl. Pop put the spoon down without stirring. I could not believe that I was witnessing this. It was exactly as my Dad had told us many times around the table when he laughingly regaled stories about his Dad's little quirks.

Jules looked at his Dad.

"Pop, instead of using up all the sugar why not use one teaspoon and stir the sugar in?"

Waiting for Einstein

In his thick Polish accent, Pop answered him with a straight face. "I don't like it that sweet."

Jules rolled his eyes in exasperation and returned to his dessert. When Pop put down the cup for the last time, I could see a half an inch of sugar on the bottom of the cup. Jules started to say something and then stopped. This time he just chuckled and could not contain himself and said, "I give up."

I had heard my Dad tell that story lovingly more times than I can count and here I had just witnessed the event in person. Is it possible that I witnessed the one and only time or was this a routine argument? I'll never know, but I was feeling grateful that I had experienced it first-hand.

It wasn't long before Adam and I had to say our final goodbyes. I knew that I would not be seeing this place again until my earliest memories after my birth in 1949 and never again if I hopefully returned to 2013. I looked around and took in the heavy floral wallpaper, the picture of the Last Supper with iridescent blue Brazilian butterflies behind Jesus and the Apostles, the French doors that separated the dining room from the living room, and the beautiful chaos that was the Majewski home.

Adam and I stood to leave. We went to Pop and shook his hand.

"Thanks for sharing your home with us. It was an honor."

He just smiled and squished our hands in his.

Grandma came over and gave me a crushing hug. She did the same with Adam but added a wet drippy kiss on the cheek. I hated those as a kid and could not imagine that my grandson was any more thrilled.

"Have a safe trip."

"Thank you."

Chapter Twenty-Nine

Jules escorted us to the door after all the girls had given Adam and I similar hugs and goodbyes.

"I'll never forget youse guys. Ya may have saved my life. I'm forever grateful. And I'm sure that my family is as well. I don't know how to repay ya."

"It was my pleasure. I'm glad you sought me out. Just stay clean and someday you just might find the right girl. I'm pretty sure that when you have kids of your own, they'll be glad to have a Dad like you. I have no doubt that you will be great like your Pop."

"That's a lot to put on my plate. I hope ya're right. I promise ya that I'll do my best."

"I'm sure you will."

I hugged him for the last time, again. He would not be waiting for me in my time. I looked into his light blue eyes for the last time. I never thought it would be this hard to lose him again. He left such a hole in my heart when he passed and it was happening again but in such a different way. I could not stop my eyes from welling up and turned away quickly. Adam and I left. I was losing my Dad for the second time in my life. I think I was able to wipe a tear away without Adam noticing as we headed down the street to where we parked the car. As I set the choke and fired her up, I looked at Adam. I could tell from his thoughtful eyes that he knew what I was going through. Thankfully he said nothing.

We returned to the apartment and knocked on the landlord's door. We had given him notice last month and he was not unhappy at the time.

"I hope you get to rent the apartment quickly. You've been a great landlord and deserve success."

"I already have it rented to an Irish family, a mother with a teenage daughter and two younger sons. A Mrs. Kennedy."

"Would that be Marguerite Kennedy?"

This was not possible, or was it? How did I not realize I had rented her apartment? I had been there enough times but never remembered the name of the side street off Flatbush Avenue where she lived. I always found her place because of the Korean Market across the street.

"That's her name. Why, do you know her? Are they decent people?"

"I know the family. They're nice people and you won't have any trouble with them."

I thought it best not to tell him that my grandmother had just been recently divorced. That might not be such an earth-shattering revelation in the 21st century but here it was close to wearing a scarlet letter socially, especially for an Irish Catholic.

"They're stable and you will not have to worry about them taking off any time soon, I think."

I laughed to myself knowing that Grandma Kennedy, my future Mom's mother, would not vacate that apartment until she went into long term care in 1990. When the apartment went rent-controlled ten years from now in 1943, she was paying seventy-five dollars a month. That meant that the rent could only go up seven percent at the time one renter left for another. No turnover, no rent increase. No landlord would make any money on that apartment any time soon. She outlived three landlords before she passed in 1991.

Adam and I finished packing just a few clothes and mementos, trying to be optimistic about returning to our time. We had no idea of how long it would take to find Einstein or even how long it would take for him to find a solution to our plight. We were anxious to get back home but we also did not want to scare him by acting like we were in a panic. I had read that

Chapter Twenty-Nine

Einstein believed in the possibility of time travel but said that travel to the future was not possible, only traveling into the past. My hope was that we could return a short time after we left and that could still constitute our past. I needed a genius to agree with that interpretation. Imagine that. Einstein agreeing with me. That could be the most amazing part of this trip if it happened.

The next morning, we left our apartment for the last time. I'd be returning as a baby in 1949 with my family to visit my Grandma Kennedy but Adam was done. We threw our small bags in the trunk and locked it. While the car warmed up, we glanced over the maps and reviewed the route to Princeton. We pulled out from the curb, circled the block, made a right onto Flatbush Avenue eventually taking a right and headed toward the Brooklyn Bridge to cross over to lower Manhattan. We had decided to take the Holland Tunnel to Jersey City and then head south to Princeton.

Strangely, I noticed a black Chevy roadster with two fedora-wearing men, follow us from the time we pulled away from our apartment. They kept a distance but I could swear the driver looked like the thug my Dad had driven with. They stayed on our bumper all the way to the Brooklyn Bridge. Was the mob still checking out all the little two-tone green coupes after that incident involving my Dad? Was switching the passenger side mirror to replace the one I broke hitting Jules, replacing the trunk and the Connecticut plates, enough to fool them? Were they looking at the out-of-place hubcaps? I glanced nervously in the rearview mirror, trying not to alert Adam to our trackers. I would know whether they were on to us if they followed onto the bridge. With my eyes glued to the rearview mirror, I breathed a sigh of relief when they turned off toward Court Street as we hit the entrance ramp to the bridge.

CHAPTER THIRTY
Finding Einstein
October 18, 1933

Crossing the Brooklyn Bridge, we made a last-minute decision to ditch the Holland Tunnel and go via the Staten Island Ferry for the view. Alighting from the car, we stood along the railing and caught the sun as it was rising. We were treated to an incredible morning light show framing the Manhattan skyline.

As we approached the Staten Island side, I told Adam how I had found the original deed to Staten Island when I was going to St. Francis College in Brooklyn Heights. It was around 1969 or 1970 and I was having lunch with Art Konopf, curator of the Brooklyn Historical Society based at the College. I was enjoying a sandwich that I had just picked up at Piccadilly's when he got a call from the archivist at the New York Supreme Court, a few blocks away on Court Street. After Art got off the phone, he shared the details of the conversation with me.

The records department had just reached capacity and it was basically a case of "out with the old and in with the new." It took little thought to volunteer to go over to the court to pick up some skids full of old documents that were going to be thrown out if we didn't want them for the Brooklyn Historical Society. Art rented a van and we went over the next day and backed up to a loading dock in the back of the building. In the hallway leading to the dock were several old-style skids heaping with boxes, books, and loose documents stacked willy-nilly almost chest high.

As I slipped the skid jack under the pin in the front, a leather-bound document slid off the top and hit the floor. I picked it up and opened it. On one side was an ancient piece of paper under a protective thin gauze of some kind and a facsimile on the right. When I read it, my jaw dropped. It was the original deed to Staten Island. I had no idea if historians knew that there was an actual document that went along with the famous twenty-four dollars in beads and stuff that the Dutch had paid the Native Americans for the island, but here it was right in my hand. IT WAS SLATED FOR THE DUMP IF WE HAD NOT VOLUNTEERED TO TAKE IT.

What other historical treasures were hiding on these skids? As it turned out, there were so many that I could not remember all of them. Most were from the Dutch colonial times. I remember that one of the most important ones was the Religious Bill of Rights, proclaiming religious freedom in the colony and that it was the first in the Americas. Historians came from all over the world to view the documents when they were finally put on display.

Adam looked at me incredulously.

"You've told me so many stories, but this one is clearly the most unbelievable. If you are ever going to write about our experiences someday, don't mention this or they won't believe anything else you say."

"Are you kidding me? That's what will kill my credibility? It's really true, I found the deed to Staten Island. I wouldn't make up stuff like that."

Chapter Thirty

"Okay, I believe you but don't mention it to anyone else. I'm just saying."

"Whatever."

I could not believe that something that I thought was pretty cool to be a part of was the thing Adam felt was unbelievable. Living in 1933 was not unbelievable. Having dinner with the Bartons, Ruths, and Cagneys was not unbelievable. Adam being friends with Julia and Dorothy Ruth was not unbelievable. Yet, my finding the deed to Staten Island was unbelievable?

The trip was much easier than I expected it to be. I had read the map carefully and it was pretty direct by following US 1 South once we hit New Jersey. I-95 and the Jersey Turnpike did not exist yet and traffic through the towns and villages along the way was not bad since it was a Saturday morning. We entered Princeton by lunch time after we had taken a right turn, off of US 1, traveling north a short distance before entering the center of town.

Princeton was definitely a college town as was evidenced by all the obvious students roaming around looking for places to eat or hang out downtown. Some were walking with visiting family or girlfriends and others in small groups. They dressed in the latest collegiate fashion and none looked like they wanted for money. Their families were weathering the Depression and still had the means to afford university costs. This was a stark contrast from the streets of Brooklyn that we had just left that morning.

I had no idea where Einstein lived when he first arrived at Princeton. I knew he would buy a house in 1935 but that would not help me now. We decided to camp out near the entrance to the Institute for American Studies since he would be showing up there pretty much on a daily basis. He had come to Princeton

Waiting for Einstein

just yesterday and it was all over the news. It was not going to be easy to get near him with all the press around and everyone trying to get his attention.

I had plenty of pocket money thanks to the Bartons' generosity and took a room at a boarding house near the center of town. Many large houses had been transformed into mini-hotels from the grand single-family dwellings of the teens and twenties when the breadwinners either lost their jobs or accepted lower pay to keep them. You could drive down any street and see "FOR RENT" signs hanging from tree branches or signposts in front of many of these stately dwellings.

Our new landlord, Mrs. Violet Sanders, said her husband had been an automobile salesman and had lost his job when sales plummeted due to the continuing Depression. He actually had a good relationship with the Hupp Motor Car Company regional representative and was offered a job at their assembly plant until the economy recovered. He took the job and was living in a boarding house in Detroit and religiously sent money home to support his wife and three children. His paycheck, coupled with the rent money she collected, barely made it possible to maintain the huge house but if anyone could stretch a dollar it was Violet. At least that's what she told us in the short walk to our room. If we stayed a week, we would have her family history back to the Mayflower. She was not a private person.

We unpacked and fidgeted because we were itching to meet with Professor Einstein. Our surveillance at the Institute started first thing in the morning. He would enter the front door every morning with reporters dogging his heels just to get a picture or one sentence of something brilliant enough to sell to a paper. It would be three days before we would finally get our chance. Adam had noticed that we did not see Einstein exit the Institute

Chapter Thirty

at five yesterday like the previous two days. The light was still on in the window that we had identified as his office, but there was no evidence of movement in the room. Slowly the newsmen gave up and dispersed. We both agreed that he might have left the light on as a subterfuge and was using a different way to exit the building to avoid all the media attention. We checked out the building for possible choices and found one that looked good. It was our best hope to get close to him without an audience and tell him our plight. It paid off big time. Tomorrow we would test our theory that this might become his new routine based on his success today.

About 5:30 P.M. the following day we spotted that big shock of crazy hair as Einstein quietly tried to sneak out the back exit. I had a plan that I hoped would keep us from scaring him, and hopefully getting his attention. We walked toward him and tried to act like we were not interested in him. I cut in front of him at the last instant and placed a dollar bill that I retrieved from under the seat of the little Chevy, into his hand. I had put all my cash from 2013 there when we knew it was useless in 1933.

"I thought you might like to see this Professor. Please check out the date of the 'Series' on the bill. You might find it very interesting."

I continued past him. I looked back to see that he was holding the note closer than moving it back and forth until the small numbers came into focus. Adam and I stopped and waited for a reaction.

Then seemingly out of nowhere, a police officer or campus policeman approached Einstein. A conversation ensued with both of them looking back and forth toward us during their discourse.

Waiting for Einstein

My heart started to sink and Adam said "Oh God," as the officer left Einstein's side and headed in our direction. Running was not an option and we waited until he was standing in front of us. He was not smiling.

"Do you have some business with Professor Einstein?" He was slightly tapping the palm of his hand with his nightstick for emphasis.

"We just wanted to say hello to a great man. We are both big fans."

"I'm not sure he is interested in your attention at this time. You need to move along. That's not a suggestion. Do we understand each other?"

"Yes, officer, sorry if we were a bother."

"Move along and let the Professor pass."

He turned and waved to Einstein to proceed. The professor walked by much closer than you would expect someone to if he was worried that you might be a danger. He even tipped his head to acknowledge us as he passed by. When he was well past us, the officer retreated back to the campus, eventually out of sight. We did not move a muscle until then and we slowly turned toward the direction Einstein had gone.

He was gone, nowhere in sight. Adam and I started to walk slowly in the same direction.

"What do we do now?"

"Not really sure. Looks like he let that officer know that he did not want to be bothered by us."

As we approached the next crosswalk, we spied Einstein as he stuck his head out from a large brick house on the far corner. Without a word he waved for us to come over to where he was standing. We jogged across the street and soon found ourselves standing in Einstein's presence after all these months of waiting.

Chapter Thirty

He held up the bill I had put in his hand. "Do I have to ask you where you got dis, Sir?" he asked in his thick Austrian accent.

I wasn't surprised by his addressing me as "Sir" since I was certain that I was older than he was at this point in time.

"I got it with change back in my time. Maybe I should say 'forward' in my time."

He thought for a moment and then spoke.

"I tink dis vill require furder investigation. Art you free for some suppa? I know a nice little cafe not far from here dat has some goot food. You vilt be my guests, yes?"

"That's not necessary but I definitely agree that we need to talk."

I presented my grandson.

"May I introduce my grandson, Adam. He also has been traveling with me."

We shook hands all around and Adam and I followed the professor to a quiet little diner a few blocks away. There were some students there and a few recognized Einstein right away and tipped their hats to him. None approached. Decorum was different here and we soon were seated at a booth in the back which afforded us the privacy we needed.

Adam and I sat across from the professor. Einstein pulled out the bill and put it on the table in front of us.

"My eyesight coot be bedder."

He pushed the bill toward Adam.

"Vhat is da date on the little bill young man?"

Adam looked at it and then looked up.

"Series 2009, Sir."

Einstein looked at me.

"You said you got dis wit your change. When vould dat be again?"

Waiting for Einstein

"I never really said but I would guess the day before we got here. That would be March 10, 2013."

"But dis is October. Did you arrive in March of 1933 or here in October?"

"We found ourselves here the same day of the year we came from but in 1933. That was last March."

"You have been here all dis time?"

"Over seven months."

"What were you vaiting for?"

This was the smartest man in the world and I had to give him an answer to what I thought was pretty obvious.

"You, we've been waiting for you."

"You know somet'ing? When I avoke dis morning I had an intuition dat I vould learn someting new today. I believe that I may be dhe student for de first time in a vhile. I vould like to hear your story now."

"I think my grandson can probably tell it better than me and maybe leave out some details and get to the point faster."

"I like detail. More to chew on, as dey say. Don't spare anytink. I want to hear it all," Einstein remarked.

We were on our third cup of coffee by the time Adam's story brought us to the present, sitting with Einstein.

"And that brings us up to date. We are having coffee with you. We've waited a long time to meet you. Pop, says that if anyone can help us it would be you. You do believe in time travel, don't you?"

"If I wasn't sure about it, I guess I vould have to admit that you make a compelling argument, . . . if your story is true."

Adam looked at me and asked.

"Pop, should we have him sit in the Chevy like we did with Mrs. Barton?"

Chapter Thirty

"Young man, are you going to make me valk all over town to see vhat you tolt me about already? I guess I will have to take your vord for it to save myself some valking, ya? This is an interesting and amazing story. Did you really meet dhe famous Babe Ruth? I'm sorry. Dis is not important right now but you must promise to tell me if he is as nice a man as the papers tell, later. I should focus on your problem. No?"

"Yes," I jumped into the conversation.

"You say you are from the future, 2013? If you are, den you must know dat I do not think traveling to de future is possible. Den again here you are from the future. I always have theorized dat it was possible to travel into de past but dhat involves traveling at de speed of light and many odder elements not discovered, well at least not yet. Do you travel at de speet of light in your time?"

"Not yet, we're working on it. However, we have sent probes into space and we have taken pictures of Mars and most of the planets from up close in space. Actually, we landed men on the moon over forty years ago in the late sixties."

"Please do not tell me any tink more. You will hurt the surprise for me. I tink you know many things that I would like to know and some that I would rather not. I believe that Hitler can destroy the world as we know it. You're being here tells me that maybe he did not accomplish this. Let's leave it at dat. Ya?"

"I understand completely. Adam and I have talked about this many times. You are correct when you surmised that we know a lot about what is coming down the road historically. We also think that it is not our mission to try and educate society to correct mistakes that are being made and will be made in the future. I think we are like travelers on a train who can see the

Waiting for Einstein

world passing by, but we are limited to what we can accomplish when we are left off at our train station.

"I think that if I shared what I know, no one would listen anyway. There are always people trying to point out upcoming disasters and no one listens. You must feel that way about what Hitler is doing. It doesn't seem like the German people are listening to you. There's a lot of truth in the old adage that 'history repeats itself.' I have a responsibility not to stand on the sideline in my time but not in yours. I will admit that I did make an attempt to tweak history with my family. We will see if that worked when we can get back to our time."

Einstein smiled and remarked.

"You are a very smart man. You have learned much in your lifetime."

Adam looked at me and laughed.

"Pop, Professor Einstein just told you that you are smart. That's quite an endorsement!"

"That's what I've been trying to tell you your whole life."

We all laughed.

Einstein looked at Adam.

"Your Grand Papa is smart because he listens and learns. Remember, it is not how much knowledge you collect but what you do wit dat knowledge. Knowledge is only important if you use it. It is not something to be collected and den put on a shelf. It only has value if you can build on it."

Einstein looked serious again.

"So vhat did you tink happened to get you to travel to the past? Did you use a machine?"

"Not exactly, as Adam told you, we were driving in my 1933 Chevy which is far from anything high tech. In our time it is eighty years old but I have a theory."

Chapter Thirty

"And your theory is?"

Einstein looked intrigued waiting for an answer. I was frozen in a realization. Einstein was asking me about *my* theory on something! I was going to tell Einstein *my* theory! Not in a million years did I ever think that I'd be doing that. This definitely topped finding that deed to Staten Island and would be just as fantastic to my family if I could ever tell them.

"I've given it a lot of thought and I think we may have stumbled upon a 'wormhole' entrance that gave us a path into the past."

"Vhat is this 'vormhole' that you mentioned. Is dis some kind of tunnel through time?"

Einstein's mind was working in hyper-speed. You could see it in his eyes and demeanor.

"Exactly. Theorists of time travel in my century think that there may be these wormholes that are like shortcuts that can be taken to travel through time and possibly space even going long distances in relatively shorter time spans. Some theorize that they have been used over the millennia by time and space travelers, but no one has definitively ever found evidence of this activity. None of these travelers has ever come forward and identified themselves.

"Well, except now with Adam and me seeking you out. I think these 'wormholes' are like tunnels that cut through complex hills and valleys of time and space. Climbing the range up and down can take months or years but a direct line through the mountains can cut the trip to a fraction of that time depending again on how close and deep they are. Some think that time and space are not linear but like ripples with these highs and lows."

Einstein thought for a moment.

Waiting for Einstein

"I've imagined such travel but in my mind we are using bridges to even out de trip across valleys and moving peak to peak. I guess I tought it is easier to imagine building bridges than tunnels but I like your idea as vell."

"How fast were you going ven you vent trough dis tunnel?"

"I looked at my speedometer and I was doing forty-two miles per hour. Not exactly breaking the sound barrier. It was only a moment before I realized that something had changed and we had ended up in a different time. I guess eighty years could be simply a blink in relation to time."

Einstein tilted his head and asked.

"Have they passed the sound barrier in your time?"

"I thought you didn't want to know things from the future?"

The genius cracked a smile.

"Ve can cheat a liddle. It vould be very nice to know."

"Okay, yes we did. Actually, you will get to hear about it in your lifetime. I don't remember when but I'm pretty sure that you will see them hit Mach II as well."

"What is dis Mach II?"

"I'm sorry. We call the speed of sound Mach I and twice that speed is Mach II. I think it's named after some scientist.

"So dey kept the name for the speed of sound after Mach. They must still keep it for my good friend Ernst Mach. He was a fellow Austrian and smart, and a great philosopher of what many of us were trying to theorize. He deserves such an honor. Another friend of mine Jakob Ackeret was the first to apply the term "Mach" in Ernst's honor. I think in a paper he wrote a few years ago in 1929."

I thought this was incredible to hear how Einstein knew all these guys, but I was getting a little frustrated since this incredible trivia from him was not getting us any closer to the

Chapter Thirty

answer of how we were going to get back to our time. I blurted out the unimaginable before I could stop myself.

"Professor Einstein, stay focused!"

Oh my God! Did I just say that to the smartest man of the 20th Century?

"I am so sorry. I should never have snapped at you like that."

He started to laugh.

"Do not vorry about it. You are not de first person to tell me dat. Many men, not so smart as you, have tried to keep my mind on topic. I do much thinking in a day. Zo den, shall we return to trying to solve your dilemma?"

"That would be nice. I'm so sorry, really."

My face was warm and I knew I must be blushing with embarrassment. Adam just looked at me wide-eyed in disbelief that I had just snapped at Einstein.

"Please, do not tink about it. Your situation is making my head spin wit many theories and vonder. I am like a kid in a candy shop right now. Dis is becoming a great day for me."

He did have an infectious and totally warm smile that calmed me immediately. There was a confidence in his voice that made you feel that there was an answer to every problem and it was just a simple case of finding it. It put us at ease for the moment.

"As I was saying, we were doing forty-two miles per hour. We went back through the tunnel a half a dozen times afterward trying to get back but it was not easy to hit the exact speed. I think I did it at least a few times but obviously with no success."

"Did you try going back up this hill in the same direction you traveled back in time?"

"Yes, at first I figured we would need to go in from the opposite direction to return to our time. But that didn't work. Then we tried the other way with no success as well. We did that many times. Do you think that the direction is important, does it matter?"

"I don't know. It seemed easy enough for you to get here. I only know, as you report, that it did not vork your way. I don't even know if de hole would stay open there or pops up in another place. Have there been stories of people disappearing before in this part of your town?"

"I'm pretty sure there have been no cases that I am aware of. So why us?"

"That is a great question. But I believe there are no such tings as accidents. Every event has purpose in life's order."

I could not believe that he just said that. He believes what I have always believed, that every event, relationship or experience in our lives has a purpose as well. Here was one of the smartest people in history saying the same thing. Could I actually be smarter than I realized? Most of the nuns at St. Hedwig's Grammar School did their best to try and convince me that I was not that bright. It surprised me that after all these years, I still felt the sting of being labeled the class dummy even though I later became an honor student in high school and earned a BA in English. This was followed by a nursing degree twenty years later. I wondered what the nuns would say now if they saw me carrying on an intelligent conversation with Einstein?

"If we go back to the old trestle, how will we know if the 'wormhole' is open?"

"You are asking a difficult question. Ve are in uncharted waters now. My intuition tells me that this may ve your only choice."

I was amazed at this reply.

Chapter Thirty

"I don't want to sound insulting but we need your genius more than your intuition right now."

"Don't underestimate the power of intuition. It is almost as important as imagination and can be more so than knowledge."

I could not believe it but I was actually hearing Einstein telling me his thoughts on imagination. I had a T-shirt at home that had a quote from him under a picture of him with dark sunglasses. "Imagination is more important than knowledge." I knew that it was a real quote but hearing it from him in person was quite amazing.

He seemed to be thinking out loud.

"What if dis portal or vormhole opened up to here because you were supposed to fix dis ting with your Papa? And now it is done and the door is sitting there open for your return? The accomplished task was the key, not time or speed."

"You think we can just go back to Connecticut and try to repeat entrance into the trestle opening from the same direction and hope for the best?"

Einstein looked at us with a wry smile and shrugged his shoulders.

"Do you have a better idea? I realize that it zounds too zimple but I do not have anoder idea right now. I zuggest that you at least try it and if you cannot get back to your time, return here and then ve will use zome of my fancy physics and try to formulate another zolution. I am already excited just by hearing about Mach I and Mach II speeds being attained. You have made me cautiously excited for the future with all dis talk of time travel."

"I am glad you feel that way but I also know that there will be much sadness in the world along the way as well."

I just had to say it.

Waiting for Einstein

"I know dis to be sure. I have already zeen de evil of Hitler at vork. Mussolini is not any better and I fear dere will be much destruction and lives lost all over Europe. I fear dat tings vill also deteriorate in the Far East someday as well. The Japanese are gaining strength and I fear it is not a goot ting for dheir neighbors as vell. However, even I cannot help you in varning the vorld. I do not believe that is your purpose here. You have secured your family's future and you need to try and go back home. I believe dat if you have accomplished de correct ting den you will find your 'vorm hole'."

We shook hands and I asked him one last question that I just had to know.

"Can I ask you a personal question?"

"As long as it is not too difficult to answer, ya."

He smiled.

"Is there some kind of a message you are sending by not combing your hair? I don't believe you do anything by accident."

He laughed again.

"It does look like an accident, ya? No. I have no message to telegraph with my hair. I just tink dat at my age it will not make me look any better so vhy vaste sleep and energy trying to control it. And it does make it easier for my friends to find me in a crowd, ya?"

He looked at my bald head clipped close to the scalp.

"I like your solution as well but it looks like a lot of vork and I fear my head may not be as vell shaped as yours under all dis."

He gave me a genuine smile with that famous twinkle in his eye.

I loved his answer.

"I respect your answer and will take it to my grave."

Adam laughed at this exchange.

Chapter Thirty

"I doubt dat my hair is dat important to carry such information to de grave. Thank you and good luck in your journey. If you ever come back, I hope you vill look me up. We can trade ideas."

Wow! Einstein wanted to trade ideas with me. If my Dad only knew.

"I'd like that."

As Adam and I walked away and headed in the direction of the car, we did so in silence both thinking that it could not be this simple.

Adam looked at me.

"Pop, do you think we wasted all this time waiting for Einstein when all we had to do was drive through the tunnel in the same direction we entered it the first time?"

"I believe everything happens for a reason. I truly believe that we were supposed to be here and for this length of time to get something done. I don't know if getting my Dad to quit the mob was the whole motive but it had to be at the top of the list."

I looked at Adam still worried.

"I can only hope that this is going to work and that we can get back to a time close to when we left. Otherwise, we are going to have some big issues and a lot of explaining to do."

CHAPTER THIRTY-ONE
Back to Cheshire?
October 19, 1933 or 2013?

We drove all day and all night. We had agreed that we were both too homesick to delay any longer. I never felt so happy to see the George Washington Bridge before. The bridge which spanned the Hudson River between New Jersey and New York is an engineering marvel. When it opened in 1931, it was twice as long as any suspension bridge ever constructed.

I took my favorite way out of Manhattan when we got to the New York City side of the bridge. We took Route 9 North, the West Side Highway, to the Saw Mill River Parkway, caught the Cross County Parkway to the Hutchinson Parkway North. This led straight into the Wilbur Cross Parkway when we crossed the border into Connecticut. We stopped at a gas station on the Parkway and caught a nap knowing that we were maybe an hour from home.

We woke almost simultaneously and went to the men's room on the side of the gas station to throw some cold water in our faces, wash up a little and relieve ourselves. We then took turns changing into the clothes that we had worn the day we left unexpectedly for the future. Adam and I had gotten haircuts before we left Princeton and made sure that they looked as close as possible as our March 2013 look, at least as we could remember, when we left for that fateful ride to Blackie's eight months ago.

Chapter Thirty-One

I hoped that Adam had not grown enough to be noticed. I had been with him daily and saw little change. How would he look to his parents, brother, and family? Would they notice the new found confidence that he showed in his carriage? He had matured quickly to survive and became streetwise in the Flatbush, Brooklyn of 1933. We both agreed that I had changed little, possibly more grey hair but with it cut close to the scalp it was pretty much undetectable. I noticed a few grey hairs in my eyebrows but maybe they were always there. When we examined each other as we returned to the Chevy, we were pretty confident that we looked as close to our 2013 look as possible. This could almost work as long as we returned close to the time we left. However, if we fell short or overshot our target date all bets were off.

I ran the gears as quickly as possible to get up to traffic speed on the Parkway. We started to get excited about the possibility of getting back home. We also could not stop thinking about all the adventures and especially the people that we met there as well.

Adam confessed that his best memories were definitely of my Dad, his great grandfather, and his family.

"I am so glad that I got to meet my great grandfather and even his Dad. I never told you this but I see a lot of you in both of them."

"I will take that as a compliment. They are really good men and were devoted to their families."

"I have to say that hanging out with the Ruth family was a close second."

Adam admitted that he related better to seventeen-year-old Julia than the younger Dorothy. They spent many nights together at the Ruth apartment while I went out with the Bartons and the girls' parents. They listened to the radio and from Adam's reports he enjoyed *The Lone Ranger* best, noting, that not having a visual of the story that a television would provide, allowed his imagination to create his own images and scenes purely based on the narrative and sound effects. He understood what Einstein was referring to about the value of imagination versus knowledge.

His appreciation of finally meeting my friend, Katie and Jim Barton was equal with meeting the Ruths. We both discussed the value and depth of that friendship with her which saved us financially and emotionally while we waited for Einstein. Life would have been different without their financial support as well as the money that Adam brought in selling papers, and then working at the Popp's Ice Cream Parlor. We had weathered the Great Depression better than most.

We talked about the Cagneys and Wiley Post's adventure flying around the world solo, the baseball games, and everything else we experienced. I knew we would be spending time alone with each other to decompress and to reflect on our time traveling and what it meant to each of us.

We were talking like our return to 2013 was a done deal. We stopped reminiscing and started to review everything we had to do to make sure that we replicated how we went through the trestle just as Einstein directed so that we could somehow reenter the "wormhole" correctly and return home.

We never discussed the "what if's" if it didn't work. I confidently told Adam that, like Einstein, my intuition told me that the professor was correct in his assumption that this simple solution would work. I thought about intuition possibly having a force all its own to make our attempt to return home a reality.

Chapter Thirty-One

We arrived at the entrance to the Mixville Pond in Cheshire mid-afternoon and sat there with the engine idling comfortably. We looked at each other, shook hands.

"Here goes nothing, Buddy."

I put the car into first gear, let up on the clutch and hit the gas. We started to race up the hill. The little Chevy did not have much off the line in that gear and I clutched again and shoved it into second gear. She took off like a jack rabbit, I looked down, thirty miles an hour, as the engine's RPMs increased. Another quick clutch and gear shift and we went into third gear just before the trestle came into view. My foot went to the floor and as we approached the tunnel under the trolley bed.

I recalled the story Babe Ruth had told us when we dined at Sardi's about his crash in 1920. Ruth was in Wallingford, Connecticut, driving through a one lane culvert similar to this one. When he entered the culvert, he crashed head-on into a Mack Truck. Ruth was sprayed with glass from the shattered windshield. His brand-new Packard was destroyed but the Babe emerged unscathed. God, how I hoped that we would not repeat Babe's mishap today.

I returned to the task at hand. I looked down at the gauges, forty-two miles an hour.

Adam yelled, "There's a light up ahead."

It was now or never. We drove through the trestle in the same direction as last March. I prayed that the light was coming from the entrance to the wormhole and not a Mack Truck. I kept my foot to the floor and the steepness of the incline kept the Chevy steady at forty-two miles an hour. We raced through the underpass and I swerved to the right as I did the first time. Nothing was coming in our direction. Whew, both of us exhaled a massive sigh of relief.

Waiting for Einstein

    A short distance later I spied a house set back into the woods on the right.

    "Look Adam! That wasn't there in '33! We drove a little further. On our left I saw the back yards of two raised ranches that were built by a crew I worked with in the summer of 1973 when I was a carpenter. Another raised ranch came up on our right just before the slight curve to the stop sign where the restored Victorian sat just as it did when we left. I continued straight onto Mathew Street where all the modern houses now outnumbered the few remaining farm houses that still peppered the neighborhood. I had not turned right onto Plank Road like we did in March because I had already seen enough to believe that we had miraculously made it back. I was sure that Blackie's was going to be where it should be in 2013.

    I looked over at Adam and saw tears rolling down his cheeks. I didn't say anything since I still had no idea if we had returned to a time close to when we left. We could be months or years off the mark and I had no idea what reaction awaited us when we saw family. That's assuming we could find them. The fastest way to find out was to simply go to my house which was the closest and just see what awaited us.

    We turned right onto Luke Street and at the top of the hill made a right onto Melissa Lane. I wanted to approach my house on the loop from the north with a long view to see if anything seemed different. As we rounded the bend, I spotted my mailbox which was leaning toward the street just as it was after the snow plow had clobbered it with wet snow in January. I could not imagine that it would not have been fixed by someone if we were years off our mark. I turned into the driveway and hit the garage door opener I had kept on the rear window shelf of the Chevy.

    It opened!

Chapter Thirty-One

Adam never said a word. A hint of a smile formed on his handsome face.

We both looked into the open garage as we entered to park and spotted my 1958 Rambler Ambassador in the first bay. Henny's '05 Lexus RX330 was in its usual spot. We both realized that we definitely had to be somewhere close in time to when we left.

"Want to come in or wait here, Adam?"

"I could never stand the suspense. I'll go in with you. I have to know."

We entered through the garage and climbed the half staircase into the house. As we approached the kitchen past the mud room, I spied Henny's pocketbook on the kitchen island. It was the same one, in the same place, as it was when I had left that fateful afternoon. Henny turned around from the computer she was doing genealogy searches on at the kitchen table.

"Hi, Adam! I thought you guys were going to the cruise at Blackie's?"

OMG! We are in the same time frame we left in. If we weren't exactly on time, we were close enough. Definitely not enough for Henny to notice.

Adam ran over to her, and as she stood up, he gave her a powerful hug.

"You have no idea how good it is to see you, Grandma."

He let her go when he realized that he was acting way too weird to explain. Henny looked confused and did not notice the tear in the corner of his eye.

"That was the nicest hello you've given me in quite a while. What is that all about?"

"Nothing. I just missed you, that's all," Adam stammered.

"Well, that's really sweet. I missed you, too. Maybe we need to see more of you. What do you think?"

"I'd like that."

Adam stepped aside. She looked over Adam's shoulder at me.

"So why are you guys back so soon? Is that old car giving you trouble?"

I was never so glad to hear her pick on my old car. I walked over to her and gave her a kiss on the cheek. She saw my tear. Her gentle hand went to my cheek

"And did you miss me too, Bobby?"

She only used that name when she was playing cute with me. It just sounded sweeter than ever.

"More than you could ever know."

"What does that mean? What are you two up to?"

She looked at Adam because she figured that if we were playing with her, he would be the first to crack and show our hand.

"Nothing, Grandma. Really. Come on, Pop. Didn't you say you had to get gas?"

I could see what he wanted to do next. He wanted to see his family.

"Okay, Buddy. Let's hit the road. "

As much as I wanted to stay with my wife, I knew Adam needed to get home more. We ran out the door and jumped in the car. She fired right up.

"You know, that culvert that the Babe ran into the Mack Truck is only fifteen minutes from here. Do you want to take a run through it?"

"Pop, you can't be serious!"

"Just kidding! Let's get you home."

Chapter Thirty-One

We sprinted over to my son's house in Cheshire in just over ten minutes. We both noted that everything we spied along the way was just as it was when we left.

"Pop, I think we exited the wormhole just moments after we entered it. I don't think anyone knows that we were gone for more than half an hour."

"I think you're right. I was thinking the same thing. Einstein's intuition was right. I cannot believe that the solution could be that simple."

We pulled into his driveway.

"It may have been only an hour or so for those left in 2013 but it had been an eternity for us."

We entered his house on Cornwall Street.

He ran in before he noticed that his father's car was not in the driveway. David and Karen were not home. When I entered the house, he was just coming down the old servant's stairs that led from the upstairs to the kitchen.

He looked so frustrated.

"They must have gone out to dinner. I can't remember if they told me they were doing that. It was so long ago. They usually take Colin out if I'm doing something."

He was getting a little hyper.

"Okay, Buddy, calm down. You know we are back to the right time and place and everyone is fine. Maybe this isn't a bad thing that they are out. We almost blew it with your grandmother. Let's regroup and decide how we are going to play this out with them. Your Dad is too good at sniffing things out and if you start acting strange, he will zero in on it. We can't tell anyone about this yet until we can figure out what it all means. Not to mention, they will just think we are spoofing them anyway. Only time will tell us when it is appropriate to tell anyone our story, if ever."

Waiting for Einstein

"Pop, I've had acting classes and I think I know how I can play this. Why don't you go home since that is what you would normally do? When they get home, I'll just tell them that the turnout at the cruise was light and we left right after we ate. I'll rehearse how I should act if I was only gone a short while and I promise that they will never know."

He hugged me.

"I knew you would get us back home. It was really scary but it was also amazing. Please don't take it personal but I'm never driving through that trestle again, especially with you. I'm okay now so why don't you go home to Grandma. I'll be fine."

"Thanks, Adam. I just want to sit on the couch and watch her putter around. I never thought I could miss someone so much. I'll be happy to return to our unexciting life in the country. I appreciate how Kitty felt when Jim died. I never want to feel that way again. Any time you need to talk just call. We may need each other to work out some unexpected issues."

"I will, Pop."

He hugged me and I headed home. I could not wait to get home and return to my simple life. No more hanging with Broadway, sports, and Hollywood legends. No more worrying about the mob and my Dad. No more people talking to me like I was Methuselah.

Did we save my Dad from a fate that might have erased my family's future as we knew it? I'll never know. The one thing I was sure of was that Adam and I would never take our family for granted. We would cherish every moment with all of them for the rest of our lives. Adam lost everyone but one from the people he met in 1933. I had already lost all of them in the fifties and sixties when my grandparents died, in 1988 when my Dad died, up until my Mom's death in 2008. In the present, only my Uncle

Chapter Thirty-One

Al and Julia Ruth were still with us. I'd plan a visit to him in Vermont as soon as possible. Julia would have to stay off limits.

There is a statement that will always be true in our lives. As Dorothy said in *The Wizard of Oz*, "There's no place like home."

EPILOGUE
Cheshire
June 2016

Over the last two-and-a-half years, Adam and I would go off to the side at different family functions and talk about our experiences in 1933. We had promised ourselves that we would support each other as we dealt with our feelings. We talked about the loved ones that we left behind.

I found it heartwarming to hear Adam reminisce about the Majewski, Barton, and Ruth families in sincere and truly loving terms. He confessed how he found himself looking up anything he could find about Julia Ruth Stevens and how she was doing. He saved *Babe Ruth Central* as a favorite site on his computer to keep up to date. He would look on YouTube to see the latest news clip about Julia, throwing a ball out at the start of games around the country. Adam knew he could never contact her since we had agreed that would not be a good idea when we discussed it back before we left her in October of 1933.

Although she was now old enough to be his great, grandmother, he was happy to have known her as a teen and cherished their time together. He told me that he had seen interviews with her and could still hear similarities in her laugh and the way she sounded when he first met her at Sardi's with her parents.

Epilogue

He'd been bugging me to visit my Uncle Al as well which I had not done since we returned. Life with seven grandchildren, not to count our own adult children with their spouses fills the calendar quickly. Plus, I was still working part time as a registered nurse at Connecticut Hospice in Branford. All that living doesn't leave much time for everything you would like to do.

Henny and I had been invited to my son David's house for a barbeque on Father's Day. It was a beautiful day and I decided to take the '33 Chevy out for a spin and drive over to their house. The car looked more in tune with the 1905 Dutch Revival house than my son's BMW and Volvo that I parked behind. Eventually, Adam and I were sitting in the living room of this beautiful home in the historic district of Cheshire. As we often did, Adam and I had separated from the family for a few moments to touch base with each other about how we were handling our secretive and shared experience.

In general, we agreed we were doing well. I told Adam that I'd like to take him up to Uncle Al's in Vermont. If he recognized us from his childhood, we would deal with it on the fly and determine if we could get away with a full denial or let him in on the secret. As we were talking, my cell phone rang. I looked at the number and immediately thought it was a telemarketer since I did not recognize the area code. I don't know why but I decided to answer it figuring I could always hang up if my first assumption was correct.

"Hello, is this Robert Majeski?" a male voice asked.

"Yes, who's calling please."

"Well, you don't know me but my name is Tom Stevens."

It still sounded like a telemarketer. I added "And?"

Waiting for Einstein

"You don't know me but I'm Babe Ruth's grandson, his daughter Julia's son, to be exact."

I almost dropped the phone.

"And you're calling me because?"

"Well, my Mom has told me this ridiculous story and I was hoping you could help me put this craziness to rest."

"I'm not sure how I can help. I'm listening."

Tom was quite persuasive and, without telling me anymore, I somehow agreed to visit Conway, New Hampshire in a couple of weeks and bring Adam along as well. Tom gave me the name of a nice motel, The Scenic Inn of Conway, less than a mile from the Stevens' home. After getting Adam up to speed, we agreed to run up there on June 22.

Henny was curious why Adam and I were invited to meet with Babe Ruth's daughter. She knew of Ruth's affiliations with the Bartons because she had also heard the stories from Katie over the Sunday dinner table at my parents' house when we were dating. I still had not told her about our adventure and could never decide when the time might be right, if ever. She loves to travel so there was no excuse that would make any sense to deter her from coming along to New Hampshire. I booked two rooms at the Inn.

Henny and I decided that Adam and I would visit Julia without her to find out what all of this was about. I would offer to take the family to dinner that evening and Henny would come along. I did tell her that I was interested to find out more about Julia's impression of the Bartons even though I already knew from my experience with them back in 1933. It still did not explain why this meeting was really happening.

Tom had told me that Julia did not get up until about noon but would be ready for company by two o'clock. After all, she was

Epilogue

100-years-old and needed her rest. We followed Tom's directions and ended up at the grey-painted country home of the Stevens family. When we got to the house, Tom greeted us at the side door and ushered us into the screened-in porch. He was only a few years younger than me but was obviously in better shape, appearing to be athletic. I'd find out later that he was an avid skier like his Mom had been in her youth.

It was perfect weather for staying outside. Before we could seat ourselves an older lady with a walker entered the doorway from the main house. She was about five-foot-six inches to Adam's five-foot-eleven-inches when he stood to greet her. She looked up at him with a big smile.

"Well, hello again Adam. I could not stand the suspense any longer and had to see you for myself. Now I know that what Kitty Barton was telling me was the truth."

"You remember me?"

"Why wouldn't I? You really haven't changed that much. A bit taller, maybe. From what I can see, you barely look any older than when I last saw you. Well, in my lifetime I think it's been about eighty-three years since we last met. Yes, I remember you. I'm Julia, Julia Ruth."

"Oh, my God!" Adam almost yelled. "How did you find us?"

He approached her and gently kissed her on the cheek. He turned to see me standing there with my mouth wide open.

"Pop, it's Julia!"

"I have been watching you on YouTube.

"Well, I *am* a celebrity in a fashion." She laughed. "I wasn't sure if you were the same Adam I last saw in 1933 but now I'm quite sure of it. If you can help get me to my chair, I think you have some explaining to do, young man."

She looked closely at Adam.

"It is amazing though. Although I can only see shadows you only seem a bit taller but otherwise you sound just as I remember you when we last saw each other. How old are you now?"

"I'll be eighteen in August, Mrs. Stevens."

Adam knew her married name from his web searches and wanted to be polite.

Julia didn't say anything until she was finally sitting in a comfortable cushioned chair on the porch. Her son Tom, Adam, and I pulled up chairs to be close to her.

"You don't have to call me Mrs. Stevens. I think we have been friends far too long for such formalities. You may still call me Julia. I'd like that."

"Thank you. So how did you find us, Julia?"

"You probably don't remember but you used to talk about being from Cheshire, Connecticut all the time and how you missed your family. You mentioned your father, David more than once. You even described your house rather well. After you and your grandfather left so suddenly, I felt that something just wasn't right about your departure. I finally hounded Kitty until she cracked and told me the true story."

She looked at me and added. "You had to know that there was no way that Kitty could keep a secret that long."

"What did she tell you?"

I needed to know.

"She told me a fantastic story about two time travelers who somehow slipped into the past from the future, 2013 to be exact. She told me that you made the trip in that Chevy coupe of yours. Of course, I did not believe her. If she was telling the truth, you would have been driving an eighty-year-old car and that was not really conceivable back then. Cars weren't old enough to be called antiques.

Epilogue

"But she went into such detail that for years I kept asking myself, 'What if it was true?' She did swear me to secrecy and I am much better than she was at keeping a promise. In the late sixties, I would see news items about people driving cars from that era and realized that maybe that part of the story could be true. I vowed to see for myself and waited until 2013 but I have such a busy life that I could not find the time to do enough research to see if you really existed in this century.

"When I lost my eyesight a few years ago I realized I needed someone else's help. My son Tom, here, would have to be told. I was afraid that when I told Tom what I was up to he might have me seeing a new doctor. Well, as you can see, I'm not getting any younger and I figured if I didn't check Kitty's story out soon it might never happen.

"I decided to give myself an early birthday present. I'll be 100 this coming July 17th. I guess I sounded credible enough and was a little persuasive with Tom. I stuck to my guns and he is such a dear. He never said I was crazy even though I know he was thinking it."

She turned to her son.

"Do you still think I'm crazy now?"

"I'm still trying to process all of this. It's a lot to take in."

He looked at me and asked me how old I was when I last saw his mother.

"I was sixty-four back when we first met in 1933. I believe Julia was seventeen and Adam was fourteen. Dorothy was around twelve. I don't remember your grandparents' but the Bartons' were forty-three and thirty-years-old. I just know that I was the oldest in the group by a lot. Jim and the Babe used to sometimes call me 'Old Man'." I could not argue with them. I was the oldest. I'm sixty-seven now."

"This is so freaky. Did you guys call each other behind my back and rehearse all this?" said Tom with an expression of disbelief as if he were a child asking a magician to reveal the secret of his trick.

Julia laughed out loud.

"Do you think we could make up a story like this and for what purpose?"

She looked at Adam.

"I always knew there was something special about you. You were just so smart and treated us girls like we were special. You were too well-spoken and always acted like a gentleman to just be some kid from the sticks."

Adam returned the laugh.

"You were royalty, to me and everyone who loved and admired your Dad. It took a while for me to realize how blessed I was to be so accepted by your family, especially when I was basically a nobody. It helped me a lot during trying times."

"You must be close to graduating from high school now."

Julia was genuinely interested.

"I did, last week."

"I assume you are going to college in the fall?"

"Yes Ma'm', I mean, Julia. I'm going to American University in D.C."

"I always knew you were a bright boy. I'm not surprised at all. Over the years I had hoped that your future would be as blessed as my life has been. You were such a nice boy back then. I guess you still are."

She giggled at her comment.

"I'm so glad I got to know you, too, but we needed to get back to our time. I hope it all makes sense to you now. If it wasn't for

Epilogue

Albert Einstein's help, we might never have gotten back," said Adam.

Tom jumped into the conversation.

"You met Einstein, too?"

"Yup. We sought him out to try and help us figure out how to get back to our time. We knew that he believed in time travel and if anyone could help us it would have to be the smartest man in the world."

I looked at Julia.

"That's when we left, telling everyone that we were going back to Connecticut. We really went to Princeton, New Jersey first. I knew from history that Einstein had just arrived in Jersey after fleeing Nazi Germany. Until today, I thought he was the only other person beside Katie that knew about us."

Tom was amazed by what Adam and I were sharing.

"I guess he helped, or you wouldn't be here talking to us."

"He was a huge help. What surprised us was how Einstein was unimpressed with his own genius and status in the world. He was easy to talk with and liked joking around as well. We liked him a lot. He even seemed impressed that we would have made such an effort to wait for his help."

"It's very hard to comprehend that your story is true, and I am not saying I'm there yet, but if what you are telling me is true, it sounds like you really had to experience some amazing things back there."

"Even though we had no say in starting the trip or 'when' in time, we would land, so to speak, if you had to time travel, 1933 was an incredible year, especially if you were living in the Tri-State area. Thank God Katie believed in us. She was the key for our survival. Because of her we lived fairly well off during the height of the Depression. It was actually Adam's idea to look her up."

"Because of Jim and Katie, we got to meet and hang out with your grandparents and great-grandmother, James Cagney and his wife Willie. We got to meet George M. Cohan and even Wylie Post before and after he flew solo around the world, not to mention all the celebrities that hung out at your house. But, we were always worried about getting back to our families. We have to say that it was still pretty cool to say the least. We owe so much to Katie and Jim and even your grandparents."

"It sounds like you really made the best of an unbelievably stressful situation."

"We tried but there was a lot of frustration as well. Think about all the future history that we knew about. The rise of the Third Reich and the Axis, the Holocaust, Pearl Harbor and all the rest of man's inhumanity to man all the way up to our time. We had all this information to save lives by the millions with no way to ever get the information to those that needed to know. And if we did, would they ever have believed us?"

Adam jumped in.

"Pop and I talked about it more times than I can count and every time we ended up with the conclusion that we were not there to try and change history, at least not on a global scale."

"You make it sound like you did tamper with it a little."

"I confess that I became very involved in my father's life and may have pushed and helped lead him in a direction that assured that he grew to adulthood, which in turn preserved my entry into the world, as well as the rest of my family for generations. Would it have resolved itself without my nudge, who can say? Either way all went well. It's a long story."

I turned to Julia.

Epilogue

"But I'm more interested in how you're doing. It sounds like you have had an incredible life since we last saw you."

"I graduated from finishing school a year after you and Adam disappeared. Daddy and Mum took me on an 'Around the World Trip' on the beautiful ocean liner *The Empress of Japan*. When we stopped in Japan, Daddy and many other American ball players who were also on the trip were invited to play exhibition baseball. The Japanese had fallen in love with the game and followed Daddy's, as well as many other players' careers in America. I guess that sounds amazing in light of the fact that their government declared war on us a few years later. I guess you both knew what was coming when you were with us. That part still amazes me. It must have been maddening to know all that and not be able to do anything about it."

"I still wish we could have warned people but, like I told Tom, it just was not feasible. All in all, the only persons I may have saved was my Dad and all his descendants. I will never know if he would have changed his job on his own or if we really had to have a hand in it. I guess we all will just have to accept the fact that this will remain another mystery. Forget about us."

I encouraged to Julia to continue, "So, after your trip?"

Julia regaled us by recounting her life since we had parted so many years ago until she tired. We could have listened to her stories all afternoon but it was obvious that she needed to rest. We made plans to take her to dinner and asked Tom to call us when she decided where she would like to eat. It would be our treat.

Adam and I returned to the Scenic View Inn to get cleaned up and changed for dinner and pick up Henny. I called Tom to find out if Julia had decided on a place to eat. We arranged to eat at one of her favorite places in North Conway called Horsefeathers at six o'clock.

We only had a half hour to give my wife an explanation and there would never be enough time to satisfy the thousands of questions that she was going to throw back at us. But she had to know.

"Henny, do you love me?"

"What kind of a question is that? Of course, I do."

"And you love me too, Grandma?"

"What is going on with you two. What have you done? You're starting to worry me."

"We have a story to tell you and you have to just listen. You're going to have a lot of questions but try and save them for when we get back. You need to know some things or you are really going to get confused when we meet Julia for dinner."

The next thirty minutes made Henny's head spin. It was easy to see that she really doubted most of what she was hearing. Most of the time her small hands were trying to cover her mouth that seemed to be open in shock at what she was hearing. I'm not sure that she blinked much either. Even Adam's verifying everything I was telling her didn't help. This was not going to get resolved before dinner and I ended up begging her to be patient and simply go with the flow this evening.

"I'll go along with you for now but the both of you are on notice. I'm not done with you."

We drove to the restaurant in silence. Henny stared vacantly out the window but I could sense her mind racing a million miles an hour as she struggled to comprehend.

While we all waited outside, I saw Tom pull into a parking space with their Mercury Monarch. I went over and helped Julia

Epilogue

out of the passenger side. While Tom retrieved her walker from the trunk, I introduced her to my wife.

"Julia, I'd like you to meet my wife, Henny. Henny this is Julia, Babe Ruth's daughter."

They shook hands.

"I'm honored to meet you Julia, I actually was quite surprised when my Bob and Adam told me that they knew you. How long has it been?"

Julia looked at Adam and me.

"I think we figured, what boys, about eighty-three years now?"

She chuckled and looked back at Henny.

"I get the feeling you still need some convincing young lady. It's really quite a story. But I'm getting hungry. Let's eat and maybe we can ease your doubts. Tom, my son here, is still stuck on the dock like you are. Maybe we can help both of you get on board."

More laughter.

Within moments we were inside and greeted by the hostess who cheerfully acknowledged Julia. I had no doubt that she was known by everyone in the area.

After we were seated, I started to read the daily specials to her from the chalkboard on the wall. I barely got through reading off the first, which was baked stuffed sole when she said,

"Stop there! I don't need to hear any more."

"That's her favorite. I recommend the Scallop Pie as well," said Tom.

Adam, Henny, and I ordered that, and we were on our way to a great meal with wonderful conversation.

Waiting for Einstein

We talked about my driving her and her family around in Jim and Kitty's huge Lincoln and she reminded me that Daddy always loved Packards and Cadillacs.

Then she stopped for a minute to think.

"You know, Daddy did have a Lincoln once. It was a Continental and his last car. The Ford Motor Company gave it to him for his support of the Boy's Club and Little League Baseball over the years. I believe it was in 1947 but the car was a '48. I loved that car. Daddy would double park it in front of our apartment building in Riverside and give me the keys when he came in. He hated going to the parking garage which was a few blocks away. I'd drive the car around the neighborhood before I would finally go to the garage. It was a beautiful car and it was wonderful to drive. I had hoped that, after Daddy had died, that I might get to keep it. Sadly, Mother sold it. I wonder if it is still around?"

I honestly did not know. I assured her that it probably was unless it had been in an accident. Celebrity cars were always highly sought after and collectible. I told her about another Continental of the same vintage that used to show up at car shows in the late sixties on Long Island that was originally owned by Arthur Godfrey. If his car was saved then the more famous Babe Ruth car had to still be around. I think she was happy to hear that.

Adam, Julia, and I related stories about our lives in New York City in 1933 to Tom and Henny's continued amazement and disbelief. You could tell they were still having trouble wrapping their heads around all of this but, as we talked, their doubts seemed to slowly dissolve. Tom filled us in about her upcoming 100th birthday party on July 17. Seventy-five close family and friends were coming from all over the country. He and his wife

Epilogue

had been planning it for a long time. Tom apologized for not inviting us but I said we barely counted as close friends since we had not kept in touch in the last eighty-three years. We all laughed. I understood completely.

When our table was cleared, we finally said our goodbyes and headed out the door. I asked Julia if we could have a picture together.

"I knew you would ask that, but I need to have my hair done first and I do not have an appointment until Thursday. But I do have something for you. Can you get it Tom?"

He went to his car and retrieved what I could see was an 8 x 10 black and white photo. He handed it to her.

"I'd like you to have this."

I took the photo from her. It was a picture of her with Dad and Babe. It was signed, 'Bob, Best wishes. Julia Ruth Stevens.'

"I think my hair looks better in this picture."

I hugged her and thanked her for making the effort to find us.

"You understand that I had to know if Kitty was telling me the truth."

Adam hugged her.

"I will never forget you and your family. You were there for me when I needed you even though you could not have known that. I wish you many more birthdays, Julia. I hope my life is half as wonderful as yours is. I would consider myself blessed."

As they pulled away from the curb, Henny, Adam, and I headed down the street to find some ice cream. Looking at my wife and Adam, and thinking about my kids, and grandchildren, I already knew my life was as blessed as Julia's. I also knew that Adam and I still had to answer a lot of questions from Henny. After our evening with Julia, it looked like it might be a bit easier.

That became evident when she said, "Stop, you two!"

We both said simultaneously, "What?"

"That day that you were both acting weird and telling me that you missed me?"

Adam smiled.

"Bingo, Grandma."

"No brag, just fact, Henny."

Epilogue

Autographed photo given to the author by Julia Ruth Stevens after an interview two weeks before her 100th birthday. Julia with Babe Ruth, circa 1934.

Katie Barton at Sunday dinner at the Majeski home with the author and his then girlfriend Henny O'Connor, January 1968.

Waterbury, Connecticut
June 12, 2019

The little Chevy shined like a new penny. Samantha, my oldest granddaughter at fifteen, had asked me to take her to a cruise night that I had raved about in Hamden. The Glenwood had the best fried clams, not to mention hotdogs and burgers. I was happy for the company. We cut through the back roads of Prospect, from her home in Waterbury. I avoided the infamous trestle in Prospect since Adam and my return to 2013. We eventually cut over to South Brooksvale Road in Cheshire and as we approached a park on our right Samantha looked up from her iPhone as I started to hit the brakes. All four tires started to squeal on the blacktop.

"What's that bright light, Pop?" as we skidded a bit more, we were totally enveloped by the light.

ACKNOWLEDGEMENTS

It was on a Friday evening, February 5, 1960, that a seed was sown that culminates in the writing of this novel. My young mind was opened to the wonders and possibilities of imagination that unforgettable night. It was two days before my eleventh birthday and my parents and I were visiting my Uncle Nick and Aunt Emmy in Seaford, Long Island. I sat on the living room floor watching a TV show on their black and white TV set, captivated by the most amazing story I had ever heard or seen, while my Dad and Uncle watched from the couch. A World War I pilot, in an old biplane, had landed at a NATO Air Base in France in our time. As the story revealed itself, there was drama and confrontation with MP's and he had to escape the Base security to get back to his fighter plane to fly off and save his Flight Commander caught in a dogfight back in 1917. He told Security that his Captain was close to being shot down by an enemy pilot. He escaped and flew off into a cloud to save him. That pilot he saved was the Commander of that NATO base in 1960. When Rod Serling finally gave his cryptic message, "And somewhere in between heaven, the sky, and the earth, lies The Twilight Zone," I turned to my Dad in true childhood wonder.

"Is that a true story? Did that really happen?" I almost whispered the question fearing that somehow, I would ruin the mood the TV show had created.

Waiting for Einstein

Dad never blinked and with a wry smile simply said, "What do you think?"

"It sounds real. I think it was real," I whispered.

"Then it was real for you." What a gift my Dad gave me that night. He let my imagination expand beyond my small world never to be bound by anything other than the limits of my own mind.

Over time I found out that it was a screen play, and later learned that it was Episode 18 of the first season of the legendary TV series, *The Twilight Zone*. It was titled "The Last Flight" and was written by Richard Matheson. More than sixty years later I still enjoy that memory and the wonder that was experienced through the power of the pen. The germ in my mind to write and read more grew out of that singular experience.

Where do you start to thank everyone who helped you accomplish the feat of writing your first novel? For me it will always start with my Dad, Julian Majeski, for nurturing my young imagination and in retrospect, Mr. Matheson, showing me a path. My Dad was an amazing storyteller and could command a room full of friends and relatives with his tall tales. It is a gift that my siblings Martha, Linda, and Raymond also inherited and that I have finally set to the printed page here as my contribution to the family legacy.

I started this project in 2013, and during that time my poor wife has suffered endless verbal outlines and review of the research that the storyline sparked. She has reigned in some of my crazier ideas and kept me true to the characters and plot as I developed them. Her endless patience over our fifty-five years together is worthy of any saint. She is my muse.

Katheryn Mullins Barton was truly one of my best friends in my youth and her stories about Jim and his Vaudeville, Broadway, and film career only fed my growing imagination. Her added tales of her friendships with Babe and Claire Ruth as well as Jimmy and Willie Cagney helped add entertaining elements to this book. I still

Acknowledgements

have a wealth of stories about Gregory Peck, Debbie Reynolds, and many more in reserve to tap in the future when appropriate. I love and miss her every day. She gave this story a richness that I could not have imagined without her.

What can I say about Julia Ruth Stevens that has not been written or spoken over her one hundred-and two-years life? I contacted her through Babe Ruth Central on the Internet, giving a short description of my project. I knew of her mother Claire's close friendship with Katie and dangled my own relationship with her as bait, hoping to get an interview. Four months later, I received a return email from her son Tom stating that she would be glad to do an interview when she returned to her summer home in North Conway, New Hampshire. My wife and I stayed over the night before we met her. It was less than two weeks before Julia's 100th Birthday! The day of the interview, Tom let me know that I had to wait until Julia woke up and dressed which would not be until late morning. Henny encouraged me to go alone and I walked the short distance from the motel to their home, armed with a notepad full of questions. My goal was to learn more about Babe as the father and the family man. I also wanted to hear about the relationship of the Ruth's and Barton's to corroborate what I had learned from Katie in my youth.

The fruits of that interview helped me learn of the Ruth family dynamics and the less public view of their lives on Riverside. It also verified the closeness of the Ruth and Barton families that extended well beyond the passing of Babe and Jim. Later that day we were dining at Horsefeathers, Julia's favorite eatery, when I asked her when she last saw Katie. She related going to NYC with her mother to meet her for a movie and dinner. She was not sure of the year or the movie but remembered the theme song and started singing "Everybody's Talkin' 'bout me." I quickly asked, "Midnight Cowboy?" "That's it!" she gleefully answered. Then I told her that would have been 1969. It was also during that interview that she told me that in those earlier days everyone called Katie, "Kitty." That triggered a lot of editing, for sure. My heartfelt thanks go to Julia and her son Tom for a wonderful day that was followed by an equally delightful dinner. I can only hope that I can be that sharp and witty when I turn on a hundred. My book is richer for their input.

I have to also give a shout out to all my family, my adult children, David, Tara, and Eileen as well as their spouses, Karen, Scott, and Kevin. My grandchildren have also been wonderfully supportive, obviously Adam and his brother Colin and their cousins; Samantha, and Ian, as well as Emma, Julia, and Kevin, Jr. Thanks goes out to friends and even co-workers at Connecticut Hospice who have endured my verbal updates during many breaks since I started this project in 2013. I am sure they are glad to see the final product is finally here. Their encouragement was much appreciated.

I must acknowledge my close friends, Nancy and Andy Johnson. First, Andy for entrusting his 1933 Chevy coupe into my care in 2008 after his ownership of over twenty-one years. Many adventures were enjoyed on trips in it by Henny, me, and our grandchildren and it gave me the spark to write this story. Secondly, thanks to Nancy for her encouragement with the project over the years and her reviewing and doing the very first edits of the earliest draft. Having her stamp of approval was the fire that helped get the engine into the station.

Joan Schulte, my son-in-law Scott's Mom, was an early believer in this effort and suggested the approach to blur the lines between reality and fiction, not unlike something from *The Twilight Zone*. I hope I came close to suspending reality for my readers, if not only between the covers of this book but maybe a bit beyond.

One of those family members who I told of this effort was my wife's cousin, John Bach, who put me in touch with Frank Amoroso,

Acknowledgements

of *simply francis publishing company*. It is this final collaboration with a true professional and eventually mentor that has raised the bar and brought my novel to a level that I could have not achieved without his encouragement, suggestions, insights, guidance, and nudging through the multiple editing that an author needs to do. You are the Master and I look forward to working with you on many books that I hope to write in the future. A shout out to all the staff at *simply francis publishing* from cover design, to formatting, editing, etc. It's been a great ride and your patience and expertise is well appreciated.

Until we meet again, somewhere in time,

Robert J. Majeski

ABOUT THE AUTHOR

Robert J. Majeski earned his B.A. from St. Francis College in Brooklyn, New York in 1972. He majored in English Literature with a focus in Victorian Prose. He had hoped to enter teaching, but the Gods had other plans. After a circuitous journey that included carpentry, furniture restoration, retail, and eventually a VP position in wholesale, he found himself unfulfilled, except for a great marriage with three children in college and high school. With the full support of his wife, he followed another dream and pursued a degree in Nursing and achieved another milestone when he obtained an RN in 1994. His twenty-five year career as a nurse was capped with the last fifteen years as a staff nurse, managing Infection Control and Wound Care for Connecticut Hospice in Branford, Connecticut. Founded in 1972, it is the first hospice in America.

In his first novel, *Waiting for Einstein,* he brings his love of literature, history and storytelling, sprinkled with more than a dash of family lore. His hope is that readers, young and old, will read this adventure and realize that, like him, they are surrounded by history with stories to listen to and hopefully share with others.

Made in the USA
Middletown, DE
28 June 2023

34042511R00155